Tales of Spooner Pond

Terry Lynn Rasner

Tales of Spooner Pond

Copyright © 2025 by Terry Lynn Rasner
10 9 8 7 6 5 4 3 2 1

Library of Congress Cataloging-in-Publication Data is available.

ISBN: 979-8-9939738-1-4 Paperback

ISNB: 979-8-9939738-0-7 ebook

Acknowledgement

My husband, Joseph, and I are together as one. We are passionately and faithfully creating our journey in life—praying, laughing, smiling, and kissing all the way! I'm truly blessed and grateful for your never-ending love for me!

My daughter, Sarah, you are the backbone of my life, and you will never stop giving and helping those who need an extra dose of the unconditional love that God instilled in you! You are an angel among all of us.

My grandson, Howard Edward IV, is why I wrote this book. My anchor in life. Never stop believing in the Lord and what hidden treasures He has stored up for you!

To all my family and friends, especially Emily, Ann, and Danny. The encouragement to assist me in finishing the book, having an ear to hear, a voice of reason when chaos broke out, and a shoulder to cry on. I'm beyond fortunate to be called your family and friend. I love you all!

Contents

CHAPTER ONE

What's All the Fuss?

"Dreams and fantasies are fine, Pippy, but a line must be drawn when *your* dreams and fantasies become *my* nightmare."

My dad said this as he paced back and forth alongside my bed. He towered over me like a stout oak tree, but his leaves were a full brownish-red beard and curly brown hair.

"What were you thinking...that this was okay?" he asked, pointing to the north-facing wall of my bedroom. "I just can't believe you would do this to your room. We *won't* be waiting until tomorrow to discuss this; I'll be back upstairs with your mother as soon as I can get her off the phone. You better be ready to explain this mess, young lady!"

I remember that night Dad was steaming like a geyser, ready to erupt. He was glancing daggers at me as he left my room. He hit the light switch with a karate chop and stormed out, slamming the door behind him and leaving me alone in the dark.

A chill came upon my room after he'd left. I pulled my covers around my neck and heard a familiar voice echo in my room. Unlike my father's voice, this voice was sweet and soothing.

"Don't be troubled, Pippy; you *were* indeed in Spooner Pond, and soon I'll show you how you can summon me and visit whenever you want."

"Truggles!" I said, peering into the darkness of my room. "Is it you?" I pushed my blanket and comforter aside, jumped out of bed, and put on my fluffy pink robe.

"It's me!" His voice was bold and cheerful.

"Shhh, my parents will hear you," I said, realizing they would never understand if they saw Truggles. After all, he was a very tall mix between a furry dog and a panda, standing in my room.

"Don't worry, Pippy," he began. "Only you, my dear, can hear my voice."

"Where are you?" I glanced furiously around my bedroom. I didn't want to arouse Mom and Dad by turning on the light, and this being a moonless night with no streetlights anywhere around our house made it hard to see.

"I'm with you always," he said, "but don't expect to see me in your world just yet."

Suddenly, the chill in my room intensified, and I started to shiver. I climbed back into bed, got under my covers, and wondered if I was imagining all this. I was talking to a voice I had only heard before tonight. But I knew Truggles was in my room, not just a voice in my mind or my dreams. And now that I was back underneath my blankets, his voice was gone. There were only twenty or thirty seconds of silence, but it seemed an eternity until Truggles' voice broke it.

"I'm still here, Pippy. I'll always be here."

For a moment, I just stayed tucked under my covers and smiled. I wanted nothing more than to be with this most extraordinary friend, but life at home was getting in the way.

"I believe you, Truggles, but what do I do about my dad and mom? They're flipping out!"

"Love your parents and listen to them, Pippy," he said, his voice seeming to come from a point not more than two feet from me. "In time, they will understand. You must be patient and accept your calling to come to Spooner Pond. Few are chosen, and few of your kind will join us at your age."

"But when?" I pleaded in the dark.

"When you are ready. When the time comes, I will accompany you to Spooner Pond. You can travel between your home here in North Star Ridge and the world of Spooner Pond. And to keep you company until I *know* you're ready to be alone in Spooner Pond, you may choose up to three other friends to bring with you."

"*Really?*" I said, thinking the first person I'd want to take with me was my best friend, Sarah Samuels. Sarah was awesome, sort of like my partner in crime. We did everything together when we could...and when our parents would allow it (and sometimes even when they didn't).

"Yes, up to three others. But for now, only your young friends, though there may be a time much later when you'll be able to bring your very stout and bushy oak tree of a father to visit us."

How did Truggles know I saw my father as a big, bushy oak tree? Gaping, I asked, "So, you know all my thoughts?"

"Indeed, every thought, feeling, and almost everything you do."

"No way."

"You will come to appreciate it, my dear. But for now...I must go. Goodbye..."

And as he stopped talking, the chill that had entered the room was gone.

"Truggles! Come back," I hollered. "Come back!"

My bedroom door flung open, the lights turned on, and my parents walked in.

"*Oh, Truggles, oh, Truggles! Where are you?*" Dad said, poking fun at me. And then, glancing at my mother, he said, "I told you, Holly. It is worse than we thought. Now she's talking to this Truggles...whoever *that* is."

Shaking his head in disgust, he led Mom over to the area of my bedroom wall that was causing all the fuss.

"Oh my gosh!" Mom said, staring first at Dad and then back at me. "Pippy Natalie Hyland, *what were you thinking?*"

It's funny to look back on it now—but not then—to think that Mom's eyes were as round as quarters, and her nostrils flared less than Dad's.

Before I could respond, Dad gave her the news she didn't want to hear, "It's the land where the Truggles live, Holly, and now it's painted all over the princess's bedroom wall."

I didn't know how to read the look on Dad's face. In one way, he looked furious, but in another, he seemed a bit fascinated. At that moment, I chose to believe he was intrigued.

"I've been chosen to go to that land," I blurted out. And then I proclaimed: "*And I may very well do so!*"

At first, they gave me a pitiful stare.

"Oh, Arthur, our baby's ill," Mom said.

"It is real, Mom. It's a world full of animals!" I sat up in my four-post brass bed, the tops of my blanket and comforter tucked under my arms folded across my lap.

"You have to understand one thing," I told them. "These animals are as human as you and I. Most have human-like faces, though they are hairy, and some even have human-like hands and feet." I finished up, even though I could tell from their expressions this wasn't going over too well, "And they speak like you and me."

"In English, I suppose?" Dad asked as he paced about my bedroom. "And do they wear their robes to bed, too?"

"Of course. I'm wearing mine—well, I got a chill on me."

Then, Mom made a move I'd always loved when I was little because it signaled story time and make-believe were on the way.

"Honey," my mom began, "your father and I love you more than anything. You're our only child, and we'd do anything for you. But we think you've gone too far with this Spooner Pond fantasy."

"But it's real, Mom," I protested.

"Not to your father and me," she said, pausing and hugging me. "I don't understand what's gotten into you, Pippy. I never imagined you'd do this to your room. You ruined this wall!"

"Gee, Mom, it's just a drawing. A map."

She conceded, but then a wave of frustration came out of nowhere: "But you've covered half the wall with magic marker!"

While Mom took a deep breath, I noticed Dad was studying the drawing on my wall. Mom stood, took a couple of paces from my bed, and spun around to face me. "I want you to talk to Mrs. Sopher this week about whether she can get you in, Pippy Natalie."

I knew from the tone of her voice, using my middle name, and the look in her eyes that her decision left no room for negotiation.

"Sure, Mom. You mean the lady at the community center?" But I was thinking of *the lady who talks to the parents about how to deal with kids. She is harmless.*

"Mary Sopher is an outstanding school counselor," Mom said matter-of-factly. "She sometimes works with children from the center in the evenings and on weekends at her home office."

"You guys think I'm crazy?" I asked.

"No, honey," Dad said as he turned away from my wall. "We're just concerned that your wild dreams have become more than a fantasy, like there's another world you think exists. This whole thing," he said, pointing to the wall, "looks like a giant map."

"Suppose it is?" But maybe it *was* a map of the Spooner Pond of my dreams, even though I wasn't entirely sure what it looked like.

"Then it's a problem, Pippy," Mom said. "Your dad and I are worried your fantasy has turned you into a daughter we sometimes feel like we don't know. Talking about your dreams is one thing, but dreams don't cause normal children to get up at night and draw maps on their bedroom walls."

"The memories of your dreams and fantasies, little princess," Dad began rather slowly, "have made one heck of a mess for you to clean."

"Right now?" I asked.

"No, *little princess*," Mom said, staring daggers at Dad, whom she mimicked. "Your walls will be cleaned and repainted this weekend."

"Sure, fine, Mom," I grumbled. I was ready to argue with her when Truggles' voice echoed: *Right now, love your parents and listen to them. In time, they will understand. But you must be patient and accept your call to Spooner Pond.*

After Mom and Dad flipped off the light and closed my bedroom door, I gazed into the dark emptiness they left behind and called out Truggles' name. I called once, twice, and again a third time, but there was no response. Disappointed and sad, I pulled up my blanket and comforter and, before going to sleep, planned what I would do tomorrow after school. Because in two days, my wall would be clean whether I liked it or not.

***

When I got home from school the next day, I used my dad's instant-print camera to take pictures of the large, comprehensive drawing on my wall. It was about three feet tall and five feet wide...the most giant thing I'd ever drawn. It would later take me four days to piece together the multiple photos and make a pen and ink drawing of what became my first official map of Spooner Pond.

I also got Sarah's older brother, Brandon, to make me a copy of the map. I hid the copy and photos of the map underneath my toy chest and kept the full-color original for framing. I hoped that one day, when this was all forgotten, my parents would let me hang it on my north-facing bedroom wall.

In her sweet, soft voice, Mrs. Sopher began the phone conversation by emphasizing how much my parents love and want to protect me. She explained why their concern for me always seemed more than that of other parents. Most of the time, it was *way* over the top.

Mrs. Sopher cleared her throat. I could hear her unravel a cough drop and discreetly pop it into her mouth without missing a word. "Pippy, when you were born, you only weighed four pounds and lived at the local hospital for several months in a plastic bubble with tubes and wires connected all over your body. The doctors informed your mother and father you would not make it through the night. But you did! When he first laid eyes on you the next day, your father affectionately whispered in your ear, 'This is my little princess warrior, Pippysqueak.'"

"I love my nickname," I interjected. Boy, did I, especially knowing that my dad lovingly first named me Pippysqueak.

Mrs. Sopher told me a story about when I was born. It may seem a bit selfish, but I love hearing the story. It often gives me courage when I must stand up against my classmates. It's a story about when I was born; I was small in stature and always needed assistance grabbing items from the top shelves and having to sit in the front row seat of classrooms so I could see. That is how I got the nickname again from my taunting classmates: "Pippysqueak."

But whenever I hear it from my classmates, I can only smile. They think it hurts my feelings, but I can only relate to my dad's affectionate voice whenever they call me it.

When our session ended, Mrs. Sopher informed me that we would pick up where we left off the next time we met. Then, without missing a second on the clock, she asked me to hand the phone to my mother. My mother spent the next thirty minutes divulging my dreams and behavior to Mrs. Sopher like I was a crime suspect. Of course, my mother had a way of slanting my suspicious activity if she thought I was lying. Nevertheless, she got Mrs. Sopher to get me on her appointment schedule. And this time, it would be *in person!*

In other words, it was pretty serious stuff.

CHAPTER TWO

Mrs. Sopher and a Noggin-Nudger Moment

"Hello, Holly," Mrs. Sopher began, greeting me and my mother at her door. It had been three days since they'd made this appointment on the phone, and I wasn't sure how to feel about it.

"Hi, Mary," my mother said, looking half-embarrassed. "Thanks for getting us in so quickly."

"No problem." Mrs. Sopher turned her attention to me. She looked taller than I remembered from seeing her at the community center. "Hello, darling," she said as she extended her hand and leaned over to greet me, smiling. "So, this is what Pippy Natalie Hyland looks like when she's not dressed up as a princess phantom."

"Yep, it's me," I said, rolling my eyes. I would never live down dressing up as the princess phantom at the Harvest Ball, complaining about her cheap candy corn treats.

"Why don't you come back in an hour, Holly?" Mrs. Sopher said.

"But I thought you'd be seeing both of us."

Mrs. Sopher grinned broadly. "Not just yet."

My mother nodded uncertainly and slowly made her way back out the door. She seemed slightly lost and doubtful as she left.

It was just Mrs. Sopher and me, alone in her spacious den. It was set up with every stuffed animal surrounding us, giving me the sense that we were being observed while talking. And we did this for almost sixty minutes.

"Tell me about these dreams, Pippy," Mrs. Sopher began. "They sound fascinating."

"You believe I had them?" I asked, awestruck.

"We all dream, Pippy, about many sorts of things. So, tell me about this place, Spooner Pond." I watched her open a yellow notepad, preparing to take notes of our meeting. She sat across from me, her legs crossed, making her close to six-foot-high frame less imposing than before. The deep red lipstick outlined her sparkling, almost opaque white teeth on her full lips, and her makeup was delicately applied to accent her high cheeks and hide her wrinkles.

"Will you tell my parents?" I asked.

"Only if you want all four of us to talk," Mrs. Sopher said almost without looking up from her writing pad.

"Really?"

"Yes, I'm sure, Pippy. Now, let us talk about dreams. But first, how long have you been having them?" Her eyes were still more focused on her writing pad than on me, which I found odd. Her long silver-gray hair was piled high on her head with a tiny red hat on one side and held together by an old-fashioned hairpin. I found it ironic that it appeared to be the shape of a stretched-out, furry, dog-like panda.

I remember being sure no adult would understand what was happening to me. Of course, I hardly understood, either, but something wild and wonderful seemed to be happening to me in my sleep, and no matter what the consequences were, I liked talking about it.

"Well," I began, "I've been dreaming about Spooner Pond for a few months. It started with hearing this butler's voice in my head. You know...*my dear, my dear,* this and that. And all the while, I found myself in this colorful place that was not North Star Ridge. Even though the place looked a lot like Chickadee Meadows, it wasn't at all dusty or dirty, and all the plants and trees were thick and overgrown and often surrounded by tall grasses. This place was almost like a picture in a perfect painting."

"Fascinating, but how were you certain you were somewhere?" Mrs. Sopher was scribbling on her writing pad.

"It wasn't until I felt myself walking on the ground in my dream that I knew I was somewhere real. I remember kicking the grassy ground to see if it made my slippers turn green, and it did, but the green was gone when I checked in the morning."

"Anything else?"

"Well, yeah, the most important thing." I smiled.

"And that was?" she persisted, making me talk like counselors do.

"I finally stumbled upon the source of the voice I was hearing in my dreams."

"That would be your friend, Truggles?"

"Not my friend at first! Hearing his voice and talking was one thing, but when I first ran into him, I wanted to run away

11

and hide. What would *you* do if you came up on a very tall and furry dog-like panda? He was impressive and handsome, but he was so big. His face, long ears, and head were all dog, and he was handsome with long, furry golden hair that looked like a blanket. His face looked like a panda. And his body, too, but it was super big!"

"What, did he scare you?" Mrs. Sopher asked.

"A little bit, but as soon as I heard his voice again, I was better."

"And that meeting was several months ago?"

"Yeah," I grinned, "dreaming has never been so much fun!"

Mrs. Sopher stood up, trotted to a lemonade pitcher, poured herself a glass, and offered me one. I couldn't resist, and she returned with two full glasses. I watched as she strolled across the room with a certain air about her—an impressive woman—all confidence and dignity.

"Well, this fellow, Truggles, is more than an interesting character, to say the least," Mrs. Sopher said as we resumed. "Your parents told me he was the one who told you to draw on your bedroom wall."

"Well, in a sorta kind of way. Truggles didn't tell me what to draw but suggested I draw what I saw in my dreams."

"On your bedroom wall?" she asked, raising her eyebrows.

"No, that was my idea."

"So, this drawing on the wall...did it represent *everything* you saw in Spooner Pond?" She removed her eyeglasses and let them dangle around her neck.

I stared at her, wondering about her fascination. I didn't feel comfortable answering that question. So, she tried again.

Her voice had a creepy fascination yet a look of adult disbelief in her eyes: "Did you see everything you drew?"

"Not really," I said. "Some of what I saw was too unusual for me to understand to be able to draw it."

"Then you drew from what...divine inspiration?"

I was caught a bit off guard by her line of questioning. Though I was only seven—well, almost eight—I'd been through my share of adults being too pushy and trying to outwit me. I would never have admitted it then. I wasn't sure I didn't have help drawing the map on my wall, but I couldn't remember.

"Truggles told me all about Spooner Pond," I said in a tone that demanded her full attention. "He took me for tours around Spooner Pond. Though I didn't always know where we were going and how it related to other areas of Spooner Pond, I can say that what was on my bedroom wall was not everything I saw. And I'm sure I didn't know everything about all the places drawn on my wall or the names of all the landmarks and other places noted on my map."

"But it is real to you, isn't it?"

"Entirely real, Mrs. Sopher. I suppose the wall drawing is a map of Spooner Pond as I saw and felt it and as Truggles described it to me. Particularly over the past five nights of dreaming and our talks on the Happy Trail."

"Talks on the *Happy Trail?*" she wondered.

"Yes, I've been on the Happy Trail with Truggles, and it's an impressive place."

"You believe it's in Spooner Pond?"

"Well, yeah. It is not here in North Star Ridge, and it's on my map of Spooner Pond."

"Was on your map," she stared, half-scolding at me. "I understand you cleaned your wall last weekend."

"Yeah," I sighed, "that's right...was on my wall." I had another map...but I thought it best not to tell Mrs. Sopher.

"So, how often have you traveled to Spooner Pond?" Mrs. Sopher asked as she scooted closer to me while I backed away.

"Just a few times over the past month, but three times this week."

"Really?" She nodded, placing the glasses on her face. My attention was also drawn to a necklace she was wearing. I hadn't noticed it earlier, but it was now apparent as she leaned toward me. It had a jagged oval burst of melted multi-colors and shapes. I found myself getting sleepy just gazing at it.

"I don't understand why your parents never saw the drawing before last week," Mrs. Sopher said.

"I don't know," I replied, a bit puzzled because drawing the map took me almost four days.

"I think I know your Spooner Pond," Mrs. Sopher mumbled, wrinkling her nose and tilting her head down to stare at me over the rim of her shiny gold and black glasses. At that moment, I thought they looked too ornate to be real.

"Your Spooner Pond," she began as she took the hairpin out of her fluffy, long, silvery-gray hair, allowing it to fall, "is it a divine land where animals are similar to humans? I imagine some even have human-like hands and feet and talk as we are talking right now, and it's not a scary place, is it?"

I'll never forget how I sat there, confused by her dramatic change in demeanor. She couldn't know Spooner Pond as I knew it, yet she spoke as if she did. I wondered if she was just humoring me.

"No, Spooner Pond doesn't scare me at all," I said. I was beginning to feel much more comfortable talking about Spooner Pond than ever before. "From what I've seen, the animals are all quite pleasant and seem to have a way about them, making each of them different from us."

"And what else have you seen?" Mrs. Sopher asked, her face aglow as she pinched her oval necklace between her fingers.

I stared at her and wondered what had happened and what was happening. I'm sure she didn't even recognize my staring because she was gone, zoned out, and all I could do was continue to stare at her and smile—a genuine smile from deep within me—a smile of joy in sharing my tales of Spooner Pond.

Maybe a full minute passed before we made eye contact again as Mrs. Sopher attempted to tidy up a bit. It was clear Mrs. Sopher was more than interested in what I was saying, but I didn't know at the time just how curious she was. That wouldn't come to me until some time later.

"When will you return to Spooner Pond, and how will you get there?"

"I'm not sure, but Truggles told me he'll soon show me how to go there whenever I want."

"And how many times have you been?"

"Oh...I don't know. Lots."

"You think the world of this Truggles, don't you?" Mrs. Sopher asked.

I paused for a moment and peered her in the eyes. I think her question was genuine, and I had longed to tell someone just how I felt about Truggles, and she had given me the opportunity.

"I love Truggles. He's like the King of Spooner Pond and treats me like a real princess."

"Like your parents?"

"No! They call me a princess but forget that when they get mad at me."

"Princesses aren't perfect, Pippy." Mrs. Sopher chuckled at her comment.

"Yeah, I know, but when it comes to Truggles, I always feel perfect."

"I think I understand," Mrs. Sopher said as she jotted a couple of lines on her writing pad.

"Now you're going to tell on me, I know," I said, a little disappointed.

"No, Pippy, I will tell your mother you're fine, that your Spooner Pond is your dream home—a place you go in your dreams to have an identity away from North Star Ridge. So, I don't think they need to be worried, and although the bit about drawing on your bedroom wall is awkward, it's not like no other kids have ever done it. But I don't think it's enough to consider you disturbed."

"You mean it?" I asked. I couldn't believe it was a real place.

"Yes." She edged closer and whispered, "I once had a place to go to in my dreams when I was young. It was a forest of flowers where you could eat them like candy. There were all kinds of tastes and textures. And they never caused cavities."

"Any giant honeysuckles?" I asked with a cheek-stretching grin.

"I don't recall any, but there was plenty of fresh, cool spring water for when I got thirsty."

"And were there any animals?"

"I don't recall any animals."

Suddenly, I got bold with her. My mom had always told me not to ask adults how old they were, but I could not resist. "So, how old are you, Mrs. Sopher?"

Just then, my mom knocked on the door, and summarily, Mrs. Sopher straightened up her glasses and hair. "It's time for us to stop, Pippy. I do not need to see you again. But please remember this: right now, love your parents and listen to them. In time, they will understand. Be patient; not everyone who's called to Spooner Pond succeeds." She smiled and added, "And I'm seventy-two."

Mom knocked again on the door and rang the door chime.

"No way you're seventy-two," I argued with her.

"Just last week."

"Well, what about those Outsiders?"

"I'm not sure what you are talking about," Mrs. Sopher said.

"But..."

"Only one more thing, Pippy," Mrs. Sopher whispered to me and smiled. "Your animal pals seem more like palimals to me."

She threw me off at first, but as she reached to open the door, I focused on her encouraging smile and thought, *Why not? At least it'd save me some time explaining that they were animals with different human traits.* Sure, palimals, and I smiled big at her and thought of Dack, one of the palimals I had recently met at her lagoon not too far from the Happy Trails. I remembered Dack's words, "Be certain to know it's a 'noggin nudger' moment every time something simple just makes good sense."

And I knew I just had a noggin nudger moment with Mrs. Sopher.

***

I was so relieved that Mrs. Sopher wouldn't tell Mom anything terrible that I somehow missed the deep connection I made with her that day. Ironically, though, I didn't speak to her again for almost five years, even though we'd smile and exchange winks with each other occasionally at the community center.

As it turned out, Mrs. Sopher was right all along, though she never actually said it this way; not talking about Spooner Pond around my home or with her was the only way I could convince my parents it was nothing more than a wild and wonderful dream. Furthermore, I learned it was an option for my parents and me to laugh and tease about the silly "palimals" of my dreams. At the same time, I never again needed to try to convince them that Spooner Pond existed.

Spooner Pond had been my private world for what seemed like a fast five years. Still, I got to know only a few of the palimals personally. Then, in my twelfth year, I discovered palimals I never knew existed and watched as they attained new powers and identities. Most of my visits to Spooner Pond were with one or two of my friends—mostly Sarah and another friend, Howie Yeary, who also made a trip with us.

And so, these tales of Spooner Pond are really about my fifth and sixth years in Spooner Pond, when I was twelve and thirteen and when my life changed forever, never to be the same, by a series of events I never imagined possible.

CHAPTER THREE

How Feathers Got His Name

I had just turned twelve, and once again, Truggles escorted me to Spooner Pond. Over the last six months, he'd been turning me loose to wander about on my own in some regions of Spooner Pond, but this day, he left me to explore the meadows just west of the area where I met this most curious cat for the first time—a cat that would soon become very close to me.

"Dun't know how ta express it, but I like brain...da taste of it. Thing 'bout Spooner Pond is da only place ta catch rabbits is halfway 'tween Tahoe's and Grandma Goat's, so dat's where I live. I gots ta catch a rabbit every week, just gots ta, and once in a while some birds and mice, too. Gross, huh, but I likes meat."

"Ughhh," I said as I cleared my throat, "nice to meet you, Kitty."

"Kitty Joe's da name."

"Yes. Truggles tells me you're quite a fellow," I said as I stared at this oversized black and white cat. "You're bigger than cats I know."

"Twenty-eight pounds, I am, and all muscle."

If anything, Kitty Joe was a slender twenty-eight pounds. When standing on all fours, he was twenty inches in height and almost fifteen inches from the top of his head to the ground when sitting.

"Well, I'm Pippy Natalie Hyland," I said, introducing myself.

"Da girl, I've heard 'bout in these parts."

"Yeah," I said, scratching my head, unsure how to take that comment. "And you're a hunter, huh?"

"Yup, I think I'm da only true carnivore in Spooner Pond. Otherwise, I'm a pur-fect kitty. I purr, rub legs, lap sit, and all dat stuff."

Staring at him, somewhat cross-eyed and suspicious of such a contrasting view of himself, I chuckled. "How does a great hunter like you settle down to be a kitty?"

"Easy," he said. "Now, catch!" he blurted out before leaping up at me sideways. I was slow to reach out to catch him, and a moment later, we crashed into the tall grass, Kitty Joe hugging me around the neck.

"Good job, Hayland," he said as he crawled out of my arms. "Yar pretty, and yar tuff."

"It's Hyland, and thank you, Kitty Joe."

He stared at me as if to size me up more as I got up from the tall grass. "Come here," I said, offering him my arms for him to jump up.

He did so gladly.

"Whoa, you really are twenty-eight pounds," I said, marveling at how heavy he was, "but you're soft, too." Indeed, his fur was thick, and his hair of medium length. He felt like one of Mom's fine fake fur coats, and as the big cat wrapped his body close to me and purred in my arms, I fell in love with the rascal right then and there.

"You're just a big baby," I said.

He reared his head and peered me right in the eye, startling me momentarily, though I didn't feel threatened or need to drop him. "I'm the only real hunter in Spooner Pond," he began. "And I like da' plump juicy bodies a Peigts dat I eats whole and then spits out dar crunchy legs."

"And your point?" I asked, staring at him down.

"Ma point is ya can't tell all da others I like ta purr and cuddle too much."

"Oh, sneaky, are you?"

"Naw, yar different," he said, rubbing his cheek against my neck.

"Okay, Kitty Joe, but I can't hold you forever. You're heavy," I smiled, wondering how such a sweet face would look chewing on a rabbit's head, the carcass of a decapitated mouse, or those Peigts about which he was so fond.

"Sure, Pippys," he said as he jumped down. "Come on, let's go ta Hangin' Branch Tree."

"Tell me if you see any Peigts, huh, Kitty Joe?" I said, remembering if Truggles had told me much about these critters.

"No Peigts this way, but I'll shows ya sometime."

We wound through tall, fresh green willows and tall grass for twenty minutes. In many ways, it was like many forests back home, but everything in Spooner Pond seemed more colorful and lusher. And the fragrances were intoxicating. Eventually, we came to a clearing that revealed a rather monstrous tree.

"Dats Hangin' Branch Tree," Kitty Joe said as he leaped into my arms and pointed to a giant tree with big, broad leaves filling its high branches. Its trunk looked sturdy and thick, and it seemed to be about thirty feet between the ground and the beginning of the branches...except for this one low-hanging branch that dropped from the thirty-foot mark to maybe seven feet off the ground. It appeared the branch was shaped like a stairway, but you'd need to be pretty tall to reach it.

"Dat branch is a great place for seein' Outsiders," Kitty Joe said.

"Outsiders?" I wondered aloud.

"All da others who come here but dun't liv here."

"But..."

"No buts. Oh great...look!" Kitty Joe pointed across the field behind us.

"What?"

"It's da big ol' hairy one."

With Kitty Joe back in my arms, I turned my head over my shoulder behind me and was startled by what I saw. I released Kitty Joe and jumped back as the hairiest-looking creature I had ever seen approached. He came forward with a swagger and an ear-to-ear grin, exposing big, long teeth!

"Is it an Outsider?" I asked.

"Naw," Kitty Joe began, "dats Furry One."

"That's a cer-tain-ty," Furry One said in a sweet voice as she neared us.

Straightening myself and looking up at this *massive* bear with long brown fur, I extended my hand. I remembered all the stories Truggles had told me about this big brown bear palimal.

"Hi, I'm Pippy Natalie Hyland."

"I was told you were com-ing. I see you're with the ras-cal," Furry One said in a slow-motion voice, nodding to Kitty Joe and smiling.

"Dats *Hy*-land, Furry One," Kitty Joe added, smiling big.

It was odd standing there next to her. Even though I had heard of Furry One, I never imagined she'd be well over six feet tall and wide. Her hair was a foot long on her body and just inches long on her paws and face. I expect if she were to stand on her hind feet, she'd be close to seven feet tall and at seven feet tall, scare anyone until she opened her mouth and smiled. But instead, she seemed to have this tenderness in her voice and smile that was calming and not scary.

"I see the lit-tle fur ball is still sheeddding," Furry One observed with her slow speech, pointing to the white hairs all over my dark sweater.

"Hey, ol' big bear, ya ought ta talk," Kitty Joe shouted.

"I don't shed no moore, and it's a good thing," Furry One chuckled, reaching down to tickle Kitty Joe with one of her massive claws, almost as big as Kitty Joe's head.

"Ya could make a blankit with all a yar fir," Kitty Joe said as he dodged Furry One's claw, hopped onto Furry One's arm, and rubbed up against her face.

Then Kitty Joe stopped rubbing and raised his nose to sniff around before focusing on Furry One's opposite shoulder: "I smells a mouse."

Talk about a shocker. Before me, a nose and eyes peeked out of the fur on Furry One's shoulder.

"Is dat ya, Barn, hidin' in da fir?" Kitty Joe said, staring at the protruding nose and eyes.

The nose didn't twitch, but the eyes glanced first at me and then at Kitty Joe.

"Come out, ya squeker," said Kitty Joe.

Still, no action, as the eyes seemed to retract back into the safety of Furry One's long hair.

"It's okaay, Barney," Furry One said, and the eyes and nose reappeared.

"Is that really you, Barney?" I asked excitedly. I'd met Barney once before on one of my very first trips to Spooner Pond. He was an easy-going, oversized white mouse a few months earlier at Tahoe's barn. Tahoe is the sweetest once wild Mustang horse you'd ever want to meet. She allows Barney to live in the hayloft of her barn.

Then, as we watched in awe, Barney slid his body forward out from beneath Furry One's hair. Attached to his head was a set of ears I had never seen on a mouse. Thin and almost transparent, each ear was about six inches long and broad in its middle.

"It's big ares, Barn," Kitty Joe laughed. "Where in da world did ya git those ares?"

"Are you heerrre to be nice, or weerrre you on your way to go rabbbittt huntiiinnng?" Furry One offered an agonizingly long interruption.

"Matter a fact, if ya two hadn't come up, I'd still be in Pippy's arms gittin' rubbed up," Kitty Joe grinned. "But then a big bear 'n a flap-ared mouse is interestin', don't ya think?"

While these two were yapping at each other, I stared at Barney and wondered what had happened to him. He was definitely not the large but otherwise inconspicuous mouse I had met several months earlier.

Holding back a giggle at the unusual sight, I was surprised to see the bravery of this little mouse, which was dwarfed as much by Kitty Joe as I was by Furry One.

"Well, either you go, K.J., or get back down with Pips, 'cause I'm gonna learn to fly today!" Barney snapped at Kitty Joe.

Kitty Joe laughed. "Ya ain't gonna fly. Yar a mouse."

"I'm a bird now, and I'm gonna be able to do things you can't do, K.J.!"

"Eeenoughhh, you two. Kittty Joe, you get down," Furry One said, and Kitty Joe jumped and climbed back into my arms.

"Barrrney has gootttten the gift," Furry One said like a proud mother.

"The gift?" I asked.

"Yup, the gift of flyyying."

And with that, Furry One reached her left hand up to her shoulder, and Barney stepped onto it. When he did, he revealed not only his big floppy ears but a set of new hind legs that were long and retractable.

"Git sum Peigt legs, Barn?" Kitty Joe chuckled, the intent of his comments having little meaning to me because I still couldn't visualize what a Peigt looked like, and that wasn't the time to ask.

"Barney," I said as he approached Furry One, Kitty Joe now back in my arms. "Mice can't fly."

"Well, just watch me, Pips!" he squealed.

I just hate it when he calls me Pips., I thought.

And with that introduction, the most fantastic thing I had ever seen a mouse do was done there at Hanging Branch Tree.

***

It had been weeks earlier when Truggles had ferried Barney over to visit Furry One; the adventure with flight had begun. Barney had always complained of how ordinary he seemed...

that he wasn't unique enough to be a palimal. Initially, he'd intended to visit the Pinenut Forest to get encouragement from the singing butterflies. However, in the Pinenut Forest, when he was alone, he met a sweet-talking benevolent wizard woman known throughout Spooner Pond as Old Hag, who offered to make a trade with him. Barney would get something spectacular of his choosing in exchange for arranging an escort across Spooner Pond for Old Hag.

Based on the story we got, Furry One quickly accommodated Barney's request and offered to give Old Hag a ride after she helped Barney. No one floats unaccompanied across Spooner Pond because they've heard stories about creatures getting swallowed up in Dark Seas—stories I had yet to understand. From what I understood, Furry One and Truggles were the two palimals capable of ferrying visitors across any section of Spooner Pond. However, Furry One was limited to ferrying visitors across the southern route, where the water is no more than four feet deep.

That day, Barney was given a pair of very long ears and a pair of remarkable back legs that would enable him to learn to fly. The trade was agreeable to both: the old Hag was escorted across the southern route of Spooner Pond to a place near High Pass, and a mouse with dreams of flying was at least a bit closer to that dream. First, however, he had to give up being the mouse he'd always been and accept the new creature he wanted to be.

So, we were in a meadow near the southwest shore of Spooner Pond—Furry One, Kitty Joe, and I watched the unthinkable: a mouse learning to fly. The mechanics were simple:

once airborne, Barney would extend his legs, grabbing the tips of his ears with his feet to form a perfect aerodynamic, gliding wing. Furry One had chosen the fields around Hanging Branch Tree for Barney's flight school because the grasses were soft, and the space was wide open and somewhat private.

"Barrrney, grab the tips of your ears with your feet, sprrreaaad them out, and hang on," Furry One said just before she tossed the little mouse into the air.

But there was another crash as Barney tangled in his legs and ears. I think there were nine attempts—some more dramatic than others—before Barney finally learned to glide. But after he did, we sat in awe of his skilled navigation and steering. His gliding maneuvers grew in length and variety, and it wasn't too long before Furry One flung him high into the air. We watched Barney do loops, dives, and complete belly rolls like a stunt pilot.

Oh yes, Barney had learned to glide.

"I'm a bird, I'm a bird!" Barney yelled, full of bliss, as he swooped by and glided to a safe landing next to Kitty Joe and me. "K.J., I can really fly!"

"Yar flyin', Barn, but yar no bird," Kitty Joe said. "'Cause ya ain't got no feathers."

"But I fly," Barney said, puffing up his chest and raising his arms.

"Yeah, I suppose," Kitty Joe said as he paced around the larger mouse. "I've never seen a mouse even sorta fly, and ya do that."

"Yeah, I fly like a bird!"

"Mosquitoes fly, and dey ain't birds."

"But—"

"Lookit, Barn," Kitty Joe interrupted him. "If ya wanna fly like a bird, ya gotta flap dose ares a yars and really fly. So ya does that, and I'll call ya a bird."

And as if driven to be what he was not, Barney tried time after time to flap his ears with his legs but made no progress until Furry One had the idea to take him and place him on the hanging branch, seven feet off the ground.

"Cliimmb up the braannch, Barrrney. Get reeeaaal high and jump off and try flap-ping your eeears. You don't have to worrry beecause if you get in troubbble, you can always fly with your eeears held out as wings like you learned."

Barney tried once and crashed really bad. So, he tried again, and the result was somehow even worse.

"No more, Barney," I said. "That's enough."

"One more, Furry One," Barney said.

"You don't have to prove yourself, Barney," I said, patting Kitty Joe on his rear.

"Lit him try," Kitty Joe added, motioning to Barney. "Come here, Barn 'n lit me shows ya a trick."

Kitty Joe manipulated Barney's hind legs and ears, showing him how to coordinate the flapping action as he thought it should be. He whispered something in Barney's ear before encouraging him to climb to the highest point on the branch and jump off.

Determined, Barney got hoisted up on the branch, climbed to the top of the branch, and stood about twenty-seven feet off the ground.

"Ya can do it, Barn!" Kitty Joe yelled.

He jumped off, falling faster and then continuing to fall faster and faster. He went straight into the ground.

"Kitty Joe!" I screamed as I ran over to check on Barney.

"I'm okay, Pips," Barney grinned. "I got it now."

"What?" I gasped. "You almost killed yourself."

"No, I had to test the fall rate," Barney grinned. "Now I know I can do it."

Oh great, I thought, *and if he gets hurt, Truggles will murder me.*

Barney winked at Kitty Joe, and Kitty Joe flashed a grin. Barney pleaded with Furry One to give him one more hoist onto the hanging branch. She did reluctantly, and Barney climbed to the branch's top and leaped off. He went into his gliding position and began to glide in extensive circles. After stabilizing himself, Barney flapped his hind legs, moving his ears like enormous, majestic wings. He began to fly.

"Way ta go, Feathers!" Kitty Joe hollered. "Yar flyin'!"

Kitty Joe was grinning from ear to ear as he gazed at the floppy-eared flier.

"Dat's it. Dat's it, Feathers!" Kitty Joe said excitedly. "I told him, Pippy, if he could fly without feathers, I'd be callin' him Feathers. And now dat's his name."

And that's how a mouse named Barney became known as Feathers, and Hanging Branch Tree became known as Flying Tree.

Reflecting on how I felt that day, I remember how convinced Barney (well, *Feathers*, I suppose) was that he was a bird trapped in a mouse's body. He never stopped believing this, and although I guess it's okay for a mouse to fly, I've never felt good about him no longer feeling like a mouse. Sure, I remember thinking he couldn't take off or hover like a bird, and with those big ears, he couldn't crawl through mouse holes nor fit very well in my pocket. But, of course, those are mouse things to do.

I'll never forget how much I wanted to meet the Old Hag who spelled him because I didn't think it was right. But much as Feathers liked it, I still wasn't sure a mouse should fly. Why, if Feathers ever broke one of his legs, not only would he not be able to fly, but he also wouldn't be able to walk or do any mouse things except eat and get fat.

Beyond that, I keep returning to a single question: Why did Truggles have me come to Spooner Pond that day to watch a mouse learn to fly when I feared heights? It all seemed befuddling to me but not as strange as it was one day with Kitty Joe in the Wooded Forest.

CHAPTER FOUR

Furgit the Roogers— A Peight Breakfast Is Worth It

"Waaellll, gotta be 'bout 5:30. Sun's not up yit," Kitty Joe yawned. "So, whata ya think, Tahoe, this a good day fur Peigt control in South Sideways?"

Peeking down at them from our hay seats in the loft, I said, "Hey, what you two up to?"

I was seated beside Barney, who I was still having difficulty thinking of as *Feathers*. It was just light enough with the full moon setting on the horizon, its glow creeping through the window in the hayloft. It was just enough light for me to read Bar—er, Feathers, a story about a circus mouse who slept with an elephant. Mice are early risers, and although I had school that day, I had called on Truggles for an early morning trip to Spooner Pond to visit with Feathers and Tahoe.

Tahoe's barn was a marvel in itself, and like most of the structures in Spooner Pond, it had been built by Benjamin Beaver. It was old and a little creaky, with some moss and climbing ivy growing, but it was sturdy and clean. Feather's loft smelled fresh, and the hay was soft, but nowhere was there a pitchfork or hay hooks. Still, Tahoe's barn had an assortment of saddles, saddle blankets, and bridles.

Tahoe peered up toward me, winked, and smiled. She then turned away to nestle her nose against Kitty Joe's face: "Our little K.J. is thinking of a Peigt breakfast, Pippy."

Scooting back to use his left paw to wipe away what he called *Tahoe's nasty nostril drippins*, Kitty Joe leaped up and perched himself on the side wall of one of the eating corrals. Tahoe's barn was set up with several of these eating corrals that had an abundance of well-stacked and easily accessible alfalfa and a couple of sleeping corrals with deep beds of hay.

"Xactly what I was thinkin'! Wanna come along, Tahoe? What's about you, Pippy? It'll be a first fur ya both."

Tahoe shook her head and pulled a flake of alfalfa from her feed. Before chewing on her alfalfa, she glanced briefly at Kitty Joe, with a mouthful of alfalfa sticking out of her mouth. "Not me," she said. "It's too early in the morning."

I approached my little palimal and said, "Aww, Tahoe, I bet our K.J. just wants a ride."

"Ride me?" Tahoe mumbled with alfalfa falling from her mouth. "Well, maybe to get over Benjamin's Boardwalk, but not into the Wooded Forest." She paused to finish her alfalfa before adding: "And anyway, Benjamin's not very fond of you right now."

"Yeah, Benny's against ma Peigt huntin'."

"Yes, and against your idiolect. It drives Benjamin crazy," Tahoe said, still chewing on her last flake of alfalfa.

"It's just da way I spakes."

"I know, but he doesn't see you often and can't always understand you."

As I listened to these two talking, I suggested that Feathers join them, but he wanted to stay in the loft and look through the pictures in my book. While listening in, I started sifting through all I'd learned about this group of characters since stumbling upon Spooner Pond.

Kitty Joe is definitely the hunter he says he is, yet he's not entirely without manners and good cleanliness. He's a tidy hunting cat who never brings his catch indoors and lives just south of the barn, alongside Spooner Pond's southwest shore, far from Flying Tree. I think he's stuck at about three years old, and I'm pretty sure he prefers an excellent rubbing over the potential for a good hunt. But based on how he acted today, an exception to this might be a Peigt hunt. It's hard to imagine his little cuddly face is the same face that terrorizes his prey and rips off their heads.

On the other hand, Tahoe is lovely...though at first, she's a little scary-looking because she's so big and strong, and her movements are so powerful. She's as gentle as my pet rabbit but not as messy. She's a two-year-old Wild Mustang horse who doesn't age, with a face as cute as a model and a mouth that's all lips. Her face resembles a stick pony I had when I was about two years old, which I called Tahoe. I used to ride Tahoe into my dad's bank and park her next to the post at the head of the teller line. Tahoe is gifted with the flexibility and strength to stand on her hind legs while her forelegs transform into arms and her forehooves transform into hands. This makes her about thirteen feet tall with about a fifteen-foot reach. Unfortunately, such anatomical adaptations are more the rule than the exception for palimals in Spooner Pond.

"Ah, that ol' flat-tailed chub's bin afta me since I took him ta Big Woods with me," Kitty Joe said.

"The time the Roogers caught him?" Tahoe asked.

"Xactly."

"Well, I'm worried about the same thing," Tahoe said, her eyes opening wide. "And you shouldn't be taking Pippy with you either."

"Dat 'ol Benny's slower dan honey drippin' from a spoon, and da Roogers were all over him in no time. Was amusin' seein' ol' Benny less than four inches tall!"

"That's mean, Kitty Joe," I said, scolding him for how he laughed at Benjamin Beaver. Of course, I had no idea what the Roogers were, so I had no real idea what Tahoe was talking about.

"Aw, nobody ever hurt Benny, Pippy," Kitty Joe explained. "We were just funnin' with him."

"Well, we don't need any funnin' with Pippy or me by the Roogers," Tahoe insisted.

"Don't worry. All we hafta ta do is git by da Big Woods Area far sunrise. Da Roogers'll be sleepin'. They sleep more than da Peigts, and 'sides, dey won't take on a horse, and remember sunrise in the Wooded Forest is always an hour later than here 'cause a da tall trees. C'mon..."

"Don't think so, K.J. I'm slow in Big Woods. If they catch me, I don't know what to do."

"Yar way too fast to git caught, Tahoe! And yur a jumper."

"But speed doesn't matter in the Big Woods; it's not the same."

"Roogers catch Kitty Joe, Tahoe, and Pippy? Don't think so," Kitty Joe bragged. "Don't worry, Tahoe; I don't think dey'd be interested in ya or Pippy. Yar too big and yar quick, and Pippy will ride ya. I'll swat 'em away before dey git ta yar ankles. And 'sides, if dey caught us, we'd only be miniatures fur a day."

"Hey, wait a minute, you two," I protested. "What are you talking about? I keep hearing about these Peigts, which I don't understand, and now Roogers. What *is* all this?"

Just then, Feathers glided down to join us. "Let me explain, Pips, before those two drive you crazy with their bantering, and don't let K.J. fool you: the Roogers can mess up your plans for the day, Pips."

"A bite on your ankle from a Rooger," Feathers began, "causes you to shrink to ninety percent of your size in seconds. And it'll be twenty-four hours until you're back to normal after being shrunk."

"What?" I said, unable to imagine something so awful in this magical place. "Not in Spooner Pond!"

"Oh yes, very much so in Spooner Pond, but the Roogers live only in the Big Woods Area of the Wooded Forest."

"Truggles never told me about creatures like Roogers. Are they big?"

"Big, huh," Feathers laughed. "They're scrawnier than I am. They're like a miniature Kitty Joe with fur like a cheetah, but it's hard to get away from them once Roogers are awake and get you in their sights. And they're swift and clever in the foggy darkness of the Big Woods! But their bite's not poisonous. It's that way for the first twenty hours; you're shrunk and awake. After that, you can't sleep even if you try. It's most dangerous right after fourteen hours because you start groggy, your mind wanders, and you can't think clearly to avoid predators."

"Sounds scary, K.J. Why would you expose us to that?"

"Ats nothin' to git bit by a Rooger. Ya just has ta fund a suitable place ta sleep off da last four hours of shrinkin.'"

"He's right, Pippy," Tahoe added, "but you need to know that the only times they can't bite you are before sunrise and after sunset."

"Well, I suppose I should be thanking you, Feathers," I smiled as I petted my little palimal.

"Yaws all warry too much. A Peigt breakfast is worth it? Think 'bout ten or so plump yum yums. C'mon, it'll be a game fur us. Kinda like sleep and seek; while dey're sleepin', we'll seek 'em wherever dey hides."

"Gross," I said.

"I don't eat Peigts, and I don't want to get shrunken by a Rooger," Tahoe insisted.

"Furgit the Roogers. Haf ya ever bin snipped by one?"

"No, but I am not interested in Peigts."

"Hey, wait," I pleaded. "Peigts? You're serious about eating them, K.J.?"

"Yes, I ates 'em all da time."

"But in front of us?"

"If ya wants."

"No, I don't want to, but I do want to know what these Peigts are," I demanded.

"Will you explain, Feathers?" Tahoe asked.

"Yes, please do," I encouraged.

"Peigts live in South Sideways or Bad East Daisy," Feathers explained.

Feathers stared at me for a moment and then advised me to sit while he explained Peigts to me.

"Peigts," he continued, "are actually baby Monpeigts. The Monpeigts of Second Level Earth are a culture of humanlike philosophers with advanced mental powers, but the Peigts of Spooner Pond are more like Monpeigt misfits stuck in time. They'll never become grown-up Monpeigts; they have short lives and look like chubby grasshoppers. Twenty years ago, seven Peigts were stolen from Monpeigt Chambers, Second Level Earth, during a leadership conflict."

"Wait, wait..." I stopped him. "What? Second Level Earth? And what...are you like the expert historian on Spooner Pond? You're like a brain stuck in a mouse's body, not a bird."

"Silly Pips. All of us in Spooner Pond know these things, and one day you may, too, but few of us speak of them."

"It will come to you eventually, Pippy," Tahoe advised.

Kitty Joe jumped down from the side of Tahoe's feeding coral and faced us, standing on the straw-covered floor. "Okay, okay, I likes their crunchiness. Now ya two got a minute ta decide if yar comin' and den I gotta git'"

Tahoe leaned down to nudge him with her snout.

"No nasty nostril drippins," said Kitty Joe.

"Okay, one lick and I'm outa here. Ya two comin'?"

"You're crazy, K.J.," Tahoe said as she lapped her tongue on his head. This caused Kitty Joe to jump off three legs instead of four, holding his right foot knee-high for style like a pointer dog.

"Crazy as da sun is, yella," Kitty Joe laughed. "Yup; 'spect ta git thar by 7:30 far da sun rises."

"Pippy?" Kitty Joe said as he looked to me for an answer.

"I've got to get to school."

"Whataya thinks, Tahoe, can we pause time far Pippy if she wants ta go?"

"I suppose, but..."

"But what? Pause time?" I asked. "What are you two up to?"

"I say, pause time and send her off with K.J.," Feathers said. "He'll take care of her. Or we'll string tie him to Flying Tree."

"So, it is," Tahoe said.

At that moment, a bright flash of light filled out the surroundings. It sort of tickled at first, and then everything seemed quiet. I grinned as I knew it had been paused for me. This was unbelievable, but I was overjoyed by not having to leave and go to school then. I was free to go with Kitty Joe into the Wooded Forest.

At the time, I couldn't explain how they could pause time like that, but I later learned whenever two or more palimals got together and appealed to High Stones, a feat like pausing time was possible. So this would be the first of many days the palimals frozen time for me—just another bit of magic this fantastic world had revealed to me.

CHAPTER FIVE

Kitty Joe's Incredible Adventure

Leaving Tahoe behind at Benjamin's Boardwalk, which we crossed without hesitation or surprise, Kitty Joe and I hurriedly struck the Big Woods Area. It was still pre-sunrise in the Big Woods Area. Purple light glimmered in the trees, and the most beautiful mist rose from the ground as the morning warmed. We made it through without seeing a Rooger, though I hoped we would. I wasn't worried because even if I got nipped by a Rooger, I'd never miss a minute back home in North Star Ridge with time paused. Traveling at Kitty's hurried pace, South Sideways is a twenty-minute walk from the Big Woods Area.

Making a great time, we strolled into South Sideways, a little village near the Wooded Forest. On our short walk, I learned this was the only place in Spooner Pond where visitors could harvest treasures and keep them when they leave Spooner Pond. The tallest ferns in South Sideways looked at least twenty, although most seemed about four to ten feet tall. I'm sure the lushness of the green ferns was because it was kind of wet, and as Kitty Joe explained, it was lit with slivers of sunshine peeking through during the day. Our target was the baby ferns growing at the base of the giant ferns. This was what he referred to as "Me huntin' zone!"

Two creeks ran through South Sideways from deep-flowing springs that begin and end in South Sideways. There's the slow-flowing Sipping Creek that provides tasty refreshments for the thirsty. I also saw Three Dip Creek, a fast-flowing, crystal clear, and shallow pool; its bottom was full of precious gems and stones.

We peered into Triple Dip Creek, and to my amazement, there were thousands of them. These multi-shaped and multi-colored stones were called Wonder Stones, and beautiful designs ran through them. I became fixated on these, whatever they were, and I'm not sure Kitty Joe was too excited about my fascination.

"What's the special thing about the Wonder Stones, Kitty Joe?" I asked. "I remember Truggles mentioning them by name once, but that's all I remember."

"Dey mighty if worn in da correct orda."

"Mighty?" I wondered.

"Powars, Pippy, big powars!"

"But they have to be worn in a certain order?" I asked.

"Orda, yep. Ya needs ta talk ta Granny."

"Grandma goat?"

"Dat's right. Now, c'mon. I gots ta ate."

We stepped over to Sipping Creek. I drank a belly full of the tasty water and sat to rest. In anticipation of a Peigt breakfast, Kitty Joe drank sparingly to quench his thirst and eyed the area around him as if scouting for hunting quarry. And that's all I remember.

I think I fell asleep because the next time I saw Kitty Joe, he had just started telling a rather incredible story. Bleary-eyed and confused, I did my best to snap awake and listen as I sat by the stream. I wondered if something about the water had caused me to pass out. My head felt swimmy, and I could have returned to sleep. But Kitty Joe was right at the story's start, and I had never seen him so excited.

"...and as I was drinking, an invisible force grabbed hold of my shoulder, and I heard a voice, '*Joe Kitty, call out for the children!*'

"I bolted to my left, away from the sipping creek, and tried to shake off what seemed to be an intruder. Then, with quick, sharp movements, I spun around to the right and left, looking for the voice's origin and finding nothing. I approached the sipping creek again, thinking it had something to do with my dizziness while gazing into the water. I began to drink from the creek again, stopping every couple of sips from looking around, thinking I might see the intruder...if there was one."

He continued, "I don't know what was more stunning, the absence of Kitty Joe's idiolect or the more adult voice that seemed to grip Kitty Joe as he told his story." Undoubtedly, he had a dramatic shift in his language skills, and I listened with amazement as he continued to share his most incredible adventure. Whatever haziness had come over me from drinking the water was gone. I was enthralled with his story.

"I couldn't get the sounds of the voice out of my head. *Joe Kitty? The children?* I wondered. I wasn't Joe Kitty; the voice must have mixed me up with someone else.

"'*All my children who have come here to find peace, Joe Kitty,*' the voice spoke to me as if answering my thoughts."

"I didn't hear any voices," I said.

"You were asleep, Pippy. Out of it!" Kitty Joe said.

"Where did the voice come from, and what did it sound like?" I asked.

He answered, "A deep male voice had to come from the air. I peered around and couldn't find a soul, but I didn't imagine that something had a hold of me. I could not move. My shoulder was in a vice grip, and the deep male voice continued talking to me.

"'*Speak to the children, Joe Kitty,*' the voice commanded.

"I demanded he let me go, and I tried to wiggle free of the grip, but I couldn't see.

"'*Speak to the children as their friend, Joe Kitty.*'

"'Hey, let me go!' I protested. 'My name is Kitty Joe. I'm a hunter. I don't like many children—sorry, Pippy—and I want you to let me go!' I demanded, trying to squirm free only to become more frustrated. 'Besides, I'm here today for Peigts.'

"'*Forget the Peigts,*' the voice said as it gripped me more. '*The children need you, Joe Kitty, and you must speak to them. It is your time,*' the voice said. '*Now, call out to the children of Spooner Pond.*'

"'But lots of children are allergic to cats,' I challenged the voice.

"'*Indeed, but you are not calling out to children's bodies, but to their spirits. call out to them.*' The voice paused.

"'*Now!*' the voice demanded, and the pressure on my shoulder was released."

"Did the voice scare you, Kitty Joe?" I wondered.

"I wasn't exactly scared, but I was shaken by the power of the voice, yet also relieved that my shoulder was free of its grip. So, Pippy, I called out your name, followed by Sarah's and Howie's, two of your friends."

"Not so fast, Kitty Joe," I protested. "Howie's not my friend, though he'd like to be friendly with me. I'm not sure about him yet."

"I shall remember that," Kitty Joe nodded.

"Back to my story, Pippy. The voice wouldn't let up. It commanded me, again and again, '*No, no! Call out to the spirits of children who are not here in body. They congregate here, eager to hear from you!*' And then it paused and ordered me: '*And no more Peigts...Ever!*'

"They'd been fighting words twenty minutes ago, but instead of arguing, I stepped away from the creek and gazed skyward. I wondered for a moment what I had gotten into. I instinctively called out, 'Children of spirit, I'm here to be with you. I'm Kitty Joe.' And then I peered around, expecting some response.

"'Is that it?' I questioned the voice.

"'*Ha, ha, ha,*' the voice bellowed. '*You are a stubborn one. Now, be Joe Kitty, and you will be Joe Kitty hereafter when talking with the children. Trust me, ha ha ha,*' the voice tapered off. All was silent."

"And I was still asleep?" I added.

"Yep, but I was resisting the whole thing. I remember how my thoughts drifted to thinking, *What the heck, I'm Kitty Joe, and I'm going Peigt hunting*, but as if the voice knew all I was thinking, it responded in no uncertain terms. '*No Peigts! Now, call out to the children as Joe Kitty. Now!*'

"'Children of spirit,' I began, 'I am Joe Kitty. I am here to be with you. Here to listen to you. Here to speak to your troubled souls.' I stared at my paws and tail and wondered where the real Kitty Joe had gone.

"'*That is it, Joe Kitty. This is who you will be in south sideways, and at all times with troubled children. As Joe Kitty, you will have powers of discernment, language, and thought that will help the children. Call them again and be bold about it.*'

"'Children of spirit,' I said, 'I am Joe Kitty. I am here to be with you. Here to listen to you. Here to speak to your troubled souls.' And then, as I lifted myself, I rose elegantly, and he sat up and peered around, confident I'd have some response. But, instead, my thoughts of Peigts for breakfast in South Sideways were replaced with a chorus of children's voices.

"'Joe Kitty, it's Macey.'

"'Yo, Kitty, it's Gene.'

"'It's Mitch, Joe Kitty.'

"'Mr. Kitty, it's Annie.'

"'Don't I know you, Kitty Joe? It's Matt.'

"And I guess this was when I woke up because I remember hearing a young girl's voice say, 'Macey.' Although the body I was looking at when I awoke was Kitty Joe's, I wondered momentarily if it was Kitty Joe because of what I had heard him say.

"'Sometimes, Macey, when you're sad and feeling lonely, like you have no friends and your dad's hard on you, you have to remember there are a lot of other places you can be and still not lose your friends or battle with your dad. I had a dad who was very strict with me. So, you must decide when to take your spirit to another place during these tough times and concentrate on how you want to get there. We'll work on this later. The important thing is not to bomb out with your dad over things you won't even care about next week or month.'"

Ain't that the truth? I mumbled to myself.

"'Crying is just like laughing to your body, Gene—both release the energy in your muscles, providing comfort when you stop. Both are triggered by emotions that grab hold of your insides and can leave you exhausted. Even though laughing is more fun than crying, ways to cry can hurt less. For example, being called names at school is difficult to understand until you realize how desperate the kids are who are calling you names. They often think they must be tough in their own worlds. We can work this out so you don't have to be so afraid at school.'

"'No sense worrying about what happened last month, Matt; it's over with; it's history. Forgive your mother and remember that as bad as it was, until you learn to forget and forgive hurtful words, they will always steal your joy and happiness when you think about what she said. Otherwise, every time you see your mother, you will think about it and never realize she's trying hard to apologize for what she did because she's learning about you as you grow older.'"

There was a pause here, and I reached out to Kitty Joe. "Have you listened to yourself, Kitty Joe? You're pretty incredible."

"The words came out without thinking, Pippy, but I still look and feel like Kitty Joe."

"But all of those voices you talked to?" I marveled.

"I believe I was more surprised than you as I responded to the voices of the spirits of children now living in South Sideways. I have no idea how many children's spirits are here."

"You're just a kitty," I said.

"Yeah, I thought so before I got here. And now there's much I must learn about my new role in Spooner Pond as Joe Kitty, the listener, not Kitty Joe, the hunter."

"And it will be sad listening," I offered.

"Not sad if I am called to help and improve the sorrow and hurt in the wounded spirits of these troubled children, Pippy."

"This is nuts! You are not the Kitty Joe I walked into the Wooded Forest with today. You spoke to each of the children without hesitation, as if you were a counselor like Mrs. Sopher." So I said to my feline palimal, knowing he would never seem the same to me again. "I'm telling you, Kitty Joe, it was like you were talking to all my friends back in North Star Ridge."

"I appreciate your kind comments, Pippy, but I'm certain plenty of Kitty Joe is still left in me."

"Well, I think that's good."

"C'mon," he urged, "let's sip some water and chat before you get your first experience of Three Dip Creek."

The rest of the morning, Joe Kitty and I sat by Sipping Creek, drinking fresh, sweet water and talking about the spirits of children who had come to Spooner Pond. Through the voice he heard within, he learned, and through him, I learned about why children bring their troubled spirits to Spooner Pond and why South Sideways is their refuge. For as long as they stayed, we learned, their bodies back at home never seemed quite the same to their parents and friends. Parents and friends know something is wrong, yet they do not realize it, which results in their children and friends being spiritless. So, likewise, we learned that as long as troubled spirits remain in South Sideways, what is left at home are shells of the children's bodies and friends they once knew and loved, but not the children themselves.

"Time you visit Three Dip Creek, young lady, and harvest some treasures to return to North Star Ridge."

And I followed my feline friend to the alluring Three Dip Creek.

As we approached, I realized things were much easier to understand from Joe Kitty than Kitty Joe, as the former explained the mystery surrounding Three Dip Creek and the Wonder Stones.

"Three Dip Creek is a four-inch-thick bed of colorful treasures covered by six inches of frigid, fast-moving water. And frigid, Pippy, is no understatement," Joe Kitty smiled. "Fittingly, visitors are allowed only three reaches into the creek to gather treasures. However, I caution you to be precise in targeting treasures because the water is so cold and the current so rapid that your fingers will freeze if you haven't aimed well and aren't quick to harvest your treasures. Those who attempt a fourth reach learn the hard way as they writhe in pain—their hand slowly and agonizingly thaws out after being frozen stiff from making a fourth and forbidden dip into the creek.

"The Wonder Stones you seek are indeed those jagged oval bursts of melted multi-colored and shaped stones you identified, and they do make wonderful beads. Depending on their color arrangement and order, they are known to bestow variable powers, heightened sensory sensitivity, and discernment for those who wear them. The degree of these powers—and there may be other powers Grandma Goat would know about—is affected by how the Wonder Stones are ordered in a necklace."

"Impressive," I grinned and studied the bottom of the creek for several minutes, targeted my treasure hunt, and made three dips. I harvested a diamond for my mother, a gemstone for Sarah, and a variety of Wonder Stones I'd take to Grandma Goat.

CHAPTER SIX

A Colorful Outsider

One of the most fun times I had when Truggles took me to Spooner Pond was when he'd leave me to roam alone. It made me feel like he trusted me and wanted me to feel at home in this beautiful new world.

"Now, Pippy," he'd say, eyeing me with playful uncertainty, "Spooner Pond is huge and full of wonders. Many of them must be explored on your own, so I often go my way after bringing you here."

"So you're sort of like my tour guide?" I asked him one time.

"Exactly!"

I got this little speech many times. It was just so I wouldn't think he didn't care about me. I could tell he loved and wanted the best for me...but he also wanted me to get familiar with Spooner Pond.

So, on another of the occasions where Truggles whisked me into Spooner Pond and let me ramble on my own, I found myself poking around in the four-foot-high wildflowers along the pasture side of Wanderers' Trail. I thought a big ball of tightly grouped red-spotted yellow flower pedals was the head of an Outsider...or *one* of its *three* heads.

As soon as I touched it with my fingers, it released an explosion of misty vapor that engulfed me, leaving me wet yet unharmed. The creature must have been sleeping because it was twelve feet tall and fully extended after it arose. Two of its three heads looked like red-spotted yellow flowers, while the third looked like a yellow-spotted red flower. All three heads were perched atop a long, skinny brown neck, which protruded from the center of its earthy-looking, squatty body, held up by a bunch of caterpillar-like legs. As it stretched its neck and head to surround me, it began grumbling in some undistinguishable words. I noticed half of what I thought were pedals were tiny eyes, and half were little mouths.

Soon, I was dwarfed by this creature, and my confidence was a bit shaken because I knew I wasn't dreaming; hundreds of little mouths were about to set upon me from all sides. But brave as I was, I just closed my eyes and screamed Truggles' name.

"Be still," Truggles' voice commanded, and I opened my eyes to see my most important palimal alongside me, standing on his hind legs with his forelegs extended above his head. I had never seen Truggles look so majestic, and with his long golden hair complete and glistening in the sun and his massive frame anchored in the earth yet projected skyward, he towered over this creature.

Again, Truggles ordered the creature to be still, and it appeared to cower at the sound of his words. Truggles looked like he was twenty feet tall, though I knew I had to be imagining that; at the time, twenty feet was good.

The Outsider slithered away, and Truggles returned to all fours and grinned at me. "Mustn't wander too far off the trail, Pippy. At least not this close to the Outsiders Thwortal."

"Forget the Outsider," I said, grabbing onto Truggles and squeezing tightly. I was more panicky about the thought of sitting there in mid-air than about a three-headed Outsider jabbering at me in some unintelligible language in a shrill, ear-piercing voice.

Speaking calmly and with certainty, Truggles said, "Let go of me, Pippy."

"No way!"

"Have I ever let you down?"

I hesitated to answer as I watched the three-headed Outsider still jabbering away, wiggling deeper into the pasture.

"Have I?" Truggles asked again.

"Not yet."

"Have I not told you I will always be with you?"

"Yes," I answered slowly, recalling how impressive he looked, taking superiority over the Outsider. It had changed my sense of just how powerful he was.

"Believe in me, and let go of my body," he instructed. "It is okay. Sit next to me and enjoy what I shall give you in return for your trust."

I smiled at him and let go.

It felt like I was sitting on firm ground, only thirty feet off the ground, and there was no fear of falling.

Wow! It was like sitting on a cushion of air next to Truggles. Of course, this wasn't the first time I was suspended in the air with Truggles as we flew about Spooner Pond on my tours. But *always* holding onto him.

It was so impressive to be sitting there, overcoming my fear of heights and lacking trust in others by believing in Truggles.

"It is time for you, Pippy, to meet Au helpair," Truggles began. "Summon him with the command, 'Au helpair, Come Now,' and he will lift you from the ground you are standing and take you to a proper observational height wherever you are."

"Au helpair?" I asked.

"Yes, Au helpair—the one who now holds you safely off the ground. Always know the Au helpair is within your summons when I am not around in this area of Spooner Pond," Truggles said to me as he seemed to be fading away and becoming transparent.

"But Truggles," I called.

"The Au helpair will accommodate you; tell him with your thoughts or out loud where you want to go, and he will take care of the rest. When you're done, ask him to set you down. You can never see him, nor will he ever communicate with you, but he can always see you."

"Au helpair, Come Now?" I asked. "That's what I say?"

"Au helpair, Come Now, Pippy. Au helpair, Come Now." Truggles vanished, his voice trailing, and added: "And only in South and West Spooner Pond."

"Wait!" I demanded, and Truggles reappeared, and I asked. "What about that Outsider?"

"Silly girl, you were wafted by a Thagwin. Its snoofin' wouldn't have injured you here in Spooner Pond, but in its own land, its snoof paralyzes its victims while its three heads suck their bodies dry."

"You're joking."

"No joke," Truggles said, his image still only half complete like a ghost.

"Because of the bathing at Outsiders Thwortal?"

"Yes, it is why Outsiders must have the blue light." And with that final comment, Truggles was gone, and I sat there with Au helpair. It finally all sunk in—what Truggles had taught me about the bathing and all I had been taught about Outsiders was so true. They were everything but human or animal, at least as I understood humans and animals. And no question, the Thagwin gave me an adrenaline rush, and I found it somewhere I never expected to find in an Outsider.

So, I set off down the Wanderers' Trail airborne with Au helpair, and though the Outsiders were unpredictable and kind of strange, I learned there was no fear of them because of their "bathing" as they passed out of Outsiders Thwortal. During the bathing, they are immersed in an intense and blinding blue light that neutralizes their powers, except when they're in the place called Points Afar. So, snoofin' by the Thagwin was real, but the bathing had neutralized the potency of its snoof. Still kind of weird, though, because the minty-smelling wetness of the snoof stayed on me for a good thirty minutes.

The cacophony of sounds and physical antics among the Outsiders below me along Wanderers' Trail was befitting the festive bazaar-like atmosphere of the trail. The Outsiders jabbered away in their native languages, trading trinkets and treasures, with a few or more of them pushing and shoving their way through more crowded sections of the trail. At times, it seemed everyone was in a big hurry, and at other times, everyone seemed to be moving in slow motion.

I became fascinated by a group of four rather exciting characters who moved along at a deliberate pace, uninterested in communicating with other Outsiders. I followed them, sitting atop Au helpair, all the way to Spooner Stream. It's impossible to cross Spooner Stream, except by bridge, because it's full of slippery rocks over which the water rushes at a furious pace. From all I've been told, anyone who falls into Spooner Stream will be swept out into the Dark Seas, where there's no escape. There's no bridge across Spooner Stream where Wanderers' Trail ends, and its forty-foot width is enough to discourage all who encounter it.

Not that I should be bothered by such a thing. With the help of Au helpair, I was safe as could be, floating in the air and watching this fantastic world at work below me.

As much as I would have liked to figure out the secret of how to get to Spooner Pond, I couldn't. I always thought I'd find a key or some secret passageway to get me to Spooner Pond, but I never did. Calling on Truggles, either during my sleepless nights or more adventurous mornings, was all I had to do. He'd do the rest, including escorting me on my adventures...most of the time. And occasionally, this even included taking some friends along the way.

And now it seemed I was about to turn thirteen, and my life was changing. And that included making my friends more important to me than they had been before. I was in middle school. My long brown hair was longer, and the boys still chased after Sarah and me, only not so much in groups anymore. Although I had a series of fascinating experiences in Spooner Pond months earlier, I hadn't returned to Spooner Pond since I used the Au helpair to observe the Outsiders.

Time in Spooner Pond and North Star Ridge was getting exciting. I felt a tug from both worlds.

CHAPTER SEVEN

"Esiarp Eht Drol, on High Stones"

Ever since my dad's birthday in March, when we went to the movies and the attendant thought I was his date, this inner voice I'd never really paid much attention to before kept reminding me that my body was changing. It was time for me to be a teenager. I'd known it was coming, but it felt odd now that it was finally here.

If I protested the words my inner voice spoke, it would taunt me: *You're just a spectator; you're really not part of the action.*

I'm sure the voice was referring to Spooner Pond because even though I had great times, I was getting bored with Spooner Pond.

Yep, the voice would taunt and challenge me: *Oh, yes, you've heard mention of fabulous treasures and supernatural powers in High Stones, but have you ever been permitted to even go there or see these powers? So Truggles and the others want you to be a part of that world, or is it all a tease?*

I wasn't sure what to think. So far, it had all been a fun fantasyland and a strange fascination that I couldn't explain to anyone but my closest friends...and even they didn't believe me.

It was my thirteenth birthday, and Mom and Dad threw me a big party down by Taylor Creek, running alongside our backlot. There were tons of kids, lots of presents, and many boys showing off, but none as conspicuously as Howie Yeary. He made sure to make a spectacle of himself by jumping from the tire swing and diving into the overflowing creek.

I was exhausted when we returned to the house, and everyone had left. I went to bed at about 11:30; it wasn't how I had planned to spend the night of my thirteenth birthday, but Sarah and I had big plans the next day. All I could think about was being a teenager and wearing the fabulous new clothes I'd gotten for my birthday. We planned to go mall crawling.

I suppose it was habit by now, but after lying in bed and crunching up my pillow, I stared at the framed map of Spooner Pond I had drawn six years earlier. It hung on my north-facing bedroom wall. For so long, I had to keep Spooner Pond a secret; as big as it was, it didn't seem to matter anymore. So that night, as I closed my eyes and my thoughts wandered to our Saturday plans, I figured I was finished with Spooner Pond... forever.

***

At about 11:50 that evening, I woke up to the feeling of slime on my cheeks. Wiping it away, I saw Truggles preparing to plant another big, sloppy dog kiss on me. I jumped up from my bed, half-tempted to slap him, but instead, I threw my arms around his neck and squeezed him. I was so happy as I ran my fingers through his long, soft, furry neck.

Suddenly, I noticed my bedroom door was wide open. I gasped.

"You broke the rules!" I said, breaking away from Truggles to close the door. "We're not in Spooner Pond, are we?"

"Weeellll...yes to the first part, and no to the second." He tilted his head and got this sheepish look on his face. It was the same expression he wore when feeling guilty or shy about something.

"You said you'd never be in my world," I reminded him.

"Over the years, that was always true."

I poked him in the rib cage and peered up at him, "And so, what? So now it's no longer true?"

"A bit feisty as a thirteen-year-old," he chuckled.

"Stop that," I laughed and then grabbed him for another long hug as we chuckled. We stared at the map of Spooner Pond and reminisced for a while before he lifted me away from him.

"It's so much more, Pippy, isn't it?"

"I don't know what you mean," I said.

"It's now time," he said. In a swift motion, he placed a spectacular black fire opal ring on my right index finger. "You'll now have access to Spooner Pond on your own, day or night," he said. "It will become as much of your world as you choose."

I couldn't believe it. I wanted to scream with joy. And just a few days ago, I'd been worried that I might be done with Spooner Pond.

"No more calling to let you know when I want to visit?" I asked.

"No. It won't be necessary. You're on your own, Pippy, and ready to become one of us. And I mean it...you're free to come and go as you please and to bring whomever you choose to

Spooner Pond. Your only restriction is that only you and three others can fit through the Thwortals simultaneously."

"Thwortals?" I wondered.

"Without me, the only way you can get into Spooner Pond is through the Thwortals. So, happy birthday, young lady," he said, almost to himself. "Now you can experience Spooner Pond." It was my imagination, but I thought he was crying a bit as he said this.

"Hey, Truggles, are those tears I see in your eyes?"

"Who, me? No, it's just the air here in North Star Ridge."

I knew he was lying. For some reason, he was crying...and that meant the world to me.

"Ready, Pippy? Want me to show you how the ring works?"

"*Very* ready," I replied with eager anticipation.

"There are four Thwortals you can use to get to Spooner Pond," he explained. "North, South, East, and West Thwortals. Each leads to a different Spooner Pond area. You might want to mark them on your map. My instructions are the same for all Thwortals, but you must say which Thwortal you intend to use when you travel to Spooner Pond."

"From wherever you are, whether alone or in the presence of two or more, close your eyes and place the palm of your left hand over your ring. Then, with your eyes closed, speak these words exactly this way: *Esiarp eht Drol, on High Stones*—then, name the Thwortal."

"That's it?" I asked. "So, all I have to do is say Esiarp eht Drol, on High Stones...North Thwortal, and I'd go to the North Thwortal?"

"Perfect! But you travel some distance through the North Thwortal to its exit in Spooner Pond."

"Is it a long journey?"

Truggles laughed. "It's so fast you can't even measure it with your sense of time."

"Wow," I thought aloud. "But what if I forget the words?"

"Your palm over the ring will ensure you remember the words, but *only you*. And you must keep your eyes closed." He spoke with careful, practiced words.

"And why?"

"Because an explosion of bright light will temporarily blind you if you don't."

"And that's all there's to it to get to Spooner Pond?" I said, half disappointed it wasn't more spectacular.

"A lot less complicated than how you got there before," he nudged me with his tail, knocking me off my feet.

"Hey, cool it with the rear end!"

"I'm not quite used to working in these confined spaces."

"Yeah, I can tell. Be sure to duck if you go through the doorway."

"Funny..."

"So," I wondered, "Can others use this ring?"

"Yes. But only after..."

"Only after what?" I asked anxiously.

"It's an 'only after' you'll have to find out on your own, Pippy. And once you do, you'll be well on your way to High Stones."

High Stones. Whenever I heard the words High Stones, a chill ran through me, sometimes causing me to shiver. But in a good way.

I gazed at my beautiful golden-haired friend for a moment, staring him up and down, and then asked what before then was the unthinkable, "How about you give me a quick guided tour of the Threshold to High Stones so I can see if all this is worth the trade-off?"

"Trade-off?"

"You know, the trade-off between being thirteen and wild or spending my extra time in Spooner Pond and High Stones."

"Hmmm…I've never received such a request. Most just want to tour High Stones to see if it's worth working to achieve it. But, unfortunately, not all who are allowed to earn their way to High Stones choose to do so." He paused for a moment, thinking. "Still, Pippy, asking to see the Threshold to High Stones without earning it is ambitious and a good part of why you've been called. Your ambition and bravery make you quite special…among other things."

"So you'll do it?"

He looked me over very carefully, and a big grin appeared. "I'll think about it," he said. "Let's see how you handle Esiarp eht Drol on High Stones."

***

I'm sure you've already figured out that trade-off or no trade-off; I immediately experimented with the black fire opal ring, and it worked. However, I found a tickling little chill in my head along with the bright light Truggles had mentioned. It was sort of like the feeling of standing next to a stereo speaker when the bass is turned all the way up.

I did pretty well on my own in Spooner Pond but found there was a lot I didn't know about it. So, I looked under my toy chest and found a copy of my first map of Spooner Pond and updated it, leaving the original drawing framed and hanging on my bedroom wall. I figured an updated map would be essential for preparing people to accompany me to Spooner Pond.

After updating the physical features and sites in Spooner Pond, I marked the four Thwortals with their appropriate compass distinctions: N, S, E, and W.

The *North Thwortal* is located in Rock Castle Mountain, a mountain made entirely of multicolored, oddly shaped rocks and hide-away rocks that can swallow up passersby who lean against them. Spiraling throughout Rock Castle Mountain are light-speckled tunnels formed by the random configuration of jagged-edged rocks dripping water. Then, there are more rounded tunnels that are dry yet so dark you can't see in front of you. Instead, you must touch the walls and sides with your hands as you listen to the voices in the tunnel walls and smell your way through the tunnels. Still, these tunnels are the quickest way to escape Rock Castle Mountain.

Not too far away is Hot Pond, where the water temperature is 101 degrees…36 degrees hotter than the average outside temperature of the northern area of Spooner Pond. The constant heat creates a steamy mist that gathers over the Hot Pond. All around its circumference is abundant growth of large exotic flowers, brilliant bushy shrubs, and a ring of thirty-foot-high trees protecting the area from winds and weather. Occasionally, you can see spouts of water swirl up out of the center of the high trees, making it look like a giant fountain. Depending on the light, the waterspouts can leave rainbow-like impressions in the skies over Hot Pond. It's also the only place in Spooner Pond where you can pick and eat sweet and juicy lulu berries, or what Sarah calls 'happy berries' because eating them makes you laugh.

Another option off North Thwortal is Back Trail—one of only two paths to the Threshold of High Stones, which I hope to visit with the transport powers of my ring this year.

The *South Thwortal* leads to the quaint but unspectacular homes of resident palimals and the area where Truggles and I spent most of our time. It's also the closest to the *Outsiders Thwortal*, where non-humans and non-palimals enter Spooner Pond. I've identified it on my map with an "O" mark. Quite a bit to the Northwest from the South Thwortal is Spooner Stream.

To the southeast, there's High Pass—a protective barrier between East and West Spooner Pond for all but those who can fly high over the Pass. High Pass is a steep mountain high-lighted by large columns of snow-covered rock that reach into the clouds. Further down the mountain are slippery and erratic sand and gravel slopes and large areas of dense tree growth. I'm not sure why the palimals stay away from High Pass.

The *East Thwortal* is the most frequently used. It's the warm-est area in Spooner Pond and the preferred way to the Flower Forest and its Bad Daisy East section, where giant honeysuckle flowers are two hundred and fifty times more significant than average—that's five feet across at the opening! It's also the oth-er home to the Peigts.

The East Thwortal is also the easiest way to get to a three-di-mensional maze leading to the southern entrance to the Pine-nut Forest, a place full of giant butterflies averaging sixteen inches across and ten inches tall. Finally, the East Thwortal is also the primary approach to Courage Cave, where I've yet to be, and one of the two ways to get to the Threshold of High Stones.

The *West Thwortal* is the least used entry to Spooner Pond because it dumps you on the outskirts of the Wooded Forest at a point that's not very appealing. Also, I wouldn't use it to get to the Wooded Forest or Benjamin's Boardwalk alone because I don't think you'd want to go to either place alone.

I don't know what's on the outer boundary of the Wooded Forest. Still, every time I ventured into the Wooded Forest on a northwest approach, I was scared away by eerie sounds and dark shadow creatures that seemed to dart in and out of the trees without identifying themselves.

You've got to go through the Big Woods Area of the Wooded Forest to get to Points Afar, just like Kitty Joe and I did to get to South Sideways and Three Dip Creek. Big Woods Area is the size of two soccer fields and twice as long, with hundreds of oaks, madrones, eucalyptus, giant redwood, and sequoia-like trees. I say 'like' trees because they look like trees all right, but they have eyes, and I'm sure some actually talk. I've heard them make sounds but have yet to engage them in conversation. All they do is stare at me and coo and whistle as I walk by. They're as old as Spooner Pond itself, and I'm sure they know a lot more about Spooner Pond than most of my palimals.

CHAPTER EIGHT

Which Was Worse for Sarah—Mannerstrom or Menacingly Tall Rocks?

A month or so after I started traveling to Spooner Pond on my own, Truggles agreed to take me on a tour of the Threshold of High Stones, and it was one I'd long remember because of this surge of confidence in my abilities. I decided to take someone else to Spooner Pond...someone I knew very well and wanted to share it with...Sarah.

Even though Sarah's a total sass freak when she doesn't get her way, she's my best friend, and as best friends, we can sass each other, which doesn't mean a darn thing. We share everything but our hairbrushes. With her long and dark brown hair, we don't like to mix the hair fibers, though we'd do about anything for each other in a pinch. Having known each other since pre-school, it's almost like we're sisters, though she's got glistening brown skin year-round, and I'm a bit fair with freckled tans in the summer.

I hate to admit it at times, but we're both princesses. Our moms are both doubting and suspicious, and our dads are golfing buddies, but that's another story. Have you ever lived with a golfing dad? What about golfing parents? It's golf this, golf that, golf ball light switches, golf club coat racks, golf cart mailboxes, golfing calendars—you name it. I suppose it's the same with tennis parents or parents who have horses, parents who love baseball, or football fanatic parents.

I've always suspected that Spooner Pond exists to get kids away from their sometimes-obnoxious parents. And I figured it was time to share that with Sarah one Saturday afternoon when our parents were golfing, and she came over.

***

"Pippy, my mom went crazy on me," Sarah began. "She wants to send me away to a prissy boarding school next year to straighten me out. She says I'm getting out of control."

"I told you parents were weird. So where does she want to send you, Mannerstrom?" I chuckled. I was already nervous and anxious about what I would introduce her to.

"Yeah, how'd you know?" Sarah asked.

"I'm sure she talked to Mrs. Sopher. That's where she told my parents they might want to consider sending me six years ago before she and I talked, and then no more mention of Mannerstrom."

"Yeah, like you're so much more perfect now," she grinned and asked, "Did your mom ever really consider sending you to Mannerstrom?"

"Yep, at first. I think Mrs. Sopher used to teach there."

"Well, there's no way I'm going to a prissy prison, and there's no way I'll give up cleats for saddle shoes," Sarah said matter-of-factly.

"They have sports at Mannerstrom, Sarah," I smiled.

"What, horseshoes?"

"No, croquet," I chuckled.

We started laughing at ourselves and knew we had had enough of this Mannerstrom talk. It took only a glance between us to know it was time for adventure...someway through the North Thwortal.

"So...Sarah...you know that place I've told you about? The magical place that I can—"

"Oh, no...not more of this Spooner Pond talk."

I smiled, able to contain myself, "What if I could show it to you?"

"You've *shown* me the map," she said, rolling her eyes.

"No, no...just...do you trust me?"

"Of course I do."

"Come here." I extended my hand to her, and she took it with ease. There was a weird, uncertain look in her eyes.

"What are you d—"

I interrupted her with: *"Esiarp eht Drol, on High Stones."*

My room was replaced by that brilliant flash of light. And after that, I never had any problems with Sarah not believing my stories of Spooner Pond.

***

"It's cold here today, Pippy; I want to go back!"

Sarah looked quite scared as we stood on the main trail through Rock Castle Mountain, surrounded by six menacingly tall rocks.

"Okay, maybe I didn't pick the best Thwortal," I said. "Just hang in there a bit longer." I wasn't upset at all. After all, she was having to process a lot. She'd just learned I had a magical ring that could transport me to Spooner Pond...a place she thought was just in my imagination until a few minutes ago.

"But what about..." Sarah said, pointing at the movement of the rocks behind me. "Let's go back home, Pippy. This is...this... I want my mom."

"What? Don't be silly. Come on and follow me. Ignore the rocks."

"Where are we going?"

"No place like Hot Pond on a Mannerstrom kind of day," I chuckled.

"You are sure, Pippy? This is...this is *crazy!*"

I glared at Sarah, much like the glances I gave her when we were about to pull a prank at school. "Come on, silly, it'll be fun."

And off we went. I led as Sarah followed behind me, constantly whining about returning to North Star Ridge. But when I heard Sarah start whimpering—which was *not* something Sarah typically did—I figured maybe I had pushed things too far.

I turned around and stopped to assess the situation. There was no doubt about it; the tall rocks had followed us along the trail and were now moving in on us.

"Ugh," I said, a bit scared myself now. "Hooded Ones."

"Hooded Ones?" Sarah wondered with a frightened look in her eyes.

"I think so. Or maybe just hide-away rock."

"I just want to go home," Sarah complained.

"Look, we're okay as long as we avoid touching them. Hide-away rocks don't come after you. Only when you touch them will they swallow you up, and I don't know what happens then."

"Terrific, Pippy," Sarah said as she clung to me and examined the now weirdly configured boulders, "let's just go back."

I had seen this stuff before and wasn't too worried, except I had always been with Truggles. There really wasn't much in Spooner Pond that Truggles feared, so I figured I could be as brave as him. So I surveyed the boulders, pointed the finger at them, and ordered them to leave us alone.

In response, the earth beneath our feet shook as one of the most prominent rock columns appeared to hop off the ground. Soon, the other rocks did indeed jump up, creating a mild trembling and rocking of the earth on which we stood. We locked arms and held on to each other as we swayed back and forth. Suddenly, the tall rocks appeared to become spongy with each jump. Instead of crumbling and falling apart, they were transformed into at least two dozen flatter, rounded boulders that fell like a rain shower, forming a bouncing ring around us.

"*Pippy...*" Sarah cried.

"Don't let them control you!" I hollered over the din of the bouncing rocks that were settling on the earth. "You're doubting everything and getting weird on me." I stared her in the eye. "Don't worry. Remember, Truggles will protect us."

"*Who?*"

I'd told her about Truggles before, but that had been back when she didn't believe me. But I don't have that problem now.

The rocks were behaving more aggressively than a hideaway rock might be, so I leaned over to one of the boulders that had come to a rest and smelled it with only one nostril, then the other nostril.

"What are you doing?" Sarah asked.

"Sniffing out Hooded Ones. The only way to identify Hooded Ones who've inhabited objects is by sniffing for their skunk-like smell." It was one of many lessons Truggles had explained in my early days of coming to Spooner Pond, back when I was just as clueless as Sarah. "I know it's weird, Sarah, but Hooded Ones can twist your thoughts to get you to believe what you don't believe and doubt what you had always known to be true."

"So," she cried, "are these rocks Hooded Ones?"

I stared at her, hugged my best friend, and shook my head. "No, I don't think so. Now come on...we'll be okay."

"Okay. But...what are Hooded Ones?"

"It's hard to explain. But it doesn't matter because I'm pretty sure those boulders are a bunch of mischievous adolescent MOTs, and we haven't the time for them."

"MOTs?" Sarah asked.

"MOTs...Monitors of Temptation," I said, pulling her close. "Shake it off; they're playing with you. Think about it: We're wearing shorts, and the air is colder than average; the tall rocks seem mean; the reshaped rocks blend with the boulders we sit on; you were happy, then scared and whining like a baby. So, forget the boulders; they're just playing with our thoughts."

"But..." Sarah began before I cut her off.

"Shhhh," I motioned to her, then whispered, "Let me show you this other trick I learned from Truggles when dealing with teenage MOTs." *Truggles, where are you?* I thought. It wasn't until then, with a friend in Spooner Pond, that I realized just how important Truggles was.

"Now, check this out, Sarah."

I bent over to admire a long walking stick lying among other sticks by the trail. Extending my hand toward the walking stick, I thought, *Dad would love this.*

"Don't!" Sarah screamed.

"But we need it," I insisted as I inched closer to the stick. "I need this stick."

"What do we do with it?" Sarah asked.

I winked. "Just follow my lead."

We paced, holding hands and talking about boys we knew back home. I know it was silly to talk about such things at the moment, but it did seem to keep Sarah calm. I spoke about Mr. Obnoxious, Howie Yeary, who I both liked and found disgusting, and Sarah talked about Louis, Emily's little brother, who had a crush on her...at eleven years old!

We kept strolling along the trail as MOTs tried to match our every step to maintain a circle around us. I glanced an active interest at that walking stick every so often, reminding Sarah that the MOTs were trying to listen to every thought we had, though teenage MOTs were pretty sloppy listeners.

I gazed at a clump of flowers, a rarity on this trail, and then at another gadget dropped by a visitor on the run, continuing my chatter with Sarah. Then, as quickly as possible, I let go of Sarah's hand and used the walking stick, and without a moment of hesitation, I started tickling one of the flattened boulders.

"Grab one, Sarah. Tickle the boulders!" I hollered.

Sarah gave me a funny look at first but joined me. In fact, she became quite a swashbuckler, using her stick like a sword fighting with the boulders, and she had a few brave jabs with her feet.

"Nothing's happening," she said, laughing, "but I'm tickling the tar outta these rocks."

"Just keep at 'em," I encouraged her.

"What if we're wrong?" Sarah asked.

"Just keep tickling," I ordered, thinking *I better be right.*

I don't remember if it was another two or ten minutes later that the first of the rocks we were tickling began groaning, but I know our arms were tired. But as soon as the grumbling started with one of the rocks, Sarah was tickling, stabbing, and slashing, and the other boulders began groaning. Within seconds, we felt the earth rumble, and the boulders started bouncing several inches into the air as we continued tickling our two. Some jumped as high as four feet, but we kept tickling them, letting our sticks do some boulder dancing. It wasn't long before their boulder forms grew spongy again, our sticks sinking into them with every tickle. Then they swallowed up our sticks and rose tall again.

For just a moment, they towered over us.

"Yikes," Sarah said.

"Oh boy," I said, peering up at this menacing group of MOTs, thinking for a moment I had goofed...badly.

Then, poof, they were gone, vanishing as if they had never been there; I wondered if the rocks could *have been illusions?*

"The MOTs are ticklish?" Sarah said with a look that could be described as only incredulity.

"That's right," I said. "But you must believe your tickling power is greater than the MOTs' will to control your thoughts, or they will forever control your thoughts."

"Is it that you have to be patient and persistent?" Sarah said.

"Not exactly. You have to believe in the power of *your* will over *their* will. And you cannot doubt the power of your belief, but if I remember, this only works on MOTs when they have possessed earthbound objects like rocks, trees, sticks, water—this kind of stuff, or when they have materialized earthbound objects."

"Okay." She dusted off her clothes and said, "But...they just disappeared..."

"Seems that way, huh?" I said. I put my arm around Sarah's shoulder and hugged her, "Precisely. Come on, let's go, MOT tamer."

I wasn't sure how this worked, but the MOTs *had* vanished. Saying you believe in something yet feeling you can't believe it until it's proven to you will never work in Spooner Pond. If I've learned anything in Spooner Pond, it's the most powerful beliefs Truggles has taught me and that I just trusted to be true even though I couldn't know they were true.

One of these beliefs was how to overcome the effect of MOTs, though doing so with teenage MOTs is, I'm sure, a lot easier with mature MOTs. Unlike the adolescent MOTs, mature MOTs were serious evil spirits with no bodies and no form that could possess you—really get inside you, but only if they could establish direct physical contact with you. That's why they read your thoughts, create and inhabit objects you desire, and then try to tempt you to touch them. If you feel the objects, the MOTs enter you at that point, and they control your emotions from the inside.

I think even then, at the age of thirteen, I was beginning to understand that Spooner Pond was more than just a place for adventures; it was teaching me so much about myself at the same time.

And I was happy to have a friend to share it with...a friend who didn't think I was nuts whenever I spoke about Spooner Pond.

CHAPTER NINE

A Helio Wrap for Sarah

After a while, Sarah became a Spooner Pond pro. Truggles would stay with us most of the time, keeping us close by. Sarah adored Truggles just as much as I did, and I think the feeling was mutual. After Sarah had made a few visits and gotten used to the place, Truggles allowed us to explore a bit on our own—a sure sign he trusted her just as much as he trusted me.

On Sarah's eighth visit, one such occurrence was on 'Ol Big Flat Rock. Or maybe it was the tenth. I honestly started to lose count after a while.

"I've never seen so many lulu berries looking so fat," Sarah said as she stood on 'Ol Big Flat Rock, a rather gigantic rock formation that shoots out of the ground just above the lulu berry fields.

"I know," I said, "They're looking juicy today, and you know what that means."

"Maniac giggles!" Sarah laughed.

"Hallelujah!" I said, and we ran down into the fields. A good dose of lulu berries was an excellent way to forget about almost anything.

Sarah took the lead, and I followed. She first went to the field section where the brilliant, bright red, yellow-striped plum-sized lulu berries grew. "Going for the peanut butter taste?" I teased.

"Yeah, peanut butter and chocolate, with a bit of honey thrown in," she said as she filled one of her pockets with brilliant, bright red, yellow-striped, plum-sized lulu berries that tasted like ground peanut butter. Next, she ran over to pick a handful of white and purple spotted lulu berries that tasted like the sweetest and most decadent milk chocolate, and then she skipped over to pick just three bright lime-green lulu berries that are known for their fruity honey flavor.

Next, it was my turn, and I went for one of my favorite licorice-flavored lulu berries. These blue-green, red-striped lulu berries taste sweet dark licorice, while the blue-green-orange-striped lulu berries taste great sweet red licorice. I filled my pockets with both, and Sarah and I went to dine on lulu berries under the welcoming tree at Hot Pond, where we sat on the grass and got silly eating these delicious happy berries.

Oh, did we ever get the giggles? After fifteen minutes of controlled eating, our feeding frenzy turned into a berry bashing. We smashed them between our hands to make lulu berry mush and fed ourselves the delightful mush using our hands as ladles. Mom would have died a million times seeing me eating like this, but then she's never had lulu berries. It didn't take long for Sarah and me to start spewing nose-tickling lulu bubbles that cause you to laugh yourself into hysteria for a good twenty or thirty minutes before coming down from a lulu berry high.

"Control yourself, peanut queen," I laughed.

"Oh, yes, madam licorice girl!"

We laughed and ate, and then, almost out of nowhere, Sarah stopped and gave me a pretty serious look. "Pippy, why are boys so weird?"

"They don't have a choice," I answered. "They're born silly, arrogant monsters with two eyes, a nose, and a big mouth that never makes sense when it speaks. Then, they turn into sweet and happy jerks at age thirteen and fourteen."

"Sounds like Pippy has some issues with boys."

"Oh, yes, one Howie Yeary would be the problem."

"Him again?" Sarah asked. "Well, I'll whoop him for you, Pippy."

"That's your lulu berry courage speaking," I laughed.

"Then you look him in the eyes and let him have it," she said, elbowing me in the ribs. "Let him have it right smack in the eyes."

"I'll take care of Howie when the time comes."

"Right smack in the eyes, Pippy!"

I stopped and stared at Sarah before moving on. At that very moment, I realized a time would come indeed, a better time than all the others. I had told Howie to stop trying to hold my hand. There'd be a time when I'd know what to say because I'd look him smack in the eyes when I said it.

"Come on, Sarah," I said. "Let's get down to Hot Pond. Sometimes a Helio Wrap is the only way to deal with parents."

"And gross boys," Sarah added.

Located just off the northeastern shore of Senter Pond, Hot Pond is everyone's dream escape from school and home, teachers and parents, boyfriends and girlfriends, brothers and sisters. It's about forty-five feet across and round. Its inside walls are supported and shaped by rounded flattened boulders, and it has a sandy bottom. It's three feet deep for the first four feet into the Pond from any of its edges, and then it slopes ten feet deep in the middle.

Hot Pond is home to Heliotroppe, the most unique among the palimals. Heliotroppe makes no audible sounds at all and is absolutely transparent in appearance. The only time anyone seems to see Heliotroppe is right after this palimal rises out of the water, and the water drips off its six-foot high by four-foot-wide shape, but there's no apparent head.

I've long felt there is some kind of thinking part in the middle section of Heliotroppe's body, but I've never seen it. Even though I never hear words by Heliotroppe, the words I feel being spoken in my head, and only during a Helio Wrap, are male-sounding, even though I never thought of Heliotroppe as male or female.

We stood, a bit groggy from the lulu berries, and peered up to see a stream of water swirling up out of the center of the high trees surrounding Hot Pond, then another and yet another. The closer we got to the Pond, the less frequent the spouts were until they ceased.

I was looking forward to a good soak in the hundred-and-one-degree water while smelling a florist's shop variety of exotic orchids and large leafy herbal bushes growing all around the Pond's edge. *Tagitter*, as Kitty Joe says, *dey produces sum great sniffin.'* So yeah, a relaxed day in Hot Pond was definitely the plan.

My favorite thing at Hot Pond is soaking in the smells while floating across the pond as I stare at the tall trees surrounding it. But unfortunately, it was a complete mental zone-out, and when the steamy mist was thick, you could not know where you were in the pond or whether Heliotroppe might grab you for a Helio Wrap.

What made the floating scary was Hot Pond's ten feet deep in the middle, but all you need to do to float on Hot Pond is lay back with your arms outstretched, fall back, and trust that you will be safe. Sounds weird, but you almost always sink if you're nervous or afraid to try to float. I think this is why most visitors float the pond's circumference because of the depth, the sandy bottom, and the steamy mist that isn't too thick around the edges. Even though not everyone agrees, the thrill of floating in Hot Pond is definitely in the middle of the pond when the mist is the thickest and the fragrances are most intense.

We sat alone on the edge of Hot Pond, dangling our legs in hot water; the scene was unusual because there's often a flock of visitors and palimals there. After a while, as I'd hoped, Heliotroppe rose from the water with a most spectacular swirl of water shooting high above Hot Pond.

As Heliotroppe twirled to dry out, we could see his six-foot-high by four-foot-wide shape, although he became invisible to our eyes in seconds.

"Heliotroppe!" Sarah squirmed like she was being tickled. Heliotroppe descended on Sarah. He began to wrap his body around her like a baby wrapped in a blanket.

"*I felt him!*" Sarah said, full of excitement.

"You're not wrapped?" I asked, expecting that she had been wrapped up by Heliotroppe because once he descends on you, you're often swept away at that instant.

"No, but he grabbed me."

"He knows you need to see him."

"That was weird," Sarah said. "I wish he'd wrap me again."

As suddenly as he had appeared to begin to wrap her, Heliotroppe burst high into the air with a swirl of water and then hovered three feet before us as he twirled to dry off, the water spraying all over us yet like never before, his shape ever so clear. Sarah reached out toward him, and within seconds, Sarah's arms fell into her lap, and she became still. Then, smiling in a trance, she lifted into the air as Heliotroppe descended, fully wrapping her.

Sarah floated motionless above the pond for twenty minutes while the birds chirped, and it seemed the flowers hummed a background chorus. I had never known there to be so much sound in Hot Pond. Then, as the level intensified, Heliotroppe began to whirl Sarah around the Pond's circumference in a spiraling clockwise motion, starting at my eye level and climbing higher with each circling of the pond. At first, they moved slowly, then quicker as Heliotroppe's swirl neared the height of the tops of the trees. Then, Sarah let out a liberating scream. Her arms flung wide open as she glided around the sky above Hot Pond like a bird, diving down and dipping into the water before streaking high into the air, hollering like she was on a roller coaster, only Heliotroppe's roller coaster had no tracks.

I had never seen this before at Hot Pond, and I watched as Sarah received attention deserving of royalty. After maybe ten minutes of soaring, Sarah was set back down next to me, but before I could say a word, Heliotroppe wrapped me and whisked me away, took me high above the trees, and then dove me into the center of Hot Pond down maybe eight feet deep, where we stayed for a full ten minutes.

He spoke to me in words I could feel as if they were being said to me, and what I remembered most was his advice and his promise: *Talk to your friend; she is ready. I will be with you as long as you believe in me. Anticipate nothing; receive all.* And as suddenly as I had been swept up in Heliotroppe's wrap, it was over, and I felt like I had just been with Truggles.

When Heliotroppe first squeezes you, the instinct is to resist and get free because he is in a mighty, firm grasp. Still, if you accept him and collapse in his understanding, you are surrendered and under his control. This is when his powers are most at work on you and in you. Like with Sarah, he may suspend you in the air, keep you on the shore, or do the whole wrap under the water like he often does with me. However, it's not until you surrender to him that he insulates you from the heat of the water and breathes for you.

Some Helio Wraps are known to last for as little as two minutes and as long as sixty. I've never gone over twenty-two minutes; that was done underwater right after turning twelve. It happened the day after I threatened to punch out my nasty, despicable classmate, Howie Yeary. I was so mad at him. He tied one end of a string to my ponytail and the other to the backrest of my desk during second-period math. So, you can imagine what happened when I stood.

I was angry when I thought about how Howie picked on me, but when I thought about how good Heliotroppe's wrap felt after going wild on Howie, I knew the power of Heliotroppe's words.

It was also significant because I'd been thinking about Howie more than usual...and wondered what he might think of Spooner Pond.

***

As Sarah and I trotted away from Hot Pond that day, I remember how envious I was about her free-flying and zooming over Hot Pond with Heliotroppe. But after she explained what Heliotroppe had told her about honoring her mother's concerns, I was happy for her. After all, she was my best friend.

"All of a sudden, Heliotroppe vibrated, and I felt a tingling all over my body," Sarah said, describing her wrap. "I swear I trembled, but I was calm as he told me to love with my heart and soul, all my strength and mind. But then, when Heliotroppe spread himself out like a flying magic carpet, I was free to spread my arms and direct him with my mind and words to move in any way I wanted within the fly zone of Hot Pond. An awe-inspiring ride!"

"Awesome. That's how Truggles describes Heliotroppe," I said. "So, you feel good about your mother now?"

Sarah peered at me, showing me her sassy look and grinning, "Think I might have her figured out."

"Really?" I offered with a grin.

"Well, I will try out what Heliotroppe said this week." Sarah nodded.

"Works for me, but it's day after day that you've got to stick with it to make it work with your mom."

"Yeah," Sarah grinned. "I need to work hard on it because you know there's a dance coming up at school, and I already know Mom and I will fight over it. But the way I feel now, maybe it won't be such a big fight."

"That would be great, Sarah," I said.

"It's worth a try."

"For sure. Hey, you up to hiking over to Big Daisy East for a taste of honeysuckle before we catch the East Thwortal home?"

"Yes!" Sarah agreed, a meandering grin creeping across her full lip, and off we went.

***

Okay, so before I go on with more stories...and some of the ones coming up are huge...we need to talk about Howie. Ah, Howie. He's the sort of guy who gets on my very last nerve but also twists my heart so that I feel sick—but on a good level. Yeah, fine, okay; I guess I have a little crush on him. I only refer to him as nasty, despicable, and annoying because I have to hide my true feelings somehow, now don't I?

But there's more to him than that. When I started bringing Sarah to Spooner Pond, I knew I'd eventually bring Howie. It wasn't a hard decision, but it was hard to ask him because it felt far too much like asking him on a date.

I caught up to him one day just before school started. I ensured Sarah was nowhere nearby...not because she'd care that I was inviting him to Spooner Pond but because I was nervous enough to speak to him alone.

"Howie?"

He turned to face me as we were walking into class. He sighed, irritated that I was bothering him. Sometimes, though, I wondered if he only acted this way toward me because maybe he was hiding feelings, too.

"Yeah, Pippy? What?"

"Do you want to hang out after school?"

He looked choked, almost mortified. But I also saw his cheeks go a little red, too. He glanced away and stormed into the classroom. "Why would I want to do that?"

"I...well, I have something cool I want to show you..."

"Where?"

"At my house." When I realized how weird this sounded, I quickly added, "Sarah will be there, too."

"What is this cool thing?" He was pretending to sound disinterested but doing a lousy job.

"It's hard to explain. I have to show you."

He frowned as he sat at his desk. But I knew I had him hooked. It wasn't until later in the day, right after lunch, that he approached me in the hallway back to class.

"Yeah, I'll come hang out. But it has to be quick. If my folks knew I was going to a girl's house, they'd flip!"

"Oh, awesome!" I said. I then realized I sounded too excited, so I cleared my throat and added: "I mean, yeah, if you can make it, that's cool."

My heart hammered hard in my chest the rest of the day, and I wasn't sure if it was because Howie was coming to my house or because I was about to reveal Spooner Pond to him. And later, when he knocked on my door, and Sarah and I answered, I still wasn't sure.

Exactly eight minutes after he came into my house and his eyes took in the sight of Spooner Pond, I got my answer: it was a bit of both.

CHAPTER TEN

Points Afar All-Universe Power & Magic Championships

There were Outsiders of every imaginable shape from lands near and far, including three of us from North Star Ridge sitting off to the side perched in a particular clearing in the woods reserved for palimals and their friends, sitting high above the arena where the competition would take place. Looking out over the arena, one can see that it was designed like a stadium, although not made of concrete and steel. Instead, it was shaped from the earth, sunken competition area, and meticulously groomed. The competition area was probably the size of a soccer field, and the arena the size of a large high school football stadium.

Sarah and Howie were with two of my Spooner Pond palimals and me. It was only Howie's third time to Spooner Pond; boy, he picked a great time to beg me to come along. He was still getting accustomed to the odd sights of Spooner Pond, but he was handling it all well.

Benjamin Beaver had shined his red boots for this occasion and was carrying a sack full of something he said we'd want to be sure to use. Grandma Goat stood there, having not missed one of these championships in over twenty years.

Grandma Goat was like the perfect grandma-type Palimal. She was considered by all the critters far and wide as a wise and witty old, long-haired Nubian goat with a touch of gray. Her ears were still long and complete, and though it was extraordinary to see, she had a superb selection of hats to wear when she'd be out strolling and enjoying the sunset over Spooner Pond.

The Annual Points Afar All-Universe Power and Magic Championships was her major outing as she grazed in her pastureland or sat on her porch swing. She's most fond of saying that one of the advantages of being the oldest in Spooner Pond is that she can do pretty much whatever she wants, and it's okay with others. There is just not a mean bone in her.

She'll get in your face with advice if you hint at a problem, but she's kind. When she speaks, she sounds like everyone's grandma at her most loving moment. I've never known her to raise her voice or hear her yelling or getting mad at anyone, but I know unless you've got something important to talk to her about, she'll nod you goodbye and get back to her grazing or swinging without exchanging words. A collapsible spine and double-jointed shoulders—kind of a Spooner Pond thing—permit her to climb onto her porch swing just like any person would, and she takes advantage of it.

She's probably the wisest Palimal in Spooner Pond. Her face is kind, and her jaw has a softness about it that permits a wide range of expressions, my favorite being the look on her face each time she puts on a new hat from the vast collection she's amassed over years of visitors giving her hats in thanks for her help.

"Welcome, everyone, welcome! Today, we begin the four rounds of the One Hundred and Sixty-Third Annual Points Afar All-Universe Power and Magic Championships."

The words echoed across the crowded arena, sounding like the baritone section of a choral group, though not as loud as the voices of the Outsiders anxious to root on their champions.

"Who said that?" I asked.

"Here, North Star Ridgeites," Benjamin Beaver said as he took the sack off his back and nodded to Grandma Goat. "And for you, Madam." As if we were going to a 3-D show, Benjamin Beaver first handed to Grandma Goat and then to each of us a pair of thick dark glasses with rainbow-colored lenses.

"Wear these paggles," he insisted, "and all you see will be as if it was happening inches before your eyes."

"This is awesome!" Howie said as he placed his paggles over his head.

Frankly, I couldn't believe it. Wearing the paggles was like looking at your hand held in front of your face without glasses. I could look anywhere in the crowd of Outsiders hundreds of feet away, and it was as if they were right there with me. I could see the hairs on their faces, and even more startling, I could hear their whispers and breathing if I concentrated on them.

"Like my paggles, Pippy?" Benjamin Beaver smiled.

"They are awesome. How come I never knew about them?"

"They work only in Points Afar; thus, this is the only time of the year I bring them out."

"I can see everything," Howie exclaimed, "I mean everything."

"They're awesome, Pippy," Sarah said. "It's like wherever my mind wants to look, they capture everything about what I'm looking at."

"And, children," Grandma Goat said, "paggles zoom in and out at your mental command. Try it; look to the stage; the origin of the voice you heard stands there."

We all stared as the speaker of the words took center stage, threw open his rose-colored robe, and, as if peering into every eye of the thousands of spectators, announced, "I am Dirlan." Almost eight feet tall, he was a muscular human-like figure, his deep rose-colored robe draped over his massive arms and shoulders. First, he raised his foot-long hands and scanned them over the arena, quieting the voices. Then, when they were still, he continued, "I will serve as this year's referee and judge." He grinned and aroused the crowd of spectators.

The spectators cheered wildly at Dirlan's announcement as if on cue, and all eyes (and paggles) were focused on him.

"Before I introduce the contestants who have made it through the two weeks of competition leading up to today's final qualifiers," Dirlan began, "I'm honored to introduce the contestants' choice as this year's Healer: my friend and our friend from the Gethian Colony, Zebteema. Oh, how mightily we enjoy her!"

The Outsiders broke into a raucous cheer as Zebteema joined Dirlan and pranced about the stage. She was a majestic woman wearing a long violet-colored gown, pulled back to reveal her muscular body. Her long, flowing dark black hair fell well below her waist and over the pouch resting on her hip.

Pointing to Zebteema, Dirlan bellowed, challenging the crowd. "Ah yes, Mistress of the elements and the mixing of potions; does anyone here know what's in the healing venoms our lady carries in her clandiram? Ha, aaayyee, not I," he said, laughing.

"Attractive," Sarah noted.

"Yeahahhh, charming," Howie groaned, prompting me to elbow him.

The Outsiders continued cheering. I don't think any of us had ever seen such a larger-than-life woman who was so beautiful. She must have been seven feet tall. "She's the best."

We watched in amazement as Dirlan approached Zebteema cautiously and, with the fingertips of his six-inch-long fingers, touched the pouch around her waist, slowly feeling the outline of its contents as she glared at him.

"What is Dirlan doing, Grandma Goat?" I asked.

"He's counting the venom vials in her clandiram. He knows each venom can kill to the touch."

"That's a clandiram hanging off her hip?" Howie asked.

"Indeed. It's a pouch made from the middle section of the intestines of a large ram," Grandma Goat explained. "Zebteema claims it is the only pouch that can carry the venoms safely while ensuring their viability."

"Careful, Dirlan," Zebteema warned him with a stare.

"I'm always careful around you, my lady. Indeed, the Leaders expect your mixed venoms will produce healing potions to soothe them." He grinned broadly, "Yes, they trust you."

She squeezed her lips together and sharpened her glare as if her eyes were penetrating his pupils. She held her steely look until the grin left his face, and the Outsiders stopped cheering. The arena grew eerily quiet. Zebteema slowly turned away from him and scanned the crowd of Outsiders, holding her icy stare for a few moments before her face yielded and her smirk turned to a smile. The crowd nervously stirred, but none made a sound until she raised her hand and twirled it above her head as fireworks spewed from her fingertips and bellowed, "Yetantino, Yetantino."

In response, the arena erupted in cheer.

"She controls him," Sarah said.

"She controls all with her charms," Grandma Goat remarked.

"The 'yetantino,' Grandma Goat, what is that?" I asked.

"It is her call. She summons and releases all her concerns and worries with that one word."

"Yetantino?" I repeated.

"Would it work for anyone else," Howie asked.

"We all have one word that will release all our concerns and worry," Grandma Goat explained. "But it must be given to you by only One."

"Truggles?" I wondered.

"The word comes from High Stones," she explained.

Sarah, Howie, and I peered at each other, our paggles reflecting off one another, and following Goat's lead, turned back to center stage.

Zebteema and Dirlan had embraced amid the cheers, prompting the Outsiders to cheer even louder. Then, separating from Dirlan, Zebteema glanced around the arena. She raised a handful of earth in one hand and, in the other, a vessel half full of blue liquid venom she had removed from her clandiram. Then, with a mile-wide smile, she taunted the crowd of Outsiders into a frenzied cheering, all eyes fixed on her. The audience, seemingly under her power, watched as she flung the earth and blue liquid into the air. As the elements and the liquid venom combined, the particles formed a flock of bluebirds, which quickly assumed a spiral formation above Zebteema's head.

"Fly and watch over the contestants," she ordered as she gazed at the birds.

"Now," Grandma Goat whispered, "the games can begin."

Dirlan took center stage and announced the rules for this year's "display and shame" competition. Palimals didn't attend the preliminary matches over the month preceding the final rounds, and we awaited Dirlan's announcement of the pairings for the first round of the finals.

Dirlan explained that by lot, one competitor draws the right to be the first to display power over the other. From there, the match would continue until one of the competitors was retired by the other or until Dirlan ruled one competitor won over the other. In "display and shame" competitions, the goal was to neutralize competitors' powers by shaming them enough to reduce the strength of their power while dominating them with your own power.

All Dirlan's decisions were final, and there was no appeal. Causing the temporary death of another was acceptable, though highly detested by spectators. Three qualifying rounds for six competitors were scheduled. The first round is three head-to-head competitions drawn by lot. The second round pits the losers of the first round. The third round pits the winners of the first round in a match. The winner advances to the finals on the following day.

"This makes for a fascinating competition, children," Grandma Goat began. "The 'display and shame' competition rules will apply only throughout the qualifying. The rules for the finals will be different and won't be announced until just before the finals begin in a couple of days."

"Today's pairings," Dirlan announced, "will be, in this order of the competition: Locka Chu versus Shardam, Kabball versus Apaska, and Rudicia Gom versus Amabona!"

Motioning to the large area off the side of the center stage where the contestants' tents were set up, Dirlan summoned the first two competitors to join him at the Afar Spiral in the arena's center point.

We turned our attention to the movements of contestants around the tents. We didn't know these names: Locka Chu and Shardam. We could only assume the Afar Spiral was the tall spiral-shaped rock in the arena surrounded by a groomed oval competition area extending forty yards from the rock in every direction. It took up about a quarter of the size of the overall arena.

"It's time, children," Grandma Goat said.

"And I'd be wiping off your paggles," Benjamin Beaver added. "You don't want to miss any of the action!"

CHAPTER ELEVEN

Lock Chu and Shardam

Locka Chu and Shardam approached the Afar Spiral.

"Locka Chu has drawn the honors and will go first," Dirlan announced.

Locka Chu was a young firebrand Trance-Caster who dressed in flashy clothes and wore his hair in long braids draped over his narrow back. Unbraided, his hair would drag on the ground of his six-foot, four-inch body. He had a moonless night sky complexion, piercing black pupils peered from his giant white eyeballs, with a tiny nose and a hollow mouth.

Shardam, quite to the contrast, was a gallant man-animal figure standing well over seven feet tall, wearing a purple robe with gold trim and tassels flowing over his highly muscular and thick frame. One look at Shardam, and you could do no more than just stare. He was magnificent and radiated a sense of calm but extraordinary power. His spectacular shape and beauty were ageless, though something about him gave the impression he might be pretty old. He had been a reigning champion of the Points Afar All-Universe Power and Magic Championships several times over the past two hundred years. It seemed all he had to do to win in the past was to show up for the competition.

"What do you think of this contest, Grandma Goat?" I asked.

"It will be curious. Locka Chu is a Trance-Caster, meaning he can create trances and use his remarkable mental powers to actually enter the minds of others and forecast death-defining moments."

"What?" Howie interrupted.

"It's elementary, Howie; Trance-Casters can make others believe events and circumstances they create are real, even when trances and forecasts are nothing more than fabrications of their thoughts."

"Trances and forecasts?" Howie asked.

"Not something used too often anymore, but Locka Chu has the power to overpower others' minds so they, and all who view the competition, see the imaginary reality he creates. With your paggles on, his creations will appear as real as the tree you're standing next to, Howie."

"No way," Howie said.

"You'll see, young man," Grandma Goat grinned. "Locka Chu will command all our minds. He speaks little yet uses elaborate and violent-looking gestures to create these trance states. Oh, yes, Locka Chu has the power, but his forecasting is the deadly part. His most famous trance is the waterfall, where he creates the sensation and physical manifestation of a powerful waterfall and the desire to walk through it. Once hooked by the trance, his victims are compelled to walk through the water. With his forecasting power, he creates illusions on the other side that allure his enemies and are real enough to kill his enemies."

"Terrific," Howie gulped.

But Grandma Goat wasn't done. "If he chooses, he could forecast the mouth of a dragon hiding behind a waterfall or a pit of venomous snakes."

Howie's color left his face, and I couldn't resist another elbow into his side.

I nudged him and said, "What's wrong, tough guy, afraid of snakes?"

Howie ignored me and asked, "Can Locka Chu *really* control his opponents' thoughts?"

"Not completely, but to a degree," Grandma Goat said. "But I don't know if any Trance-Caster could control Shardam, whose physical skills are impressive but not as imposing as his powerful psychic skills and command of the Lusean Arts."

"The ancient warrior powers?" Howie wondered. "What's that?"

"Shardam is the Master of Lusean Arts, and he has an uncanny knack for outthinking his combatants and using just enough of the Lusean Arts to overcome his adversaries." Grandma Goat offered Howie a grin. "He's the one to watch!"

The competition began with Locka Chu waving his hands and throwing fire from his eyes. He crafted a violent swirling wind trance and placed Shardam in it; simultaneously, he forecasted a moat of boiling water and fire surrounding the swirling wind. He artfully shielded the moat from view by making its surface look like calm blue water. Because it was the rule of the competition, Shardam had no other choice in the qualifying round but to accept Locka Chu's trance and thus was forced to struggle against the virtual tornado. After some time, however, it appeared Locka Chu's spell was strong and impressive, and Shardam struggled to escape Locka Chu's will.

But oh, how little we knew of Shardam's command of the Lusean Arts! As Grandma Goat explained, he called on Fourth Stage Lusean Arts amid the whirling winds to become thin like a knife and cut through the wind's resistance. Then, he organized his body and mind's energy and focused on the calm blue water. Locka Chu willed Shardam to see the blue water as freedom from the increasingly violent winds, so at this point, Locka Chu had Shardam exactly where he wanted him, although not as quickly as Locka Chu had hoped.

Still, it was the perfect set-up to get Shardam to seek the calm blue water and lose the match when he was burned in the moat of fire. This was Locka Chu's plan, and it seemed it would work, except Shardam, unbeknownst to anyone, used his power of transmigration and created a duplicate of himself to follow the knife through the whirling winds. All the Outsiders we saw was an image of Shardam walking out of the swirling winds unscathed and stepping onto the calm blue water.

Shardam's transmigrated manifestation was an exact copy of the gallant man-animal figure he was. As if orchestrated to make it all believable, Shardam's manifestation disappeared into the fake blue water—a moat of fire into which Shardam sank and from which smoke and steam spewed into the air as Shardam sunk deeper into the moat of fire. The crowd was shocked and began booing Locka Chu. The bluebirds hovering above the competition congregated over the moat and chattered. Yet even they were fooled by Shardam's power.

Uncharacteristically for this brash young trance-caster, Locka Chu, who would seek to extinguish his enemies, he terminated the swirling wind trance. He neutralized his moat of fire forecast to prevent further injury to Shardam. After all, it was a competition to shame one's opponent, not to kill him, and what had happened thus far appeared to everyone in attendance to be a successful demonstration of Locka Chu's power.

Although most of the Outsiders were booing, and the dust was still adrift in the air, Dirlan had no choice but to request the crowd's silence, peer through the cloud of displaced soil, and check on his old friend, Shardam. We could all see the image of Shardam, and although tattered, he was alive. Dirlan turned to Locka Chu to raise his arm in victory, but as he prepared to do so, the dust cleared, and the tattered image of Shardam was replaced by the regal Shardam, who stood there in all his glory.

Shardam approached Locka Chu and Dirlan, excusing himself as he dusted off his robe with extended fingers and bursts of air from his mouth. Then, grinning, he said only, "Don't believe everything you see, Locka Chu and Master Dirlan. I am surprised you, too, were fooled."

With that, Dirlan stared questioningly at Locka Chu and then glanced back at Shardam, eyeing him up and down.

"Seems you have been shamed, Locka Chu," Dirlan said, releasing his hand, and a big grin grew on his face as the crowd began chanting, "Shar-dam, Shar-dam, Shar-dam!" Then, without hesitation, Dirlan stepped over to Shardam and raised his hand in victory. Defeated and dispirited, Locka Chu retired from the competition. The match was Shardam's.

"What is he doing with Locka Chu?" Howie asked Grandma Goat, commenting on what seemed to us to be a friendly exchange between the two on the judge's stand.

"It is Shardam's way," she began. "For over a hundred years, he has comforted and advised his competition."

"A hundred years?" I asked Grandma Goat. "How do you know that?"

"I have observed him doing so."

"You mean," I hesitated, not believing what I was about to ask. "You're over a hundred?"

"Remember where you are, Pippy, and remember there has *always* been a Spooner Pond."

Sarah, Howie, and I just gawked at each other. My palimals appeared unphased by Grandma Goat's comments and more interested in the next pairing of competitors.

"Tighten your paggles," Benjamin Beaver advised. "This next competition will be one to watch with wide eyes."

CHAPTER TWELVE

The Contest Continues

Two contestants approached the Afar Spiral, one looking more like a giant, disheveled Bengal tiger and the other more like a dragon man of modest height who wore armor plates over his chiseled frame. Each moved cunningly like animals in the wild, circling around the Afar Spiral as Dirlan approached.

"Kabball has drawn the honors and will go first," Dirlan announced.

"Which one's Kabball?" I asked.

"Permit me, Granny," Benjamin Beaver said, getting a nod in return from Grandma Goat.

"That rascal of a dragon, he's Kabball. I've worked on his armor before, and he's a hot-head fire-breather. You bet," Benjamin Beaver explained.

"What is his magic skill?" Howie asked.

"Granny..." Benjamin Beaver deferred to the much wiser of them.

Grandma Goat smiled and explained. "Kabball does indeed breathe fire, but more importantly, he is a Mentorian and Summoner of past spirits. He can read an opponent's past thoughts and fears, summon past spirits from his opponent's life, and materialize them immediately. As a result, he has been successful in regional magic and power challenges outside of Spooner Pond."

"Really?" Howie wondered.

"Oh yes. Kabball is very skilled, and the regional challenges are quite fascinating," Grandma Goat answered.

"But they do not take place here in Spooner Pond."

"No, Howie, but we share in other places in this universe."

"Awesome," Howie said. "It'd be mighty to have such a power."

"Or perhaps the power of illusion that Apaska has," Grandma Goat added. "It will be a fascinating contrast of powers."

Kabball first merged his mind with Apaska's as he yawned, showing his saber-like teeth. Of course, there was no knowing what he saw in Apaska's mind, but Kabball summoned a trio of spirits out of Apaska's past to stand aside him to face off against Apaska. Shocked by their presence, Apaska changed forms, growing very tall and taking on more human-like traits, creating an illusion of those spirits Kabball made, turning on Kabball to destroy him.

Kabball repelled the hostile spirits and summoned three more spirits from Apaska's past. Apaska entombed them in his illusion. Now, all six souls were turning against Kabball. Reaching into his armor sleeve, Kabball retrieved a flat, shiny dagger, held it before his eyes, and chanted, "Teg ni il! Teg ni il!"

Suddenly, the spirits turned toward him and lined up like soldiers, prepared to take their commands. Apaska began morphing into different shapes and sizes, appearing tall, growing short, looking human, looking Bengal, donned in clothes, or pure wild. He threw up the shield of illusion and dismembered himself into thirteen parts, spreading about the arena's competition area. Some features were human and other tigers, but no part stood before Kabball and the spirit warriors.

"Apaska controls the moment," Grandma Goat observed.

"What is Kabball doing?" Sarah asked.

"He calls on Apaska to reassemble and fight. However, Apaska cast three-dimensional shadows around all his parts, and Kabball cannot locate his energy source." Grandma Goat paused. "Marvelous dodge; Apaska has immobilized Kabball's attack."

"Kabball's not paying attention," Howie said as he pointed. "Look, Apaska's energy source has gotta be his illusion nearest the Afar Spiral. The bluebirds have all congregated over it and not over any other parts."

"Very astute, Howie," I said, admiring him with a twinkle in my eye.

Kabball could not descend on Apaska to overpower him. Kabball appealed to Dirlan to overrule this illusion, as his opponent had abandoned the face-to-face competition. Dirlan declined the appeal and signaled them to continue. Apaska, it seemed, had reduced Kabball's offensive. There was a pause in the action.

"I have never seen this before," Grandma Goat said. And then, just as soon as the words came from her mouth, Kabball rose tall and summoned twenty-three of the fifty-three demon-devil spirits, pledged an oath to him and an additional five spirits from Apaska's past.

"Speak to me!" he ordered Apaska's spirits, and the spirits resisted until they were surrounded by his evil souls. Then, they began to recount their times with Apaska, telling every detail and revealing every vulnerability he had as a warrior and Illusionist.

Apaska was uncovered, and his mystique was diminished by the spirits. The loss of mystique to an Illusionist is as lethal as the loss of life itself, and the only way to stop the spirits from talking and revealing all was to capitulate to Kabball and concede the match, which Apaska did. Zebteema was called to mix venoms to assist Apaska in retrieving his parts. After twenty minutes under her care, Apaska was reassembled again in a humble human form to accept his defeat. Dirlan raised Kabball's hand and declared him the winner.

"You were right, Howie," I said, half hating that he was right. "I watched Zebteema attend first to the part nearest the Afar Spiral."

"Ah-huh," he grinned, "I watched Zebteema as well."

"Just what is Apaska anyway?" Sarah asked Grandma Goat.

"Believe it or not, he's not one of a kind. Apaska and his breed are more animals than humans, yet their animal side comes out only when hunting and in deep conflict. Today, he was a Bengal tiger, yet on another day, he may become a giant Anaconda snake, always with the potential to separate into many different parts, shapes, and dispositions, all with the aid of his powerful illusions."

"Awesome," Howie remarked.

"As if you understand, Yeary," Sarah said, acting a little irritated by his adoration of Apaska.

"Thanks, Sarah," I began, eyeing Howie. "I was just beginning to think the same thing."

***

Rudicia Gom and Amabona approached the Afar Spiral.

"Finally, we get to see the ladies in action!" Sarah said, admiring the two impressive contestants.

"This won't be a soccer match, Sarah," Howie quipped.

"Ha, ha," I said sarcastically.

"Amabona has drawn the honors and will go first," Dirlan announced.

"She is the one with no hair," Grandma Goat said, "that way from a curse placed on her when she was a child."

"Then the older one is Rudicia Gom," I noted. "She looks like my mom in a way; just a bit taller, but she has the same great long dark wavy hair and incredible complexion as my mom."

"She's just like your mom," Howie said, "but look at her eyes—they must be four inches deep and an inch around."

"You're right," I said as I focused on her eyes, real eerie looking.

"And she will take on the Amabona," I said. "It doesn't seem fair."

Amabona was head to toe a brilliant bronze color, her eyes an emerald green, and her lips big and full. Grandma Goat explained she was what is known as a Spellbinder, a power that permitted her to concoct spells with elements and other instruments that bound her opponents in the intent of the spells.

"Among Spellbinders," Benjamin Beaver explained, "she's a looker, and in the elemental world, she's got red appeal with thick deep skin like a tough acting firefly who glistens like a rainbow."

I laughed at Benjamin Beaver's explanation, but I had to agree that Amabona was like a model. Not quite six feet tall, she was wearing what Grandma Goat said was her trademark off-white sheepskin garment. It hung over her hip, exposing long muscular legs, and slashed across her upper body, showing very prominent and well-developed shoulders. Strewn about her waist were sacks and pouches.

"A modern cavewoman," Howie suggested, prompting glares from Sarah and me and a scolding from Grandma Goat.

"Quiet!" Grandma Goat ordered. "Use your paggles!"

Grabbing a pinch of worm casings and a pinch of dried alfinweed, Amabona rubbed them together and breathed moisture into them until they congealed. All the while, Rudicia Gom was required to wait for Amabona's first action, and she did, mumbling something to herself that none of us understood: "I fin a la."

Moments later, Amabona put the congealed substance in her mouth and soaked it with her saliva before removing it.

"Listum, manctum, grafta manctum," Amabona said as she displayed her potion to the spectators' boos and then reached out and pasted it on Rudicia Gom's forehead.

Rudicia Gom was considered the most expert in working with the elements, and Amabona was really playing with fire by challenging Rudicia Gom with an elemental spell. Still, Amabona's youth and brashness had gotten her this far, so few were surprised by her approach. Moreover, her spell was thought-binding, making it so that Rudicia Gom couldn't think or reason without assistance from Amabona.

A thought-binding spell is one of the most potent for controlling another. Still, it's also an all-or-nothing spell because it's not all that effective unless the recipient is dehydrated or feeling a great deal of mental pressure.

"She guessed wrong," Grandma Goat commented.

And so, it appeared, as Rudicia Gom seemed to reverse the spell by taking the potion off her forehead and spitting on it before throwing it at Amabona's feet.

It was pure splendor that this regal woman of old age was so fantastic-looking. Something about her eyes made everyone crazy with envy or fear, but not Amabona. None of us, but maybe Howie, didn't care to see the classy Rudicia Gom humbled by the sassy Amabona.

"I want Amabona to win, and I want to see more spells," Howie said with a grin.

"You haven't seen enough?"

"Quiet, you two!" Grandma Goat scolded us.

We watched as Rudicia Gom offered Amabona her hand.

"She's surrendering to Amabona," Grandma Goat said.

"No way," said Sarah.

"How crafty of her," Grandma Goat mumbled. "Yes, it's her surrender, as in Points Afar competitions; offering a hand signifies one has given up. So Amabona will be declared the winner."

Dirlan offered a strained look at Rudicia Gom, paused, and then raised Amabona's hand and gave her the victory. Then, as the crowd booed, Amabona strutted about the staging area, taunting the spectators and flashing her muscular body at them, sweat dripping off her hairless head.

"She's awesome," Howie said.

I stared daggers at Howie, being reminded why I didn't want to bring him along first. I asked Grandma Goat, "Why did Rudicia Gom do that?"

Grandma Goat also had a big grin as she chuckled aloud. Then, finally, she gazed at me with her crafty eyes and said, "Rudicia wants Shardam in the finals. She knows what she's doing better than everyone except Shardam."

"But—" I argued.

"No, no," Grandma Goat interrupted me. "Rudicia knows how to compete. This year's competition rules favor her plan very nicely. She expects Shardam to win the third round, so to compete against him, she must win the second round, which can only happen if she loses the first round."

"You really think so?" I asked.

"It is how it will be this year at Points Afar," said Grandma Goat.

CHAPTER THIRTEEN

The Finals

Over the next two days, two groups of three contestants battled. Locka Chu, Apaska, and Rudicia Gom competed on the first day, and Ruducia Gom annihilated the two within twenty minutes. On the following day, it was Kabball, Amabona, and Shardam. It was not as swift a victory for Shardam. Still, he was quick to dispatch Amabona to the raucous cheering of the spectators, in part because of her arrogance and, I think, because of how she humiliated Rudicia Gom. Shardam's staccato power volleys with Kabball and his demon-evil spirits were sheer entertainment, during which Shardam hardly bothered while Kabball worked to defeat him. Ultimately, as Grandma Goat said, Rudicia Gom and Shardam would vie for the Points Afar All-Universe Power and Magic Championships.

Dirlan stood facing the overflow arena wearing a metallic-looking suit of armor as if he were competing, including all his combat regalia and weapons.

"That's why they chose Dirlan," Grandma Goat said. "He's the showman and a final of the kind we're about to see needs a good showman."

"Ha, ha, ha. I am pleased!"

Hurriedly, we cleaned the lenses on our paggles and inched as close to the competition as possible.

"Welcome!" Dirlan announced, whirling his Yanlookie above his head as the crowd cheered his ax-like weapon's slashing movements. "In today's finals, we have the Yapsule Queen herself, Rudicia Gom, our reigning three-time champion and former twenty-time champion," said Dirlan as he introduced Rudicia Gom for her walk onto the stage. She wore a fitted green metallic garment with a bright gold cape tied around her neck and bright gold boots, her hair woven high on her head, and her quiver of Yapsule Spears slung to her side. She looked like a fashion model; at age two hundred seventy-one, that was magic. The crowd was deafening in their approval of Rudicia Gom, whose Yapsule Spear disciples filled the stands.

Calming the spectators with the waving of his Yanlookie and raising his hands, Dirlan announced, "Competing against Rudicia Gom is the former twenty-seven-time champion, Shardam, Supreme Wizard of Montrose." Dirlan paused to glance at Shardam for verification.

"Thirty-seven," Shardam noted to Dirlan.

"That is, thirty-seven-time champion of the Points Afar All-Universe Power and Magic Championships, Sharrrdam!" The crowd applauded at first and then broke into bedlam when Shardam transformed himself before their eyes into four different shapes and sizes: man-animal to animal, animal to animal, animal to man, man to man-animal. But, in the end, he was the same man-animal who was presented to them, wearing a shiny brown body garment over his muscular body with a purple cloak that changed colors as he waved it, going from purple to gold, or blue, or pink, or red.

Looking at him, Dirlan commented, "Aaayyee, I see Shardam is eager to reclaim his title again after decades of not competing."

"Why, that old cabbage head, wolf-faced Shardam is Cloaker Montrose," Benjamin Beaver chimed in. "He and three of his cabbage head, wolf-faced children came across my Boardwalk some months ago to get ready for this championship." Benjamin Beaver paced back and forth, glancing at Shardam and Rudicia Gom, mumbling to all of us, "I knew he was a wizard all along."

"Ah, Mr. Benjamin Beaver," I teased him, smiling, "that's not exactly what you told me."

"Okay, Pippy, well, not at first. In fact, I thought they were an odd bunch of hairy long-nosed robes. Actually, never imagined he could be a wizard."

"The old cabbage head had some powers," Benjamin said.

"You hadn't talked about Shardam before," Grandma Goat commented as she edged herself next to Benjamin Beaver.

"I only told Pippy. I knew him as Cloaker Montrose. I didn't think anything of it."

"What's this wolf-faced thing, Benny?" Howie asked.

"The whole bunch of them had big cabbage heads and wolf faces, Yeary. I didn't know any better."

Benny, Yeary—isn't that cute, I thought.

"Hundreds of outsiders crossed my boardwalk over the past few months, but Shardam differed from the others. Oh, yeah, he had the power to know my thoughts, and then he used physical power to rescue his child."

"A major physical power?" Grandma Goat asked, surprised by what Benjamin Beaver had said.

"Yeah," he paused. "Elongation."

"He was granted 'Alata' as we once were," Grandma Goat said, raising her eyebrows.

"Yes, he talked about Alata. He was different." Benjamin Beaver said.

"So, this is the one High Stones has selected to work through." Grandma Goat pursed her lips and nodded agreeably.

"What do you mean, Grandma Goat?" I asked.

"Shhh, it's time for the competition."

"Is Shardam the Lusean Master?" Howie asked.

"What do you know, Howie?" I said, irritated by his interruption.

"Shhh, you two. It's time for the competition."

***

"Then let us begin," said Dirlan. "The rule for today's final is only one: that the winner is chosen by the concession of the other. You are to walk side-by-side to the Afar Spiral and stand beside it when you open your hands and hearts to High Stones, who hosts this competition each year and permits the display of your powers. Then, pledge fair play to each other, and watch me; your competition will commence upon the raising of my Yanlookie."

Rudicia Gom, standing five feet ten inches tall, walked alongside Shardam, who stood seven feet tall, their capes flowing as they took the seventy-five-foot stroll. It didn't look like a fair match, but Rudicia Gom had taken down men of equal size to Shardam on many occasions, and her disciples knew it as they cheered her on during the walk to Afar Spiral.

Dirlan raised his Yanlookie.

Rudicia Gom was quick to strike first with a teasing trick. Picking up a handful of earth from the ring, she used her Summoning Power to bring up the memories of a distant past near defeat of Shardam that occurred on the planet on which they stood over a hundred years ago. She cast the summoned earth at him, creating a virtual movie screen image of the past event before his eyes. Then, she showed him down on the ground, fighting the Maquade—a giant of a beast that had been the nine-time biennial champion some two hundred years earlier. Shardam, then a young warrior and immature wizard, was almost defeated in the finals of this same competition.

Rudicia Gom's ploy worked, and Shardam was distracted by the images and the memory—a rookie mistake he should have never made. Rudicia Gom seized the opportunity to pull a Yapsule Spear from inside her cloak and plunge it into him, igniting an explosion of electricity and a shrieking sound that shook the stadium. She was going for the instant kill; the bluebirds were active, and Zebteema was quick to her feet.

No one who knew Rudicia Gom thought she'd resort to a Yapsule Spear this early in the competition. These are the spears of the darkest power with tips made of seven points. They are arranged in a four-inch spherical shape that ignites upon striking objects or beings and sends a shrieking sound to accompany an intense fire-like electrocution. Although none are actually burned by the electrocution, it alters the nervous systems of those struck and places them under the mind control of the thrower. In times of group conflict, all who hear the shrieking sound of the explosive strike of the Yapsule Spear become subject to the mind-control of the spear's bearer.

Shardam was stunned; his big body wavered and shook as if he were trying to rid himself of the effect. At one point, he looked into Rudicia Gom's red eyes, in which he could see his humiliated form, went to his knees, and bent his head forward. She grinned and raised her cloak to signal a quick victory—her rookie mistake—and her disciples enthusiastically cheered. Rudicia Gom had relaxed her mind control for just a moment, but enough to release her grip on Shardam. Then, he summoned his power of elongation and began his assault on her from his knees.

As he had done in Spooner Stream when Miquarto had fallen into the rushing water, he uttered, "On-Raef-Esir," and four fingers extended out of his hands. They moved swiftly and purposefully along the ground like fast-growing vines wrapped around her boots like tentacles. With a swift and forceful pull, Shardam removed Rudicia Gom's boots and flung them in the air, distracting her and further relaxing her mind control, sufficient for him to stand tall and invoke the warping power that permitted him to travel in and out of time and space.

Now, he had the spectators cheering, for none had ever seen Rudicia Gom's boots removed, revealing shriveled, rather unimpressive feet. Her disciples, although not quiet, became more reserved. Shardam had captured the spectators' widespread interest and fought her weakened mind control efforts. He warped himself in and out of time and space, appearing and disappearing in the competition area around Afar Spiral and frustrating Rudicia Gom.

"I call on the element of fire to still you," she commanded, and fire rained from the sky above them and upon Shardam every time he was in the present time and space.

"Alata," Shardam mumbled to himself as he attempted to dodge the streams of fire.

"Bring on the hail," Rudicia Gom commanded, and hail stones the size of walnuts fell from the clouds above, replacing the fire.

Shardam threw off his cloak and ordered it to hover over him and shield him from the hail like an umbrella, and he then began shaarring her with lightning bolts, not from the skies but from the palms of his hands. Finally, Shardam resorted to using one of the highest Lusean Arts against her, flinging lightning bolts to control her in ways she had yet to know, a power Shardam had never used in these competitions. First, he struck her with a bright blue bolt that restricted her vision, a yellow bolt to immobilize her hands, and a green bolt to restrict her feet.

Just as he was about to fling a red bolt to constrict her breathing and move in for the victory, she arched her body to point her fingers at him and spewed nerpon liquid from her nails, striking him in the chest, paralyzing his upper body. The effect of nerpon liquid would last for forty-five seconds. She had forty-five seconds to recover and called out for more fire and lightning bolts, but Shardam's cloak protected him. She couldn't muster a practical challenge to the shaarring, and all they knew was they had witnessed the beginning of a new level of competition now that Shardam had returned to the arena and returned with new power and magic—that of the Lusean Arts.

Her boots were gone, her hair was fallen, and her hands and feet were in spasm. Rudicia Gom uttered the words that would give victory to Shardam. They would be the exact words she spoke when she realized she must lose to Amabona. "I fin a la."

Shardam moved close to her to release her from his power, and as he did, Rudicia Gom, still disheveled and apparently aging right before our eyes, reared up and pumped her hands high in the air and let out a vicious ear-splitting scream, yelling "Anta-quanta!"

Dirlan stopped short of approaching the competition area and retreated to the stage as a thousand demons stacked on each other. Then, Rudicia Gom's army of wrath filled the entire arena and marched on Shardam. We hid, and many of the Outsiders watching the competition started running away. Yet, as anyone could imagine, Shardam summoned the power of transmigration to create a thousand manifestations of himself to match one for one the demons and to create shadows for each of the three hundred weapon-carrying soldiers in her army of wrath.

Upon his command, his shadows enveloped the three hundred soldiers, encapsulating them in delicate woven cocoons. Then, he summoned new Stages Eight and Nine powers of the Lusean Arts to smother the demons with the earth of their past lives. Unfortunately, so much earth was displaced in the process; the arena grounds were blanketed with dead monsters and wrapped wounded soldiers.

Shardam stood alone at the center of the arena, Rudicia Gom down on the ground by his feet. She conceded the match as Dirlan approached, weaving his way through the carnage in the arena. The spectators remaining and those returning cheered as Shardam was awarded the victory and the championship. Then, as Dirlan lifted Shardam's hand just a bit above shoulder high, the arena grounds trembled, and the tall and impressive Afar Spiral rocked back and forth.

A hush fell over the arena as shocked spectators gawked at the Afar Spiral as cracks streamed up and down its entire height. Then, in a matter of minutes, the rock structure split open and fell apart, revealing the unimaginable—the entombed but awake body of Afarantibo, a monster of a man-like Ancient God.

"I don't believe this," Grandma Goat grumbled. "Afarantibo...alive again. It can't be."

"Who is he?" I asked. "He looks awful."

"Awful," Grandma Goat said. "He was an expert worker of spells and magic who once commanded all the forces of Rudicia Gom and was known throughout Spooner Pond and the greater universe as a magnificent teacher until the day he doubted the power and authority of High Stones overall in this universe. He challenged High Stones when there was no such thing as an Outsider in Spooner Pond, and all forms of being roamed throughout this land, their powers intact and functional. It was a time of respect, harmony, and abundance. No palimals, animals, or rational beings feared one another until Afarantibo and his legions of followers sought to command all in Spooner Pond and overstep the authority and power of High Stones. Afarantibo's act changed Spooner Pond forever and to this day for all who followed."

"What happened?" Howie asked.

"There was a major confrontation between Afarantibo and High Stones two hundred and fifty-one years ago," Grandma

Goat began. "Shardam was twenty-one at the time; Rudicia Gom was twenty. Both witnessed the entombment of Afarantibo by the mightier hand of High Stones right here in this then-unnamed clearing in the Wooded Forest. Afarantibo was cursed and confined in the spiral rock. Forced to observe all that had been created and enjoyed for the good of all creatures. Yet to have had the opportunity to interact with it. It was his prison. Yet of the contestants here, this day in Points Afar, none but Shardam and Rudicia Gom knew of Afarantibo's actual confinement within the Afar Spiral, where I thought he was to remain for all eternity or until a mightier power came upon this place. And so, some two hundred and fifty-one years ago, this place was named Points Afar, and Afarantibo's tomb named the Afar Spiral."

"Then why hold the championships in this place? Why let Afarantibo see anything?" I asked.

"High Stones is mighty and is good, and it would be forty-four years after the entombment of Afarantibo that semi-annual All-Universe Power and Magic Championships would commence. They were held every other year for forty-four years until they became annual, thus inaugurating the Annual Points Afar All-Universe Power and Magic Championships." Grandma Goat's eyes seemed distant and in a quandary.

We all hid and watched as Afarantibo groaned, stretched, and cast away the remnants of rock that had confined him. So many in the arena ran, and only the most notorious, muscular, and skilled in their powers remained close enough to observe a most remarkable event. It seemed like the moment's intensity had caused my paggles to fog, but I found it was my sweaty forehead.

"Shardam," Afarantibo spoke in a deep, scratchy voice as he came to life, grimaced, and stretched his face to a broad grin. "You have gotten stronger. I watched as you defeated Rudicia, but she lives."

Afarantibo stepped out of the mass of crumbled rocks and approached Shardam, continuing, "You haven't the instinct to command life and death. Maybe you are not ready to be my general," he said, eyeing Shardam from his feet to his head and across his broad shoulders.

"Go back, Afarantibo," Shardam ordered. "Spooner Pond has changed. I will never be your general or serve you; you are no longer welcome here."

"Changed?" He laughed, the harshness of his voice all the more apparent. "Why? Are you in charge now?" he taunted Shardam. "What happened to High Stones?"

"I give you fair warning, Afarantibo," Shardam said, raising his left arm high as his cloak floated onto it like a force.

"My student warns me?" Afarantibo roared. "I don't think you can scare me with parlor magic, Shardam," he said threateningly. "Remember, I made you and Rudicia all you are, brought you from boyish young fancy to maturity and power. Yes, I, Afarantibo!"

"You gave us tools, but we've used them differently." Then, he challenged Afarantibo by stepping closer. Shardam said with authority. "You have nothing to do with who I am today!"

"But Shardam, I could give you and Rudicia all the power..." Afarantibo pleaded with him, moving closer to Shardam as Shardam approached him as well.

Afarantibo flung four fire bolts out of nowhere from his hands at Shardam's midsection.

As quick as lightning itself, Shardam spun his cloak before him to block Afarantibo's offensive and reflected the lightning bolts back at Afarantibo, creating a blaze of fire around the crumbling Afar Spiral.

"Still throwing flames, teacher?" Shardam grinned, mocking his one-time teacher. "I'm no longer a student who is impressed with such folly."

"But Shardam," Afarantibo said as he shook off the electrical spikes.

"Don't step any further!" Shardam ordered.

Afarantibo paused.

"You never believed in the Lusean Arts, Afarantibo, and I am now the only surviving Master of the Arts. I cannot let you return to Spooner Pond, nor can I allow you to threaten High Stones."

"Hah," Afarantibo grunted and stepped clear of the rubble within several yards of Shardam. Afarantibo was a foot taller than Shardam. Rearing his head back, Afarantibo bellowed in a threatening voice, "Where are your High Stones now?" stretching high into the sky, Afarantibo let out a cry of freedom.

The crowd of spectators left in the arena stirred. Then, as if revived by her old Master's tenacity, Rudicia Gom greeted Afarantibo. This gave us a closer look at him; he was one giant mean creature.

Shardam, however, appeared unmoved by Afarantibo's antics. Instead, he flung his cloak over Afarantibo and commanded the elements using Stage Ten Lusean Art powers. "Commune, collide, and cover!" he ordered.

A combination of earth, wind, fire, boiling water, and air swirled about Afarantibo, and he could not move beyond the force they exerted. Then, as Afarantibo yelled and screamed to be free, the boiling hot elements congealed and began entombing him again, starting with his feet and moving up his body as he wreathed with pain.

Afarantibo could not free himself, and when the congealing mass reached his head and steam was burning his eyes, Shardam halted the elements with the outreaching of his hands and said, "Afarantibo, it is over for all time for you in Spooner Pond. I will cover your head, and never again will you see what you have lost, but I will spare your ears so you must forever hear all you can never see."

Shardam lowered his arms, and the congealed mass continued to cover Afarantibo. The spectators sat, waiting for Shardam to move. The Supreme Wizard of Montrose had stilled the moment, something that had never before happened in Spooner Pond, and Shardam beckoned a cessation of the elements with a voice command and swirling of his cloak.

Rudicia Gom approached the newly formed Afar Spiral, reaching out but unable to touch the rock as it was still boiling hot. It was as if she wanted to say goodbye to her old teacher, but we didn't know. She surprised us, though, as she asserted her will on the day's events, stood next to Shardam on the rubble, and, without Dirlan's agreement, raised Shardam's hand in the victory gesture. Indeed, Shardam was victorious in the competition. However, few understood he protected tyranny and horrors of a world in which the will of the likes of Afarantibo was permitted to exist alongside the intention of High Stones.

It was clear to us that Shardam and Rudicia Gom had whispered something to each other after the competition, and their body language said they were probably good words. All the while, I noticed a deep, intense sparkle in Howie's eyes.

He was obsessed with whether it was the magic, the history, or the event itself. And I couldn't help but wonder if bringing him to Spooner Pond had been a mistake.

CHAPTER FOURTEEN

The Pinenut Forest

"'A scallywag of a butterfly' they called me for a long time. But yeah—the scales had worn off my wings, I lost my color, and I looked pitiful. I was an embarrassment to the pretty butterflies, and it was a time when no butterfly ever talked or communicated with other resident animals or visitors."

A colossal butterfly said this to me...just another amazing sight of Spooner Pond. Deep down, I wondered if I should be worried that such sights no longer surprised me.

"So that was before *the day*," I said.

"*The day*? Never quite said it that way, but yes, Pippy, it all changed the day after that *awesome night* when the wind from the north swept through the Lush Forest, and we were all reborn."

"But there are no others like you," I said. "Aren't you B.C., butterfly colorful?" I asked, looking at this magnificent, marked giant butterfly.

"B.C. is indeed colorful, but the B.C. is short for my name, Bee Cee. So, I am also known as B.C. Butterfly," he said as I gawked at this mannerly, kind of smart-mouthed butterfly palimal.

I had learned in school that butterflies rely on flowery plants and trees for their daily food and drink, and it was rather odd to think of this almost human-like giant butterfly as anything like the butterflies back in North Star Ridge. Still, the flowers and trees there in the Pinenut Forest all had largeness to them as well. I recalled stories in which Truggles told me about the conversion of the Lush Forest to the Pinenut Forest, but being here and seeing it was believable.

Truggles referred to the change as the night Spooner Pond oozed, though I never quite understood the use of such an expression. As he told me, the skies grew eerily dark over the land, and the wind that swept through the Threshold of High Stones and swirled down Back Trail to calm the raucous demons continued into the Lush Forest, bringing much turbulence.

The ordinary butterflies of the Lush Forest were flushed with the power of High Stones, causing them to grow larger and more brilliant in color. B.C., however, was not affected. Instead, an intense and pulsating light engulfed B.C. the day after the mighty wind, igniting a chorus of undistinguishable sounds as the then-still haggard butterfly was transformed into this creature I was talking with.

B.C. emerged from the pulsating light, standing twenty inches tall and sporting a wingspan of thirty-two inches instead of ten inches tall and sixteen inches across like most of the other butterflies that had been transformed that night. In addition, B.C.'s once drab brown color was changed into a brilliant mix of green, yellow, black, and red colors and shades.

Looking at him, he appeared flawless in every respect, like a butterfly, but he had a palimal look. His mouth was anything but smallish; he sported a pair of thin artistic arms, and what you'd think of as his antennae looked like the open ends of trumpets.

"We are eternally youthful in the Pinenut Forest," B.C. said as if reading my mind's bewilderment over the dramatic change to him and the then Lush Forest.

"It's hard to imagine how such a change could occur."

"It's the power of High Stones," he said. "At first, we were shocked and scared of the voracious wind. It had enough power and force to root out and destroy all the plants and trees in the forest, but the wind had a mind of its own and only rooted out the imperfections of the forest while not harming a single life or destroying anything beautiful. It was like we blinked a very long blink, and all the wild and ugly things about the Lush Forest's wild plant growth were replaced with beautifully groomed and naturally scenic forest and fauna. Then, the wind quieted, and we saw the result; the butterflies burst into song and have been singing ever since."

"But you did not?" I asked.

"No, not immediately, but I had no idea what would come the next day."

"The pulsating light?"

"Yes, and wasn't it *awesome!*"

"Yes," I smiled, admiring this splendid, proud, yet humble butterfly. "So this forest is enchanted because butterflies sing here?"

"It's not exactly that we sing, young Pippy, but we were anointed with the power of High Stones, and not only do we sing, but our music also soothes sorrows and heals emotional wounds of those who come to us and to whom we sing."

"But otherwise, things are normal?"

"Little is normal here, Pippy. Has our golden leader taken you to the Maze at our southeastern entrance?"

"A few times. I know of the Maze, but I've never gotten through it."

"Really, and you always had Truggles with you, huh?"

"Yep, but he'd never help me."

"Pity...did he tell you of the origin of the Maze?"

"No."

As if I said the worst thing possible, B.C. darted up and away from me, fluttering about me in a half circle while staring at me like he was sizing me up. Then, as he had begun, he stopped, stared me in the eye, and said, "I thought you would have conquered the Maze before I was called to work with you."

"Work with me?" I wondered.

"Yes, work with you, but you've never gotten through the Maze. Odd, but they want me to work with you?"

"Big deal—so I haven't ever gotten through it. Why's it so important?" I asked. "Because really, it's kind of dumb."

"Dumb? No, young Pippy, the Maze was created by the powerful wind of the Threshold of High Stones, but the day after, the Pinenut Forest was born. The wind swept in again, but only this time, lightning bolts and fiery tentacles streamed from the sky, reshaping the landscape to create a three-dimensional area called the Maze. In its own right, it is a spectacle of nature with a primary brain that tests your wit and readiness for the challenge you are about to face."

"Challenge?"

"Are you not here to get to High Stones?" he asked.

"I suppose, but I'm also here in the Pinenut Forest to relax and escape pressures. I've never really found the Maze to be a relaxing place, at least not based on how many times I've been stuck by the giant thorns."

"Scratch, scratch; scratch, scratch P-I-P-P-Y got stuck," B.C. broke into song. "Scratch, scratch; scratch, scratch P-I-P-P-Y-s got stuck. Next time, young lady, try patience and persistence, and never rely on physical luck."

Again, B.C. fluttered a half-circle about me before pausing to hover four inches from my nose. Then, looking intense and professional, he said slowly, "When you capture the faith to see a vision of the challenge the Maze offers, you will become that vision, and the Maze will become play. You must get beyond what is obvious to succeed in the Maze, just as you must get beyond what is obvious to get to High Stones."

"Capture the faith?"

"You will learn the feel of working with me," he said.

"Hmm? 'Capture the faith' sounds very B.C.-ish, but if you say it works, I'll keep trying."

"Good." He laughed. "Yes, B.C.-ish is good."

I'm sure it showed that day that I was disappointed I hadn't been able to master the Maze of the Pinenut Forest, and it kind of bothered me, but I never considered it that important. All the while, B.C. peered at me with a stare I had yet to see from him.

"Be still," he said, flying up and around me, touching my right shoulder, then my left with his thin, artistic arms, before landing on my head. He then wrapped his arms around my cheeks and temples, holding me for a moment. Then, he flew down to the log to sit next to me.

"I may have misjudged you, Pippy, now that I have seen inside you," he began, "the Maze may not be necessary at all." He grabbed my hands and held them. "They say you are ready, Pippy."

"Ready for what?" I asked.

"Ready to be taken into Mystasanctim?"

"What about High Stones?"

"No, no, no, no...not High Stones. You are not ready, but few visitors ever enter Mystasanctim, and not all who enter return from Mystasanctim. Before we go, you must promise to fully trust me no matter what you see or feel and to do exactly as I say...*exactly.*"

"Mystasanctim? Sounds a touch weird to me, and I have plans to go to the movies with some friends later today," I said, wondering what Mystasanctim was.

"You really do not know about Mystasanctim? I assumed you already knew," B.C. stared at me with a questioning look. "Mystasanctim is the most ancient part of the Pinenut Forest, maybe even of all of Spooner Pond, and only visitors who are invited ever gain access."

"Well, that's great, but I'm more concerned about the trust you're discussing. You're an awesome butterfly, B.C., but I've never trusted anyone but Truggles to take care of me in Spooner Pond, and this Mystasanctim place sounds like a Truggles kind of place."

"It's definitely a Truggles kind of place, but Truggles instructed me to guide you through Mystasanctim. So, he knows better than anyone if you need to go there at this time in your life here in Spooner Pond."

"Ah yeah," I muttered. "It won't take too long, will it?" I asked, knowing our big plans for the movies included much more than the movies.

"Should it matter?" B.C. questioned me. "You don't have school today, right?"

"Right, there's no school. It's the teachers' last institute for the school year, so we're off."

"Good, then, no worries, but your movies. The movies will not go away." B.C. chuckled.

"Well, I don't know why Truggles didn't tell me about Mystasanctim or that you would by my guide. He tells me everything," I said in a whining voice.

"You're now coming and going about Spooner Pond as you please. Haven't you found out you don't need Truggles like you once did, and didn't you go the Points Afar Championships earlier this year?" he asked.

"Yeeesss...but I can only get along without Truggles because he's taught me so much about Spooner Pond. This Mystasanctim you talk about sounds much different; maybe even dangerous, even like a place some of the Outsider warriors would hang out," I said, nodding.

"You don't need to worry about outsiders, Pippy; it's only about listening to me and trusting in what I tell you to do." B.C. fluttered in a circle about my head.

"Guaranteed?" I sought more certainty.

"It's absolutely guaranteed," he hovered right before my face. "Truggles instructed me to guide you to Mystasanctim, so why are you so nervous?"

"I've never quite had this kind of offer, B.C.—follow me into danger and listen to me, and only me, and you'll be okay. And from a butterfly?"

"Well...?" he mumbled as he stared at me, his antennae drooping. "Maybe you aren't ready."

"Oh, no," I protested. "If Truggles said I'm ready, then I'm ready, even though I have no idea what I'm ready for."

"You trust him, don't you?" B.C. said.

"Completely, whether here in Spooner Pond or at home in North Star Ridge," I said.

"Then you must trust me. Part of the accomplishment of the challenge Truggles has given you is having faith to step out into the dark or onto the tumultuous water of Mystasanctim without him and to instead trust the hand of the one he has entrusted to guide you."

"So, there are no Outsiders there, but is Mystasanctim all dark and full of water?" I asked.

"No, Pippy. You're hearing me with your worldly eyes and imagination, not your twishloc."

"My twishloc?" I wondered, having never before heard this term.

"Did you not observe Shardam's use of his twishloc?" he scolded me.

"Well..." I confessed, not really thinking anything more than Shardam was one mighty warrior with a magical cape.

"Truggles has not told you of twishloc?" B.C. gazed at me.

"Never."

"But he told me you were ready, yet no successful Maze and no twishloc?" B.C. mumbled.

"*Pippy is ready*," a deep voice spoke to B.C. Butterfly. "*It is time for her to learn of Mystasanctim. We await her.*"

"Okay," B.C. acknowledged.

"What?"

"C'mon, Pippy, we've got to get going. Your twishloc awaits you."

I was confused. Outsiders and their wild powers meant everything to me, but twishloc and Mystasanctim meant nothing. Still, B.C., at Truggles' request, I imagine, was telling me the Outsiders were not really a concern, yet my twishloc and Mystasanctim were most important. After seven years in Spooner Pond, why had I never heard of these things? It didn't make sense, and although I trusted B.C., I wasn't sure if I could trust him to guide me alone deep into the Pinenut Forest. After all, he was a butterfly, even though a giant one, but Truggles... he was like a massive force. I was never afraid of anything with Truggles. Also, after tasting the Outsiders' powers, I wasn't sure if Mystasanctim was another Points Afar place where they had access to their powers. It kind of felt like it should be that kind of place.

I can tell you now I had some doubts at the time of this strange encounter. I even wondered if the B.C. before me was a Monitor of Temptation who had somehow escaped Rock Castle Mountain. Then, I used the Hooded Ones' power of materialization to create this illusion and then possess it, intending to entrap me in a Mystasanctim full of Outsiders like Locka Chu and Apaska. I would have been sure he was an illusion if this butterfly hadn't known all he knew about Truggles and me. Then again, at this time, I didn't realize there was a deep voice only B.C. was hearing because, at the time, I didn't hear anything.

We began to leave our log, with me walking, B.C. flying and leading the way. Then, suddenly, as if someone poked me in the head, I blurted out, "Maybe we should go to the Maze first?" All the while, I was uneasy about two things I knew nothing about: twishloc and Mystasanctim. To tell you the truth, the Maze was adventurous, even though it always defeated me.

"I don't go into the Maze," B.C. said, "and I thought you'd given up on the Maze. Besides, we're on our way to Mystasanctim... now!"

"Let her chill out, H.A., H.A., H.A., H.A.," the voice commanded B.C.

"Taking another look at this," B.C. began, having stolen my opportunity to influence him with my well-developed pouty look. "Apparently, the Maze is on your itinerary today."

Itinerary, I mused, staring askance at him. *Weird butterfly...*

CHAPTER FIFTEEN

Through a Talking Three-Dimensional Maze

Not too far from Happy Trail, yet pretty far from where B.C. and I were standing, is the southeast entrance to the Pinenut Forest and the place known as the Maze. If you could imagine flying over it, it'd appear almost fuzzy to the eye—a mixture of rock and plant configurations that look like a giant wart magnified millions of times. It's not like the rest of the Pinenut Forest—at least as much as I've seen of it.

I've never had the patience, nor did I really take the time needed to find answers to the most outlandish rhymes and riddles posed to me by the talking rocks, trees, and bushes in the Maze. The only way you can get through the Maze's three-dimensional passageways that meander through and under some of the rocks and trees and among dense growths of all sapling species is by solving these rhymes and riddles and answering the questions. It's the only way to use the Maze to enter the Pinenut Forest.

Most of the Maze is a remarkable display of incredible formations of nature. The three-dimensional look leaves you kind of dizzy if you do not focus on where you're going. You also need to pay close attention to the objects from which voices come and that challenge you with rhymes, riddles, and questions. Although it seems the Maze can be a place to goof off on three-dimensional slides and rubbery tunnels, these thick hedges are placed about it to remind you it's not really a playground; it's serious business. These hedges have ten-inch thorn projectiles. Each is about an inch in diameter at its base and like a fine needle at the other end. If you trigger them, they stick you and inject venom into any object they touch. The poison causes itching within seconds, and nothing but time gets rid of the itch. I won't soon forget the first time I got stuck by one!

Solving the rhymes and riddles and answering the questions permits you to progress safely through a matrix of open and enclosed passageways interspersed in and about the rocks and trees and the tall, thick hedges of the Maze. Some passages are brightly lit, while others are dark and eerie, yet all are passable if you've gotten permission to pass...from the rocks, trees, and bushes that talk to you. However, how you pass will depend on how well you distinguish the surreal distortions of the actual paths or objects in the Maze created by its three-dimensional layout.

I learned the hard way that when you're in the Maze, you've got to avoid the dark, sinister-looking hedges. They're hiding the ten-inch thorn projectiles, and if you brush up against them, you'll get pricked unless you're wearing a suit of armor because the thorns' long, thin stingers can penetrate almost everything else.

I don't think the Maze was ever intended to be scary. Still, it can seem that way when you get lost in it and can't seem to find a way out, and if you get pricked too many times by the hedges, your itching is so distracting you won't concentrate on getting through the Maze. Although it's most humiliating at these times, it's pretty hard to go on because scratching yourself leads to more thorns and even more itching. The way out is to summon an escort of five giant butterflies to fly you out of the Maze. With one on each of your feet and hands and one holding the back of your collar, they fly you out facing down, giving you an incredible view of this mysterious Maze as they fly you back to the entrance.

B.C. said the Maze requires patience and persistence, not physical prowess. Although I didn't understand exactly what he meant by capturing the faith to see a vision of the challenge the Maze offered, I had gotten the message that conquering the Maze was not just a physical accomplishment. It's not like a haunted house or fun zone, B.C. would say. Another bit of his advice played in my head: You must get beyond what is obvious.

So, on our way to the Maze, I challenged myself repeatedly, wondering, *How I rely on faith; how do I believe in something totally unknown to me and then capture a vision of it so I can conquer the Maze?* That was my challenge going into the Maze—definitely not trying to overpower it. Wouldn't this be a great way to get through some classes at school—capturing a vision of the course rather than making it or the teacher a challenge that had to be overcome or else...be a failure?

I think that was my original problem: unsuccessfully working through the Maze. I viewed it as a challenge I had to overcome, or else I'd fail. All I could recall on my way to the entrance that day with B.C. were the other times I tried the Maze. The first time I tried the Maze, I handled a couple of riddles with no problem but struggled with a third riddle and got pricked about eight times by the giant thorn projectiles. Having the option of going back in and trying the Maze again, bruised ego and all, or taking the very long walk around to the northeastern entrance to the Pinenut Forest, all itchy and sore, I took a walk.

A pretty painful memory, and I'm sure B.C. knew what I thought when we approached the entrance to the Maze, and he said once again, "You must get beyond what is obvious."

Get beyond what is obvious. Get beyond what is obvious, I said to myself as I entered the Maze by ducking under a three-dimensional rock archway and crawling through a three-dimensional hole bored through the trunk of a rather large, disfigured tree. On the other side of the tree, a jagged rock outcropping as natural as life got things going.

"For the way to be clear around me," the rock's pitched voice began, "you have only to tell me the height of an iceberg sticking up a hundred feet above the water."

"That's easy," I said, having always heard that 90 percent of a whole iceberg is below the surface.

"The entire iceberg is 1,000 feet," I said, certain of myself.

"Not bad, but not entirely correct," the rock answered. "The range could be seventy to ninety percent underwater; thus, a more correct answer would have been three hundred and thirty to one thousand feet. Understand nature follows the rules, but the rules aren't always so exact. You must go around me to the left, princess," the rock said as it shifted, exposing me to a narrow passageway through thick hedges. "Be on your way, princess," the rock encouraged me.

I stood there and shook myself into a loose noodle-like state, repeating: *Get beyond what is obvious.* I wormed through the hedges as I watched the thorns darting out of their hard casings. No pricks, no sweat, but it took a lot of concentration. Finally relieved, I found myself atop a deep three-dimensional trench lined with soft grass. A perfect slide illusion, I figured, so I was ready to avoid it when the tree next to me poked me with one of its branches and challenged me in the sweetest and alluring of voices: "What do you call a ten-inch red ant, princess?"

Oh, yeah, I remembered; *some of these riddles had silly answers.* "RAT—red ant trouble," I said, grinning.

"Can you do better?" the tree asked.

Better? I blurted, "How about RATTY—red and tall trouble?" I grinned. "Yep, that's it."

"Quaint enough," the tree agreed. "You may go by." The landing on which I was standing gave way, and I was whisked down into the trench, bouncing from side to side in the track's rubbery, gooey second and third dimensions. It was like a slide, but given its three-dimensional look, I had no idea a five-second slide would last thirty seconds. The next thing I knew, I was sitting in a bed of pine needles in a very dark area of the Maze.

I glanced around and could barely make out my surroundings. Again, I thought, *Get beyond what is obvious,* and I began to recognize the darkness was itself three-dimensional. Surrounded by the sinister-looking hedges, their thorn projectile casings glistening like shining silver bullets in the dimmed lighting, I felt panicky.

As I stared away from the hedges, I saw the lively and color-ful part of the Pinenut Forest, perhaps fifty yards out. I could see myself leaving the Maze, though still unsure how.

The hedge spoke to me in a most studious voice sounding very much like the deep, slow-talking voice of the research li-brarian, Mr. Buzz, at the public library in North Star Ridge: "What is the sound of being pricked by a thorn?"

"Ouch!" I said.

"Not even close," Mr. Buzz Hedge replied. "Think this through, and you will be released to enter the Pinenut Forest."

I reasoned and said proudly, "Click, chu-wah, ouch!"

"Chu-wah?" Mr. Buzz Hedge remarked.

"Chu-wah—the sound of the thorn being projected out of its casing before it pricks you," I explained.

"Ah, inventive, but no, princess, you're actually getting cold-er." Mr. Buzz Hedge chuckled. His laughter still resonated, the hedges around me began to close on me, and the thorns got closer. The lighting was still dim, and I couldn't see anywhere to go. *Get beyond what is obvious*, I thought. *Get beyond what is obvious.*

I closed my eyes and didn't move. Dad had taught me this sort of weird thing to do when I was not focused and needed to calm myself down. So, I stood still with my eyes closed, hands to my sides, and the backs of my hands facing forward. Then, I began breathing slowly. After about five breaths, I just let my arms and hands rise on their own, palms facing down, my arms lifting in front of my shoulder high, not to the sides.

Keeping my eyes closed, my arms floating in the air, I felt for the thorns. Then, miraculously, I could touch the sides of the casings holding the thorns, not their tips, and pet them like calming down a dog. The more I rubbed them, the less prominent they became, as if they were retracting into the hedges. My eyes were still closed; I felt the thorns moving away. Then, all of a sudden, it came to me.

"Resistance," I shouted with certainty. "That's the inner sound of being pricked!"

I could hear hundreds of thorn casings completely retracting, a cascading cacophony of 'wah-chu, wah chu' sounds. Then, the Maze illuminated itself. The hedges opened to reveal a colored flower-lined trail leading into the lush Pinenut Forest. Butterflies were flying, and there was much joy in the air.

"You did very well, princess," Mr. Buzz Hedge said. "Enjoy the Pinenut Forest."

CHAPTER SIXTEEN

This Is Mystansanctim

It wasn't until later, when I rejoined B.C., that we approached the area of the Pinenut Forest known as Mystasanctim. I looked at B.C., recalled the riddle in the Maze about the ten-inch ant, and wondered about this big insect thing going on in Spooner Pond.

As we stood on the hillside overlooking Mystasanctim, B.C. explained that Mystasanctim was the only area of the original Lush forest left untouched when the Threshold of High Stones wind created the Pinenut Forest. Oddly, the perfect beauty of the Pinenut Forest was not at all visible in the Mystasanctim I was gazing at. Instead, I saw only a dense, overgrown forest of trees, flowery bushes, and tall reeds growing near the body of water. It possessed a rugged and ancient beauty, yet there didn't appear to be any life in Mystasanctim. Its eerie quiet complemented the glassy calm of the body of water but accentuated my impression of the place being lost in time and lifeless.

Remembering what he had said to me earlier in the day, I asked about the 'tumultuous water' because the water I was looking at looked like a mirror. It was so still, and our reflections were deep and crisp. It appeared fake.

"Didn't mean to mislead you, Pippy, but this is the only water in Mystasanctim," B.C. said. "It is only after we have summoned the spirits that the water is challenged and expresses its energy in sometimes tumultuous ways."

"Who are these spirits?" I wondered out loud.

"Some are teachers of the way to High Stones."

"But I always believed Truggles was my teacher."

"He has taught all of us. Never forget his words. Always be steadfast in his ways and his teachings. He has called you to follow him—to be the first of your age to become one of his teachers."

"Like you?"

"Yes, like Dack and me, Beaver, Furry One, and all the others. Grandma Goat was the first, and Joe Kitty was the latest to be called. So, it's now your turn, Pippy."

"But I'm not an animal."

"Indeed, Pippy, you have yet to claim High Stones as your home."

"Everyone in High Stones is an animal?"

"Ha, ha, ha," he bellowed and sang to me. "Silly girl, silly girl, silly girl. You're not meant to be an animal, and I'm not meant to be a boy."

"Then what are you meant to be?"

"Simple; I'm your teacher, Pippy, and you'll never get to High Stones without me." He stared me down.

"Oops." I smiled. "Why didn't you say that when we started?"

"It is our way. Remember, I'm here at Truggles' request. He will no longer teach you because he has called you to him, and you will not see him again until you have successfully journeyed to High Stones."

Maybe I should have been honored or overjoyed at this news, but it saddened me. Tears came to my eyes, and I sat, doubted myself, and wondered about what I had gotten into and what had just gotten into me. I'd be fourteen in two months and have come to Spooner Pond for almost seven years. So why was Truggles so removed and remote?

I wondered if going home and trying to forget about Spooner Pond would be the best thing for me to do. So, I did not move from there momentarily, B.C. beside me. Glancing at him and into Mystasanctim, I reconsidered the idea of High Stones for the first time since my thirteenth birthday. Spooner Pond had always been just fun, but now it was becoming a task, and I wasn't sure I was ready for that.

Then, at my lowest point emotionally, my face was in my hands, and a wisp of wind blew through my hair.

"Not now, B.C.," I said.

"It's not me, Pippy. They have come for you."

Then, yet another wisp of wind blew through my hair, blowing it off my face and ears. An intense, invigorating chill ran through my body, standing the inches up on my arms. It was my feeling when everything felt great in my life—like when everything was perfect.

"It's time to further prepare you for the journey," B.C. said, pulling me from my private emotional moment.

"Huh?"

"It will not be easy; you must command a way to get past the Howlers and into High Stones."

"Oh, *really?*" I said, laughing, still feeling a bit giddy. "And how would I be doing that? Before getting to the Howlers, there are the Ghosts of Courage Cave, the Hooded Ones, and the MOTs." I shifted to my well-rehearsed whine. "There's no way I can get through them."

"Ultimately, you must, and if your heart is steadfast in trusting in Truggles, you shall be able to overcome all fears and challenges. Also, since Truggles has called you as a teacher, you will be able to have some companionship on your way to High Stones. I just don't know what Truggles has in mind."

"I don't know if I can do it," I said as my fingers drifted and twirled my hair. I felt a touch overwhelmed.

"You will learn new tools here in Mystasanctim," B.C. said. "But it's up to you to use them wisely. We know that all these tools and teachings work together to achieve good for those who seek High Stones with a pure heart and mind, even if they never get there. Yours must be pure, Pippy, because you have been called to High Stones."

"These tools you talk of, like the powers of Outsiders?"

"Wondrous tools, but only if you are ready."

"Well, if I've been called, then why all the work to get there?"

"Good question," B.C. said before flying a couple of loops around my head. "All I know is that you are becoming well-known here and part of the plan of High Stones."

Part of the plan? I wondered. *What about my on-and-off plans to go to college, have a career, and maybe have a family?*

"No plans are changed, Pippy," B.C. began. "However, plans are made better by having Truggles in your life here or in any world at any time."

"And so, you read my thoughts?" I said, feeling exasperated.

"Oh yes, most of us do, as may you."

"Oh," I lit up, "sign me up. Let's get on with the lessons. I want to read a particular boy's thoughts, and I have a teacher who no one can figure out."

"Wait, Pippy, the power to read thoughts and all the powers here are not meant to be used to create a gain for you but to promote the ways and teachings of High Stones."

"I suppose I knew that. But the thought of knowing what the heck is going on in Howie Yeary's head is rather enticing." I grinned, feeling ever so relaxed now, knowing I was ready to learn from B.C. "And I know that's just what you want to hear, B.C."

"Exactly," he said with a chuckle. "It seems you're already reading my mind."

CHAPTER SEVENTEEN

Trust in Your Twishloc

It's difficult to describe the feel of Mystasanctim. If dinosaurs had been running around, everything would have fit. But, instead, it was like time started and stopped there as I sat under a canopy of fragrant flowers and soaked in B.C.'s teachings.

"Foremost, never ever close your eyes when faced with adversity on the way to High Stones. The challenges created by the Ghosts of Courage Cave, the Hooded Ones, the Monitors of Temptation, and the Howlers are to be observed, not feared. It is your fear from which they draw their power to control you."

"Trust in your twishloc," he said forcefully. *"You have been called by High Stones and will be protected by your feelings, belief, and faith.* Then, with your twishloc, look them in the eyes and say, *'Be gone, I resist thee,'* and raise your hands above waist level, staring them in the eyes. This may be enough to disrupt their actions.

"They are demons and evil souls who will not want to maintain eye contact with you. They fear all who have twishloc with High Stones. If they do not respond to resisting them, aggress on them if you must until you feel the power of High Stones flowing through your arms and hands, creating a tingle. At this moment, you must *fling your fingers* at your adversaries and say with authority, '*Be gone, we resist thee,*' and the energy emitted from your fingers will quell their power."

"That's it?" I said.

"This is the way to deal with the obvious frontal attacks from these demons and evil souls, but they are much craftier than this. Remember, once they had twishloc but lost it when they traded their loyalty to High Stones for the power and magic offered them by the great forces of evil that challenged High Stones and lost."

"You mean Afarantibo?" I asked.

B.C. stared at me, fluttered right then left, and said, "You know the wicked one?"

"I know of him. I watched Shardam take on the ugly monster at the Points Afar Championships."

"So, you were the one who was there?"

"Yeah, me and two friends from North Star Ridge."

"Ah huh—Sarah and that boy, Howie Yeary."

I peered at him as he nodded with a chubby butterfly grin. "How'd you know?"

"It is not too hidden in you, Pippy. Do not run from it; use it."

"So, what do my friends have to do with Afarantibo?"

"Little right now, but they are the only two of your kind who have seen the ugly monster for a long time, as you say so well. Others think he is dead, but you know better."

"I know only that he is encased in the Afar Spiral."

"Indeed, his demons and evil souls are condemned to seek him forever through the spoils of their power and magic. In answer to your question, the Ghosts of Courage Cave, the Hooded

Ones, the Monitors of Temptation, and the Howlers know all the powers, yet fear those who know how to use them and who are in High Stones' favor."

"They know this '*Begone, I resist your power?*'" I asked.

"Most certainly they do."

"So, they'll be expecting it?"

"They may not expect it from you, Pippy, because you are so young. Their doubt in the ultimate power of High Stones doomed them to their lives today. They are prisoners in a world where they must create discouragement, distress, doubt, and disbelief to have life. Their joy comes from others' suffering, but to High Stones, suffering exists to be overcome. If your belief in High Stones is strong and certain, your resourcefulness and the use of your powers will overwhelm the evil souls and demons."

"Well, they'll get no joy out of me," I said.

"That will be our hope, but you must always remain aware of their presence and know they are skilled at using their powers."

"I'll just stare them in the eye."

"Yes, you must, to Beget them. I don't expect any of it will be a game for them once they find out you have been called."

"What if they come at me with no eyes at all?"

"An excellent question! They may." B.C. paused, grinning. "Yes, it appears you are ready, Pippy. Just remember...if they do not manifest eyes, or what you think of spherical shapes used for seeing, focus instead on their effort. You want to capture that with your attention, and you can only see this when you are in the will of High Stones. So, use their eyes if you can, but remember they are heads of deception, so you must be able to discern when and in which form they are present to identify their focus. You can discern if you remain in the will of High Stones and carry Truggles in your heart."

"What about those Howlers hiding in trees?" I challenged him.

"You can Loofit to them."

"Loofit? What's that?"

"It's one of the basics; you know it as flying. I flap my wings for effect, but I really do Loofit around. It is a simple willingness of your body to lift itself to where you imagine you want to be. Heliotroppe is an expert in the Loofit."

"I just will my body to lift itself where I imagine I want it to be."

"And why shouldn't it be so?"

"It's just not done, except maybe by Outsiders."

"And what about the Au helpair?"

"Oh, yeah. Of course, but Au helpair did all the work, not me."

"You summoned the Au helpair," he pointed out. "Now, just do it, Pippy."

"Just do it. Sure," I grumbled. "Okay, body, lift up to that tree," I said rather obnoxious, still not believing. Nothing happened. "See, not so easy."

"They did say you were stubborn, which can be a blessing and a curse," B.C. said. "For now, it's a curse because you need to listen and learn. So, listen! Now, there are about seven trees in the area you just looked at. Focus on only one tree and at an exact place in that tree, and imagine you want to be there. Then, go ahead...and believe."

Believing was not as tough as getting over my stubbornness, but it was fleeting, and as sure as the sun shone in the sky, I could Loofit to the exact place I imagined I wanted to be in the tree.

"Wow!" I exclaimed.

"It's quite a power, huh, Pippy?"

"Really," I grinned, somewhat intrigued by it. "Sorry about my bratty side."

"Forget it for now, but it best to overcome it before heading to High Stones."

"Can I practice in North Star Ridge?"

"Not yet, but there will be a day after you have been to High Stones that you may use some of your powers in North Star Ridge."

"Really?" I wondered excitedly.

"Can a butterfly talk?" He chuckled.

"Okay, okay," I said, biting my lower lip as I imagined using some of these powers back in North Star Ridge.

"But only for good," B.C. chided and then refocused me. "Now it's time to take your new powers out onto the water."

He motioned me to follow him down to the water's edge and called out to spirits with a deep bellowing, "Nom, summa!"

Suddenly, the water stirred with tiny ripples, rolling waves, swirling pools, and slashing spouts. The water was coming alive, forming shapes that looked like dark, ghoulish monsters. Even as the water monsters swallowed the air around us and as far up as we could see, the shores never got wet or disturbed. It was a most unusual sight, though the smell turned up by the churning water was similar to week-old gym socks.

TALES OF SPOONER POND

"You must step onto the water, Pippy," B.C. instructed me.

"You're crazy!" I said, looking at a raucous assortment of every sort of ghoul before me on the water.

"Trust your twishloc," B.C. coached me. "Step onto the water and Loofit above them as high as you can see. You must believe it. It will protect you and cast authority over the spirits, permitting you to summon the power of Begetting and stilling the water."

I wasn't calm, but somehow, I wasn't afraid. I stared at B.C. for a moment. He looked peaceful and relaxed. I touched him, grabbed his thin arm, squeezed it briefly, and then turned around. I walked right into the tumultuous water and towering water monsters.

Instinctively, I performed Loofit like a pro and found myself riding atop the whitecaps of the waves and the ghoulish shapes of the spouts and shoots of water. Where I sat was pure calm, though, beneath me, it was absolutely violent. I guess Begetting them was appropriate if they were spirits from who knows what B.C. had said.

With as much confidence as anyone could muster, I looked to the mass of violent water below me and proclaimed, "Be gone; I resist you."

I did a lousy job because the water stilled only the slightest bit. But I remained calm and remembered B.C.'s teachings.

"*Be gone; we resist you!*" I said, flinging my hands and fingers at the water. Sparks flew from my hands and out into the water, with long tentacles of electricity wrapping around the necks and arms of the water monsters. It was like I was lassoing them in a corral. Within minutes of the fireworks, the

147

water's surface became glassy, and I sat twenty-five feet above the water on a cushion of air.

"Loofit to me," B.C. called from the shore.

I did as he asked, returning to his side.

"You are almost ready," he said.

"Yeahh…" I said, grinning. I felt like I had a handle on some tremendous power. "I think so, too."

"But there's more."

"More?" I asked, astounded. I wondered what more there could be than Begetting and Loofiting.

"There is a song you must learn, and in time, you will learn more about the powers of Loofiting and Begetting. Right now, though, you will learn the song."

"I can't sing."

"Everyone can sing, but not everyone is a performer," B.C. said. "This song, however, is a necessity for your journey. Whether or not you'll ever use it, I don't know, but if a certain situation presents itself, it is the only power you can use to overcome the demons and evil souls."

"And what is that situation?"

"I don't know, but you will know from your discernment. It is different for each person because the constellations of our fears are different, and for this power to be used, you must sing the song exactly as written."

"This is starting to feel like school and Ms. Charlene's history class or Mr. Dunbar's government class," I said, thinking of how much I hated memorization assignments.

"I don't think Ms. Charlene or Mr. Dunbar know about this." B.C. chuckled.

"Well, if it's anything like Loofit, I'm willing," I said, smiling.

"Here are the words that will, if sung as given, provide you with full immunity to the power of the Hooded Ones and Monitors of Temptation:

Lift your eyes to the skies,

from whence on high does my help come.

For the skies so high, I made all here known,

I will not let your feet be harmed.

I will not ever slumber or sleep.

I will be your keeper and protector.

Lift your eyes to the skies;

from whence on high does my help come.

For skies so high, I will keep you from all evil.

and keep you going forever."

"That's *long*," I said, feeling a touch overwhelmed.

"It's more powerful than all you have learned and ever will learn. It will give you dominion over the Hooded Ones and Monitors of Temptation and place you on even footing with the Howlers. So, practice this, Pippy; you may one day need it and desire dominion over the demons and evil souls that haunt this world."

"I will learn the song," I said. I was starting to feel a conviction that was no longer under my control but consuming me.

"I will learn the song," I repeatedly said, my eyes closed, trying to pound it into my memory. "I will learn the song."

"What are you talking about, Pippy? What song? Not another of those whatever songs you listen to."

This was my mother's voice. And somehow, I was no longer in Spooner Pond. I was not with B.C. in Mystasanctim.

"What, ah, ah, sorry, Mom, I must have been dreaming."

Sometimes, the transition out of Spooner Pond was fast and jarring...but never quite like this. Even stranger, as I came around, she offered to share a plate of cookies and some hot chocolate with me. We were sitting by the fire at the bay window, watching the spectacle of a late spring thunderstorm on a Tuesday afternoon.

I took a cookie and munched on it, doing my best to ignore the strange look my mother was giving me.

CHAPTER EIGHTEEN

Gramma "G," the Flying Goat

"Wake up, Pippy."

"Truggles?" I wondered aloud, half asleep as I stirred in my bed.

No response. I looked about my bedroom, saw no signs of anyone, and tried to go back to sleep, sure I had been dreaming.

"You're ready! East Thwortal, Pippy!"

Still, there were no signs of anyone in my bedroom, but I knew that voice. It was a voice of authority, and I remember responding to it like in the old monster movies where emotionless corpses crawled out of their coffins at the chiming of a bell. It was like I was in a trance myself. I got up, dressed, and transported myself to Spooner Pond's East Thwortal in the middle of the night.

But it wasn't Truggles who was there, waiting for me. I was pretty surprised, but in a good way.

"Grandma Goat?" I said, shocked to see her waiting for me at the East Thwortal. "I didn't think you ever got over this way." I looked her over suspiciously and added, "Maybe you're not Grandma Goat."

And before she could respond, I sniffed her, knowing very well how well Hooded Ones could duplicate almost any character in Spooner Pond.

"Convinced?" Grandma Goat grinned as she raised her eyebrows.

"Sorry, Grandma Goat, but so much has happened here, and I wanted to be sure."

"Certainty and caution do not require an apology at this time of your journey. In fact, certainty and caution are essential to your successful arrival in High Stones."

"But seeing you in this part of Spooner Pond is weird."

"You can thank Furry One for my presence," Grandma Goat said. "The darling hoisted this old body of mine up on her shoulders and carried me across Spooner Pond to be here for you, princess."

"Why, Grandma Goat?" I was still confused about what was being orchestrated by the forces in Spooner Pond. For so many months now, I had been in control of things, but the look in her eyes and this planned meeting, of which I had no genuine part, made me wonder about the power I thought I had.

"First, young lady, from this day forward, call me Granny or Gramma G. No more Grandma Goat formality going on; it will never be the same for us, Pippy."

She looked and smelled like the same old alfalfa-chewing Grandma Goat, but this Granny also had an attitude...and I liked it.

"Come, Pippy, help me tighten my bonnet, for we are on our way to Mystasanctim together to study and prepare you for your journey to High Stones." She paused to stare at me, and at that moment, I was sure I looked confused and half asleep, though it was daytime in Spooner Pond—perfect in every way. "I will guide you throughout your preparation. Are you ready?"

First B.C., then Gramma G., I thought. *It's another treasure Truggles never told me about.*

"Sure. Why not?"

I tightened the tie strings on her flowered bonnet, which looked like something Mrs. Sopher would wear to a picnic. I figured I couldn't say much about it by this time in the conversation anymore. Then, as usual, I wondered if Truggles had arranged this visit with Grandma Goat because, just the day before, I was planning everything I would do this coming summer.

"Thank you, princess," Grandma Goat said. "Now, it's your turn."

She handed me this awful-looking pink and red bonnet and insisted I put it on. So, reluctantly did, and under her careful gaze, I made it so straight and snug.

"Now," she said, "hold my ear."

Why not? I thought and grabbed onto her right ear, which coincidently looked like Feathers' right ear.

"You ready, Pippy?"

"Ready as ever, Granny," I grimaced.

"Good."

"It's an awful long way to walk. Should we go through the maze?" I asked.

Again, Grandma Goat smiled. "No maze just yet. Besides, your Granny's got a much faster way to get to Mystasanctim, but you must first let your mind be free. You worry about the silliest of things, princess."

And with that, Grandma Goat took two steps and lifted off the ground like floating in the air. Alarmed, I let go of her ear and fell two feet.

"You okay, Pippy?"

"Yeah..."

"You must hold on to my ear." She half-scolded me, staring at me like I had failed a trust test. "Just secure your bonnet and hold on!" She smiled at me and added, "Nothing can ruin that hair of yours."

Whew, something that relaxed me. *Okay, so I couldn't fake the bonnet-over-the-hair look very convincingly.*

Whoosh!

Away we went, holding on for the ride of my life as Grandma Goat took off straight up like a helicopter, and we flew, me holding her ear all the while. It was the first time I had an actual aerial view of Spooner Pond where I could see myself flying by treetops, rock outcroppings, hills, and the eastern shoreline of Spooner Pond, if only partially. I could almost see Dack's Lagoon and her home where this sort-of-duck-like palimal lived with her little dacklings.

This flying was something else. I recall many occasions with Truggles over the years when we overlooked Spooner Pond from above, but it was always the sense of dream-flying. Not now, though. We were flying, my hair and clothes blowing in the wake of our flying, and I saw Spooner Pond like no other. My perspective of Spooner Pond changed from awe to *awesome*.

I remembered my not-too-long-ago flight hanging from my butterfly escort as we flew over the Maze. It wasn't the same this time, not at all. Instead, I marveled at how intricate and artistic it was while recognizing its sheer vastness and appreciating the real dangers entangled in certain areas where its three-dimensional framework was mysteriously blurry.

Soon, the sights of the Maze were gone, and we were making a soft landing in the Pinenut Forest on the outskirts of Mystasanctim. We settled near the ridge of land that divided the manicured beauty of the Pinenut Forest and the rugged and wild beauty of the Mystasanctim.

I couldn't concentrate on being there because I couldn't stop thinking about Grandma Goat flying. Why didn't she do this before? And why hadn't anyone ever told me over the past five years? Maybe she had the power of Loofiting? It just didn't make sense. If she could fly anywhere she wanted, she could tow palimals and others all over Spooner Pond. All that talk of her needing to stay around her pastureland because of her age wouldn't be necessary.

Once we hit the ground, my relaxed mind started pondering its curiosity. "Why don't you always use the power of Loofiting, Granny?"

"Oh, sweet thing," she smiled. "I do not Loofit at will like B.C. and some others. I only accommodate Truggles' requests and trust in his word. Today was ours to get here to Mystasanctim to continue your training as the hour of your journey draws near. I simply did as instructed. I was told we would be transported to our destination if you wore the pink and red bonnet and held onto one of my ears. That we flew surprised me, but I have learned over the years to accept these surprises from Truggles, and there was an urgency to get you here. It has been a long time since time mattered so much in Spooner Pond."

"You've never flown before?" My jaw dropped open for the second time that day.

"Well, no," she said, straightening her bonnet with its broad pink and red ribbon tie. "I've flown before here and there, but as I recollect, not for about forty-nine years. That was with a little girl named Patty, I believe."

"But you were so calm."

"I trusted Truggles' word."

"Didn't you worry?"

"That would have violated my trust in Truggles' word. That he chose to have us fly to Mystasanctim was his will."

"Should I understand all this?"

"Not yet, but in time." She began to walk toward the spirit waters of the Mystasanctim, leaving me frozen in my tracks as I contemplated what had been said.

Chasing after her, I asked: "So why are we here? I know Mystasanctim."

"Oh, yes, you know the Loofiting."

"And the *Be gone*," I asserted proudly.

"But do you know patience?" she asked with a grin.

"Sure. I can wait in line at the theater and wait for my dad to gather together his stuff, whatever it is, before we go anywhere."

"And can you sit quietly for an hour?"

"Who'd ever do that?"

"One who aspires to get to High Stones one day must be able to do that." She raised her eyebrows and gazed into my eyes.

"Okay," I said, feeling I had walked into a perfect set-up trap. "What do I need to do, Gramma G.?"

"Just stay with me."

Instead of feeling like she was laughing at me like most adults when they give a phony, condescending laugh, I thought hers was a loving chuckle. Frankly, I never knew the meaning of an affectionate chuckle until that day in Mystasanctim. Adult laughter had always been hard for me to understand in North Star Ridge.

"There is a time yet to come, Pippy, and as you move toward that goal which you are predestined to achieve one day, it will come, no matter all the delays and challenges."

"It doesn't make sense, though," I said as we walked along the trail to the spirit waters. "If something's supposed to happen anyway, why doesn't it just happen?"

"Some things happen, and other things cannot happen until other events and circumstances have come to pass. Even those things that are evil and hateful have existence, sometimes longer than the good and stronger than the hope to overcome them. Therefore, you must believe in the future, which is your destiny."

"I don't get it."

"Truggles has sent me to be with you today because he watches and judges your readiness. So you will know his timing is perfect even though you may not understand the calendar he is using."

"So, be patient?"

"Be *very* patient. There is a time of preparation that all must go through."

"But I don't know what I'm being patient for. What's the goal?".

Grandma Goat stopped on the trail and stared me down. "The goal is and will always be to get to High Stones. But, for now, knowing you are a part of Spooner Pond and that something grand will happen in your life because Truggles has placed you in his will is sufficient." She paused, sighed, and said, "Come on, we're almost there."

"Part of Spooner Pond?" I wondered, chasing after her.

"You became one of us when you were taken to Mystasanctim by B.C. and learned of Loofiting and Begetting, but you have more to learn of Begetting to be fully achieved, and I will teach you. You can resist but not turn away from your destiny. Now, here...sit with me."

I did, and we gazed out to the water.

"Know these things, Pippy," she said. "A lack of patience can cause you to stumble and miss your rewards. The more patient you are, the more the thoughts of Truggles will enter you, and you will know how powerful a feeling has been for you. Imagine how you receive Heliotroppe's thoughts and how patient you must be to hear them...the more patient and quieter you are, the more you hear. Right?"

"Yes, exactly right."

"Well then, this is what patience is all about. You will need to be patient during all your trials, and your patience will be essential for you to make all the critical decisions you will face later today and tomorrow. If you doubt yourself and feel you are losing your patience, focus on High Stones and all it means to you, and as often as possible, patiently observe around you. You will learn from what you observe, but only if you have the patience to see the good things about you."

"And now what? What's next?"

"We're done," Grandma Goat said. "For now."

"Done? What'd we do?"

"You have the tools; you must learn how to use them over the next two days. I will be with you again to go over the next two important steps in your preparation, but first, you must go to the spirit waters and wait to hear from Truggles. Go on."

She eyed the path toward the spirit waters and cocked her head in that direction, making it very clear I had to get going *now!*

So that's what I did, realizing more than ever that I had some work to do when it came to patience.

CHAPTER NINETEEN

Spirit Water Speaks

I sat on the shore of the spirit water for about an hour, listening to an occasional gurgle of spirit energy. The water was as calm as possible, and I spent part of the time thinking about what Grandma Goat had said, but I spent most of the time wondering what I would do that summer. I know it's just one year, but fourteen seems so much bigger than thirteen, and I expected that meant even more opportunities for adventure in North Star Ridge and anywhere my bike or my parents would take me.

As my mind meandered through images past from North Star Ridge and Spooner Pond, I dwelled on Howie Yeary and what had happened at Points Afar. I had a different feeling about him now but was still as confused as ever about his motives. With my thoughts on Howie, an explosion of spirit energy broke the silence of Mystasanctim. The waters in the middle lifted high, forming what looked like a throne of water pulsating energy and sounds. The spectacle lasted three minutes, and I sat there overwhelmed by the sheer force of the demonstration of the spirits. Then, as quickly as it began, it stopped, and the water became still.

"Be strong in your love of High Stones and in the strength of my might, Pippy."

"Truggles?" I glanced around.

"It is I."

"Where are you?" I said. "I can't see you."

"I am with you, but I will not see you again until you come to join us."

"In High Stones?"

"Yes. You are ready, but trust your teachers, for much preparation is yet to be done. First, you must wear the armor of the powers you have learned and have yet to discover that you can stand against the evil souls and demons and all that harbor them. Your challenge is not against what you can see but against their legions, powers, and the doubt they will create in you to bring darkness and wickedness to your life as you try to get to High Stones.

"Pippy, come to me, but take the whole armor of your powers so you can withstand the evil by being truthful, patient, persistent, and resourceful in applying these powers. Then, step out on the tumultuous waters. Do not waiver in your commitment and your quest. Yours is more than a peace mission; it is one of courage and faith. Together, these will protect you from all the fires, illusions, and acts of spirit that the evil ones use to keep others from High Stones.

"Finally, be wise in choosing those palimals and friends you take with you on your journey. They, too, must wear the helmet of courage and faith for you to succeed. When in doubt, never stop asking for me or calling to me, for I am always with you, though there may be others more suited at those times to your relief. Never stop believing and asking."

He paused for a moment, his voice growing quiet and more penetrating.

"Now listen, it is known in High Stones that you shall enter if you are willing and obedient. Yet if you refuse and rebel, you shall be devoured by the powers of the evil ones."

"B.C. said you would permit others to travel with me to High Stones. Can I have palimals with me?"

"That would be up to you and them, but only three palimals, no outsiders, and only one friend. Now go; Rullen awaits you."

"Rullen?"

But there was no response.

"Truggles," I called out. "Who is Rullen?"

Nothing. Several attempts later, still nothing. I was now alone in a place of spirits and bizarre water with powers I still hadn't perfected and many things to remember.

I walked around the body of water, listening to sounds and thinking about what Truggles had said, particularly the part about wearing the armor of the powers I had learned. I have yet to discover how to stand against the evil souls and demons and all that harbors them. I'm sure Truggles was referring to the Hooded Ones, MOTs, and Howlers, but I think I'm more worried about the Ghosts in Courage Cave.

Just then, I rounded the bend in the trail around the body of water and came upon Grandma Goat.

"Oh, Gramma G., am I glad to see you. I'm supposed to see a Rullen. Do you know where I find this Rullen?"

"You've spoken with Truggles?"

"Yes, and Truggles said Rullen was waiting for me."

"That is good news. Rullen will be waiting for you, but not here in Mystasanctim. Instead, he awaits you if you ascend to High Stones."

"Right, it's like what you said about waiting and patience. But, of course, he spoke about a time *when* I got to High Stones." I hesitated and looked at Grandma Goat, "Do you believe I can get there?"

"Most certainly. Now, let's walk and talk about your time with Truggles."

"Can't we fly and talk?" I asked, remembering how thrilling and peaceful it was to fly into Mystasanctim.

"I suppose," Grandma Goat said. "Let's see if I still have the power."

We joined as before, and she summoned the spirit to fly. We were off! After getting over the sheer spectacle of flying high over the Pinenut Forest, we got down to business as we glided through the valleys below.

Deciding on Three for My Journey to High Stones

"So, you can take three palimals," Grandma Goat said. "Have you thought about who would be best to accompany you?"

"I thought right away to take Tahoe because she can be ridden, and it's a long way to High Stones."

"Interesting and wise choice," Grandma Goat said.

"Then I thought about Feathers often because I could fit him in my backpack, and maybe his small size and different look would be useful."

"Feathers is an unusual choice."

"I know, but there's something about the bond between him and Tahoe that I like."

"Hmm," Grandma Goat said, looking me over. "Okay, a provocative choice, but what about the third?"

"This is the hardest one. Benjamin would be great for me in building solutions to physical challenges. But Truggles suggested I would be challenged by legions and powers I cannot see, creating darkness and wickedness as I try to get to High Stones. I don't think Benjamin would be quick enough for those challenges."

"Okay," Grandma Goat said.

"Then there's Furry One, who'd have great power but would have less agility and speed." I paused a moment, smiled at Grandma Goat, and continued. "Same with you, Gramma G."

"Yes, darling, I know, but thank you for considering me." She was teasing, of course, knowing better than I that she'd be a poor choice for the journey.

"Then there's Dack, who can't leave her dacklings, and B.C., who can't leave the Pinenut Forest, and Heliotroppe, who's totally a mystery to me."

"And so..." Grandma Goat urged me on.

"And so, the third palimal I plan to take with me is Kitty Joe because he'll never leave my side and always be comforting. Besides," I stomped my foot and nodded in a symbolic show of certainty, "the three of them do very well together, and I think they'll be a fantastic team. And you know Tahoe and Kitty Joe are pretty witty."

"You shall have a wonderful adventure." Grandma Goat smiled and reset the bonnet on her head.

"I think so, but I still have to pick a friend to accompany me," I said, twirling my right hand's index and middle fingers through my hair.

"That should be easy. Why not take Sarah? She's your best friend."

"I thought so at first, but then I thought about what Truggles had said about my mission, and I'm not sure," I said, pacing back and forth.

"What are you concerned about?" Grandma Goat said, nudging me.

"Sarah is the coolest and very physical, but she's more impatient than I am, which worries me. But, on the other hand, I'd trust my life with her." I sat, holding my head and eyeing Grandma Goat to gauge her response.

"You have to work this out by tomorrow," Grandma Goat said, rubbing me with her head and neck. "What's your biggest concern?"

"Well, it's more than one. Truggles said to withstand the evil I will face, I must be truthful, patient, persistent, faithful, courageous, and resourceful in using my acquired powers. Four out of the six aren't a problem with Sarah," I said, standing, "but the other two are major problems." I gazed skyward as if I expected a solution to be rained down on me.

"What other choices do you have?"

"That's my problem, too. I guess I could ask my total athlete dad, but that's just too weird, and I think he'd be more into the adventure of it and not realize I had a mission. I can't ask Lou or Emily because they'd freak out and go blabbing to everyone." Then I looked at her, half-embarrassed by all the annoying stories I had told her. With a sigh, I added, "The only other possibility that recently came to mind is Howie."

"That smart-mouthed boy at the Points Afar All-Universe Power and Magic Championships who's been after you for the past few years?" Grandma Goat stared at me suspiciously but with a curious grin slipping across her face.

"Yes, Howie Yeary," I said with half a smile.

"Well, that is interesting, isn't it?" She gave me a look that reminded me of my mom. "You of all persons to fall for that rascal?"

"No! It's not like that at all," I asserted. "I wonder if he'd be a better companion on the journey?"

"How is he with your six areas of concern?"

"He's mighty in courage and faith, but Howie's truthfulness concerns me. Courage and faith are the most important in protecting us from evil one's acts of fire, illusions, and possibly death to keep me from High Stones."

"Which of your friends will wear the helmet of courage and faith best?" Grandma Goat emphasized, peering at me over the rim of her eyeglasses.

"I really don't know. I know my lack of trust in Howie's truth-stretching is a big problem, but Sarah's lack of patience and persistence is equally worrisome."

"Come on, follow me," she said, motioning me to walk along a trail.

We trotted on for another twenty minutes after arriving at a very tall tree, much taller than Flying Tree and easily as wide. The shade of the large-leaved tree nurtured the growth of a soft, light green grass at its base. Grandma Goat encouraged me to sit on the tree.

"You've got the weight of Spooner Pond on your shoulders, Pippy, and that won't do. Are you certain Sarah or Howie even want to come with you?"

"Oh, I'm certain Sarah would want to go. And after the Points Afar Championships, I got this feeling from Howie that he really liked *and respected* me." I glanced at Grandma Goat rather pensively and asked, "So, what do I do?"

Grandma Goat stared at me for a moment, looking almost like she was ready to chuckle. "I think the answer is quite el-

ementary: Take your two friends with you through the Maze...
together, all three of you. The process will allay your concerns
about either, sufficient for you to make the proper choice. You
must be attentive to their ways and use your twishloc as you
look them in the eyes. Then, you will know who to ask to join
you."

"Okay," I said, "but how can I get them to go in the Maze by
tomorrow?"

"I'll take care of that," Grandma Goat said. "Plan to meet
them at the Maze tomorrow at ten o'clock. And be sure they
know what to expect...if you can."

CHAPTER TWENTY-ONE

Will It Be Sarah or Howie for the Journey to High Stones?

Sarah and Howie were thrilled to come with me, as expected. Howie seemed incredibly excited when I told him about the Maze. We arrived at the Maze at ten o'clock and began scanning the entrance to the Maze. Each of us knew this was a get-together to determine who would accompany me on my journey to High Stones, and without hesitation, we winked at each other and entered the Maze.

"First, my ladies," Howie said, hiking his jeans over his hips. "Let the man protect you from any danger."

Oh, brother, I thought.

Howie led us into the Maze under the rock archway and through the hole bored through the large, disfigured tree. Sarah and I followed. Convinced Howie was taking the wrong direction through the three-dimensional hole in the tree, Sarah attempted another approach, only to get tangled in the rubbery gooey substance. Twenty seconds in, I was already worried about my choice to accompany me.

"Come on, Sarah," I said, encouraging her. "Just follow Howie."

"He's just as cocky as ever, Pippy!"

"Yes, and you're way too competitive," I said. "We need to work together. Now, come on."

"Hey, ladies," Howie interrupted as he faced the jagged rock outcropping. "I think we've got our first challenge."

"I think you're right, Howie, but lose the 'ladies' talk." I admonished him, thinking, *One of these two better get it together, or I'll be in deep dew fast.*

A pitched voice challenged us as we stood before the rock with no apparent way to turn. "Welcome, princess," the voice began. "Two friends with you today?"

"Ah, yeah," I said, glancing at my two companions. "This is Sarah and Howie from North Star Ridge."

"Hmm, Sarah and the obnoxious boy," the rock chuckled. "This will be fun."

Great, I thought, already worried that my plan was unraveling.

"Well, I'm sure my description is correct," Howie grinned and flipped up his long hair. "How 'bout you, Sarah?" He then bowed before Sarah as if she was a queen.

Sarah's body language made it clear she had a response at the ready, but before she could utter a word, the pitched voice of the rock intervened. "No time for play, children. If you want to pass, you've got to figure out this little formula riddle: Nychthemeron x 14 = 2 x sennight = _____. Your answer must be only a single word."

The rock's challenge silenced Sarah and put me on edge. But Howie seemed eager for the challenge as a smile slowly started forming on his face. "It's not that difficult," he said. "Nychthemeron is the equivalent of a twenty-four-hour day. So, four-teen times a day is fourteen days or two weeks. A sennight is seven days or a week. Thus, two times a sennight is fourteen days or two weeks." His grin widened as he nodded and, after a few seconds, said, "I've got it figured out."

"No way," Sarah protested.

"Yes, way," Howie said with a slight smirk.

"Wait," Sarah said desperately out of character. "Let me try to figure it out, and you tell me if I'm right before we announce it."

"Sure, go for it," Howie said.

I suspect Sarah looked at me for approval, and I was pretty much to the point with her, giving her a thumbs down. I nod-ded approval to Howie, and he announced the answer to the jagged rock.

"The answer is fortnight!"

The jagged rock applauded us in a clunky sort of way and instructed us to pass. We found ourselves sitting atop a rela-tively high overlook that I hadn't remembered before, and I wondered if the Maze had shifted and changed to accommo-date its different visitors.

We glanced to each side, before and behind us, and saw there was nowhere we could go. The trail leading us to the over-look had disappeared, and it seemed the area we were stand-ing was getting smaller and less stable. Then a giggly scratchy voice came out of the air: "Take the 'p' out of him, and you at-tract him."

We stood there on a smaller piece of land and were stymied by the riddle. I could see that the longer we stood there, the further away Sarah became emotionally. Maybe she was in deep contemplation of the problem. I didn't know, but we weren't getting anywhere, and I was ready to call for a butterfly escort. I began to doubt the idea of Grandma Goats as a way to select my travel companion to High Stones.

Then, as if struck by lightning, Howie asked, "Is Heliotroppe a boy?"

"Yeeeaaa," I said, staring at him and shaking my head. "I've always thought of Heliotroppe as a 'he' because his voice seems like he. But what..."

"And is B.Cee Butterfly a guy?" Howie interrupted.

"Of course, silly," Sarah quipped. "B.C. is a guy's name."

"Good," said Howie confidently. "Then I've got the answer."

"No way!" I marveled.

"No way, for *sure*," Sarah insisted.

"Oh yes. It's rather easy," Howie said. "Heliotroppe is the first 'him' in the riddle, and B.C. Butterfly is the second 'him.' Are you with me?" Howie asked as yet another smirking smile beamed from his face. "Take one 'p' out of Heliotroppe's name, and you get Heliotrope, a flower that attracts butterflies."

Upon completing his sentence, the overlook upon which we stood flattened out and spread out. A patch of thick grass awash with brilliantly colored wildflowers was laid before us with a clearing in the wildflowers that appeared to look like a trail to follow. Then, again, the voice came from the air about us, urging us to follow the carpet for one more stop.

Wow, easy trip this time, I thought.

The three of us strolled down the carpet of grass, noticing that the path was growing distorted, and the three-dimensional flowers were growing more brilliant in color and depth, as was the carpet of grass. It was as if the path was alive, with colors and textures flowing together like fluid. Watching it was mesmerizing, but following it became less play and more skill as we neared its end.

There before us was a confusing crossroads. Vines and assorted climbing plants grew abundant in the area, with a scattering of medium and tall trees, misshapen no doubt by the forces of nature that created the Maze, yielding three distinct directions in the trail. We debated the best direction to go. I thought we should go left, but Howie insisted we go right, and of course, Sarah couldn't agree with Howie, or me for that matter, and she wanted to go straight. At first, Howie argued with us to make his case, but my gut said to go my way.

As we approached the left direction, Howie halted us. He stooped to examine the plant growth at the center entrance, the one on the right and the left.

"Sarah's right. The center path is the right one."

"See, I told you," Sarah said, jabbing me in the ribs.

"How are you so sure, Howie?" I asked.

"It's simple," he said, pointing down the plants' features. "Look at the plants' organs—those tendrils or long fingers," he said, pointing to the center entrance. "The tendrils are growing and grabbing onto the vines and trees. The other very real-looking plants on the right and left don't have any tendrils. It's simple; it's the principle of thigmotropism. It must apply, and the trail to the right and left don't have it in evidence."

We were so blown away by Howie's explanation that nothing was uttered, and we just took off down the center path.

Then, forty feet later, we arrived at our final riddle. Before us was a small body of water and thorns and casings larger than I had ever seen in the Maze. They looked like they were two feet in length and about two inches around, and were they ever noisy, going in and out all around us but not really threatening us.

From the water came the riddle in a deep, hollow voice: "Chemoautotrophic bacteria are to *what* as grain and vegetation are to locusts?"

"Okay, Howie," I said, ignoring Sarah, "can you get us through this one?"

"Wow, this is a tough one," Howie said as he thought about it, peered around, and stared at the water. "Maybe not."

"What's wrong, Mr. Science?" Sarah taunted him.

"Be still, Sarah," I ordered.

"Chemoautotrophic bacteria are found deep in water where the sunlight can't get through," Sarah began as Howie and I did a double take. "Like this water here; it's almost black. I can't remember underwater life, particularly chemical self-feeding." She paused for a moment, uncertain.

"Come on, Sarah," Howie encouraged her, "run with this."

"Think, Sarah," I said.

"Pippy, you think, too. Remember that video you saw in Dr. Daniel's biology class last year."

"Yeah, I remember, but that was so long ago."

"Something about giant worms, but not just giant worms," Sarah said.

"Tube worms. That's it, giant tube worms!" I said.

"That's it, Pippy," Sarah smiled. "Giant tube worms and, and, and mollusks and crabs. Yeah," Sarah screamed, "the answer is giant tube worms, mollusks, and crabs!"

Nothing happened.

"The answer is giant tube worms, mollusks, and crabs!" Sarah said again.

Still nothing.

Then it hit me; it wasn't just any old crab but vent crabs.

"The answer is giant tube worms, mollusks, and *vent* crabs!" I said as I hugged Sarah. Indeed, that was the correct answer, and with Howie in tow, we were transported to the Pinenut Forest, where B.C. and Grandma Goat greeted us.

"And have you made your decision, young lady?" Grandma Goat asked.

"Kind of, but I need to talk with my friends alone."

"Very well...join us when you've decided," Grandma Goat said as she strolled off with B.C. riding on her head.

I pulled Sarah aside and sat with her. "Sarah, you are my absolute best friend, and I can't think of anyone I want to be within North Star Ridge more than you. This will be quite a journey, and I think it'd be good for you to be with me."

"Stop, Pippy. This is your best friend talking," she said, tapping me on the shoulder. "Take Howie, not me. All emotions aside, he'll do a better job than I will. And I think he'll get you to High Stones. But you're going to need to learn to trust him. As hard as I tried, I couldn't get him to crack in the Maze, and after what happened in the Maze, I'd definitely trust him." She smiled and hugged me.

"Sarah, you are my best friend," I said as I returned her hug with a bear hug.

"Yeah, something happened to Howie out there in the Maze. He was exceptionally cool, but I think it began at the Points Afar Championships, don't you?" I said.

"Without a doubt, it's more than he's really a smart guy; he adores you, Pippy," Sarah teased.

"Yeah, maybe." I blushed.

"Ah, come on. Sure, Howie does, but that's okay because he'll do everything to impress you. So, as long as you stay focused, he will be focused and do wonders for you. It'll be like having your own Superman with you, only you'll be chaperoned by a horse, a mouse, and a kitty."

"I will tell Howie; ask him if he wants to go with me."

"Don't accept a nod for an answer. Insist Howie say it boldly: *Pippy, I will go and protect you from all evil!* Or something like that." Sarah laughed, and I joined her to relieve the stress that had descended on me. The time was near, and I had to talk with Howie.

I walked over to where Howie had joined B.C. and Grandma Goat. Apparently, they had been exchanging words and songs.

"Your friend is quite a lyricist, Pippy," B.C. said.

"Is he?" I said with a twisted smile.

"He's quite good."

"We could use him here," B.C. said as he fluttered about Howie's head.

"I hope not too soon because I will ask Howie to accompany me on my journey to High Stones."

"Well, I'll be...I mean, I'm overjoyed. Yeowee!"

"Your boy is obnoxiously happy about this." Grandma Goat laughed.

I stared at Howie acting all boyish and happy and thought, *What have I gotten myself into?* Then, we grabbed his arm, excused ourselves from Grandma Goat and B.C., and led Howie to an area several feet away, where we stood amidst a field of fragrant purple and yellow flowers.

"There must be something special about you, Howie Yeary. You were most spectacular in the Maze; now Gramma G. and B.C. have taken to you. What's happened to you? I noticed even Shardam had a fondness for you." I paused to look over this *new* boy in my life. "I *really* want you to go with me on my journey to High Stones because I like the idea of having a smart, witty, pretty good-looking super boy with me, even though you're only fifteen."

"I'm thrilled, Pippy, but can you trust me?" Howie gazed at me like he had so many times before when I had doubted him.

"Absolutely. But first level with me."

"Sure. What?"

"You knew about the giant tube worms, mollusks, and vent crabs, didn't you?"

"This is about trust, huh?"

"Yes, Howie."

"Yeah, I did," he said, smiling sheepishly.

"But you wanted Sarah to succeed, didn't you?"

"She's your best friend, and I was preoccupied with looking around."

"Sure. You know, you're really something, Howie Yeary."

"So, it's just you, me, and your palimals off to High Stones?" he asked.

"Yes, just us and *our* palimals—Tahoe, Kitty Joe, and Feathers." I stared at his eager face for a moment. "And no, this doesn't mean we're together."

"Good, I'd hate the pressure of working on a relationship while fighting evil souls, demons, and monsters," Howie said, chuckling. "Especially with only a horse, mouse, and cat to help me."

"Ha, ha. I'm glad we understand each other, then. Because we've got a lot of work to do before leaving."

CHAPTER TWENTY-TWO

Evil Souls, Monitors of Temptation, and the Ghosts of Courage Cave

Howie and I spent the week strategizing over my approach to High Stones. He felt our best route would be through Back Trail, where we could take on the Hooded Ones and MOTs. He based his assumption on the kind of powers I had acquired, figuring they would be most effective against the actions of the evil souls and demons so abundant among the Hooded Ones and MOTs. Comparing the Back Trail route to the Courage Cave route, Howie reasoned Back Trail challenges would better prepare me to confront the Howlers who lived in the Threshold of High Stones, but I wasn't so sure. I thought Courage Cave was the way to go because there wasn't too much I was afraid of since the Ghosts of Courage Cave didn't elicit much concern...except maybe my death.

I didn't have the same confidence as Howie about taking on the Hooded Ones. They were the "evil souls" of Spooner Pond. When they're their usual selves, they appear haunting, wearing dark hooded robes with their hoods covering what you think would be their heads and bodies. But it's not so. They don't walk; they float in the air. They have no feet, and although their hoods are up and their hands and arms appear to fill the sleeves, there's nothing there either.

Hooded Ones have the power of absolute thought control. If you need proof of their ability, they'll materialize objects and treasures, move things that appear unmovable, like rooted trees and huge boulders, and create situations involving people, objects, and sounds that appeal to you and convince you to follow them. Moreover, they have an affinity for twisting your thoughts so that you start believing in what you don't think, doubting what you had always known to be true, and desiring the supernatural powers they tempt you to sample. The only catch in exchange for their powers is that they expect you to surrender your will, and from what I hear, visitors are up there bargaining with them all the time for forces they seek to use against others and to please themselves.

Then there are those Monitors of Temptation we call MOTs for short. Not only do they have the ability to use the Hooded Ones' powers, but they also possess their own more specialized powers. They, too, are bodiless and even more formless demon spirits than the Hooded Ones because they have no physical identity except when they express through objects they inhabit or materialize. MOTs conform to your wants by possessing objects of your desire. Once you've made physical contact with the objects, they can enter you and begin to control your emotions by influencing how you feel. Whether you're feeling happy or sad, fearful or brave, they *must* control how and what you think.

I'm sure we'll find MOTs all over the Back Trail, and I know it's dangerous to like or desire anything too much if you're anywhere near a MOT when they can materialize things like Sarah's Wonder Stones to entice you. I suppose they could even inhabit the rocks you sat on, the tree you leaned against or climbed, or be in the water you drank, but I doubt they'd be in a candy bar that was in your knapsack or in a piece of sweet root growing wild along Back Trail. The good news about the MOTs is that they're not marauders and are principally found in only the northern part of Spooner Pond in Rock Castle Mountain, the Back Trail, and the Bend of Back Trail.

Weighing the threats of the Hooded Ones and MOTs, it seemed the better way to High Stones was through one of the five tunnels in Courage Cave. Still, that's no party if you've got some fears because the Ghosts of Courage Cave inhabit the walls of the five tunnels and deal out their unique Spooner Pond demonizing. But, of course, the Ghosts only bother you when you fear something in your life. So, no fears, no Ghosts—they don't bother to come out of the walls!

In the presence of fear, however, the Ghosts can sense all your spoken and unspoken fears. Upon doing so, the Ghosts materialize from the walls through various sounds and visual images, transforming to create realities that force you to confront your fears—even those you hide very well from your parents and friends. Nothing is hidden from the Ghosts of Courage Cave, and to get to High Stones through Courage Cave, you cannot ignore your fears and unresolved conflicts.

Hundreds of Ghosts inhabit the five tunnels in Courage Cave, and they are grouped to have specific identities, though no form, with particular specializations. To name a few group-ings, the *Frampie* group deals with fears related to darkness and shadows, and the *Pulwings* group deals with worries relat-ed to the unknown. The *Bisree* group favors scary sounds and objects, and the *Termogs* group confronts your inner demons.

There is no mistaking it; the Ghosts of Courage Cave can transform themselves and the tunnel they inhabit into whatev-er stage and arena they choose. It depends on what they must do to gain control and dominate you. Once in the tunnels, you can't turn around and backtrack to the entrance. Either you endure or outwit their attacks, or you do what Lou did when he was ready to give up and holler "Sa, Jo!" to liberate you from the Ghosts. Once you've been transported to the entrance of Courage Cave, you are free to choose another tunnel, yet you are forbidden to use the tunnel from which you sought escape ever again.

The Threshold of High Stones is a short five-minute walk from the exit of Courage Cave. The direction is obvious—a lazy, winding trail marked by small yet increasingly more sig-nificant boulders leading to an unimaginably massive wall that appears limitless in height and breadth. It's like standing at the bottom of a giant dam and seeing a concrete face that reaches high into the sky, only at the Threshold of High Stones; the massive wall is rock, not concrete, and neither its top nor sides can be seen. Gazing up, the face of the wall is at least as high as the bank building in town, and that's eight stories high, and then it disappears into the clouds that hover over this part of Spooner Pond.

At the base of the massive wall, this boulder-lined trail leads you to the Threshold of High Stones, a ten-foot high, maybe seven-foot-wide triangular opening in the wall. Step through it, and it leads to a steep, narrow trail that drops you into a valley teeming with lush plant growth amid spectacular gold columns. This is all part of the Threshold to High Stones, home to the Howlers, who possess the magnificent power of physical illusion and the ability to control the elements of nature. They are more powerful than the Hooded Ones or MOTs, more illusionary than the Ghosts of Courage Cave, and they rely on these powers to find weak points in your personality and spirit to attack.

The good news is that the "Sa Jo!" command works in the Threshold of High Stones and Courage Cave, but if you use it to escape the Howlers, you are transported to the Bend of Back Trail, and the joys that await you there. Usually, the winds that precede a Howler's presence are so violent you need to anchor yourself to something solid, or you'll blow away. Then, the tortuous gusts come roaring through the valley and either descend on you in the valley or sweep up upon you.

Sadly, I know this from experience.

The memory is clear enough most of the time—thanks to Truggles. It had been a less-than-spectacular Halloween with my friends, but Truggles turned it into one I'd never forget... because I spent it in the Threshold of High Stones.

We were in the Threshold of High Stones, striding down the trail into the canyon, when the strong tornado-like wind approached from below. I felt my feet and legs lift off the ground as I held onto Truggles' neck. He remained stable through this, but I was being tossed about like a rag doll.

"Is it time to say 'Sa, Jo?'" I trembled, fighting to hold on.

"Be still, Pippy," he answered.

"Be still?" I whined. "I can barely hang on."

"The wind will stop."

Be still? Is he crazy? Hollering "Sa, Jo!" makes more sense to me. And at that moment, the wind ceased, and I fell limp against Truggles.

"Stand up, Pippy," said a thundering voice.

I twisted, squirmed, finger-combed my hair to untangle it, and stretched before peering up.

"Yeow!"

I grabbed Truggles again and glanced up in the direction of the voice to see what appeared to be a forty-foot-high genie with a mean scowl on his face and wearing a decorated robe. His left hand, five feet across, was outstretched toward me.

"Truggles," I pleaded for help, squeezing his neck, yet feeling drawn to the genie's hand but not wanting to surrender.

"The genie is a Howler. It is your destiny, Pippy."

"But you're supposed to protect me!"

"No, I am supposed to guide you," he retorted.

The genie extended his hand toward me, and I climbed aboard. Why, I don't know. It was like I was in a trance, but I remember sitting in his palm, shaking like crazy, but I wouldn't holler, "Sa Jo!" Is that weird, or what? Truggles there, I felt safe, even though he was down there, and I was on my way up.

"Well, young lady," the genie said in a deep, almost deafening yet controlled voice as he held me to his face. *I was freaked out, sitting in the palm of a Howler genie with foul breath nearly forty feet off the ground and realizing I hadn't overcome my fear of heights.*

"You're trembling, Pippy," the genie said, laughing at me. "So big and so little, aren't you, Pippy?" He taunted me with his slow-paced words, then paused and held me inches from his face, so close I could see my reflection in his eyes. His belly laughter almost blew me off his hand. "Miss your daddy, little princess Pippysqueak?"

"You put me down!" I demanded.

"Sure." He laughed, then dropped me like a hot potato.

Freefalling, I closed my eyes and yelled Truggles' name. A moment later, I was on Truggles' back, shaking and out of breath but safe.

"The Howler was playing with you, Pippy," Truggles grinned. "You did well."

"That was the play? I'm relieved." I paused before tugging on Truggles' neck and scolding him. "You were sure a big help."

"Did I ever leave you?"

"No," I said, hesitating. "But will you ever leave me?"

"Not as long as you continue to believe in me."

"But you let me get attacked by a Howler," I protested.

"That was no attack." He chuckled. "Just a demonstration. Howlers' attacks are full-scale, without teasing, and occur along the valley floor."

"Will you be there if I am attacked by a Howler?" I said, giving Truggles my sweet and innocent, never-fails-me smile.

"Young, sweet. I will be with you as long as you believe in me, but you must take on the Howlers yourself to get to High Stones.

"Mind you, their attacks are the most brutal of all demon souls and spirits in Spooner Pond. Full-on attacks by a Howler of the size that confronted you can be fatal, but would you rather have one Howler to contend with than a shower of monstrous snakes or spiders some receive?"

He stopped long enough to hug me in his Truggles. "Come on, and know I will always be with you, even when the Howlers show no mercy. Remember, they know if you get by them and make it to High Stones, they'll never again be able to control you, and in fact, you will have dominion over them because each time you get past these creatures, you demonstrate a power stronger than their own. Know further that each success you have enrages them, and they will use whatever power needed to diminish your will and thereby defeat you."

"Like, how intense would they get?"

"They will do whatever they must to diminish your will to control you. *Anything!* Controlling you increases their power by one. However, success asserting your will and using your resources and powers to overcome their powers is a victory for you that decreases their power by ten while increasing your power by one hundred."

"I can't imagine what I'd do with all the power," I said.

"That's your choice because once you have mastered it, your powers will be active in North Star Ridge or here in Spooner Pond...for as long as you choose to continue to believe."

CHAPTER TWENTY-THREE

On Our Way to High Stones

Kitty Joe had yet to join us by the time we began our trek to High Stones by way of Courage Cave, and the remaining four of us rode on Tahoe's back. Benjamin had made a saddle for us suited to our long adventure. It had a broad saddle horn for added stability, over which I'd hang my backpack, and a long double seat to accommodate my team. Howie sat in front, and I was behind with Feathers in my favorite backpack slung over the saddle horn or my shoulders. I had taken this backpack on camping trips with my dad several times, and it was very roomy—plenty of space for goodies. Howie had a long samurai sword slung across his chest and rested on his left side; beneath it, a clandiram slung across his chest and rested on his right side. Beneath the clandiram, he wore a ten-inch hunting knife secured in a handcrafted sheath. I had on my best running shoes and Howie's favorite trekking boots. We both wore loose pants with plenty of pockets.

As we were riding along, my curiosity got the best of me. "About that clandiram, Howie?" I wondered. "Did you get that by honorable means?"

"Right from Zebteema."

"It's empty, right?" Tahoe asked.

"You mean, did she take out her venoms?" Howie patted Tahoe on her neck and turned to smile at me. "Of course, she did, but I think it's a righteous pouch for carrying stuff."

"What, like gum and candies?" I said.

"Yeah, so?"

"Whatever."

"You've got the strangest habits, Howie," Tahoe said.

"I picked them up from my grandpa."

"Well, speaking of picking up," Tahoe said, staring ahead to her left, "there's K.J."

And there, another twenty feet along Happy Trail, Kitty Joe sat waiting for us, a sack full of something beside him.

"What's you got there, Kitty Joe?" Howie asked.

"Snacks fir ya 'n Feathers," he snapped.

"Oh great," I said. "All these guys can think of is eating snacks."

Kitty Joe hopped aboard, and Howie stuffed the sack in the backpack along with Feathers, who now sat higher in the backpack, substantially increasing the overall weight.

"You'll now be carrying this backpack, Howie, when we get down and walk," I ordered.

"Yes, ma'am," he chuckled. "Want me to just put it on now and sit behind you and put my arms around your waist to hold on?"

"Nice try." I glared at him. "You can put it on as soon as we reach Courage Cave. In the meantime, you keep riding in front of me."

Kitty Joe climbed onto Tahoe's head for the remainder of the trip to Courage Cave, teasing his friend, "No way I'm getting near yar nasty nostril drippins, Tahoe."

Inside the entrance to Courage Cave, Howie yelled, "Howie is a Rock Star!" and the walls started rocking. It didn't take me long to choose a door to escape the pounding beat, and we went. The tunnel was generous in size. With a nine-foot ceiling twice that width, there was plenty of room for all five of us. Kitty Joe and Feathers remained atop Tahoe, and Howie trotted alongside them as I led the way, this being *my* journey through Courage Cave. This meant I would be the one on which the Ghosts would focus their attention.

"Bam bam baloo, bam bam baloo, bam bam baloo!"

A cacophony of scary sounds from every angle of the wall and ceiling stopped us in our tracks. And then, as quick as that, animated drums and cymbals floated around us, playing themselves loudly and obnoxiously, accompanied by a chorus of giant whistles and trumpets marching toward us, tooting out the calvary charge.

Instinctively, I plugged my ears even though it didn't help much. I looked to Howie for help as if he knew what to do. He, too, had his fingers in his ears. Still sitting on Tahoe's head, Kitty Joe stared at me like I was hopeless, and by now, Tahoe had seated herself on the cave floor with Feathers tucked in beside her neck.

"You're all a big help," I complained, yelling in Howie's ear.

"They're Bisree," Howie mouthed as he placed his mouth so close to me I could smell his bubble gum, prompting me to make faces at him because I absolutely loved bubble gum, and he hadn't offered me any.

He grabbed my hand, briefly pulled my finger from my ear, and said nonchalantly, "Just endure them."

"What, you're the big expert now?" I offered as the shrill sounds grew far more annoying.

The Ghosts' sounds vibrated through my head, making it feel like my eyeballs were dancing in their sockets. Yet, simultaneously, it felt like the bones in my joints were scraping together, bone to bone, as the whistles and trumpets marched over us like we weren't even there. Looking at him like I thought he was nuts, I watched as the marching whistles and trumpets blanketed my palimals and passed over them.

With my fingers still in my ears, I glanced again at Howie, looked at the obnoxious Bisree, and yelled to my palimals, "How about some help here?"

My friends didn't move, but the Bisree did calm down...for a bit. So I yelled again, even louder, only this time I screamed at the Bisree. "Bisree, be quiet!"

It helped a little, but they continued on with their loud sounds. So amidst their chatter, though not nearly as noisy, I convened my troop and gave them a quick lesson on how to Beget the Bisree as a group, figuring it'd be the only way to be loud enough to get the Bisree's attention.

Tahoe stood. Howie stood on one side of her head, and I was on the other, as Kitty Joe and Feathers sat on her. Then, on my cue and in our loudest voices, we demanded, "Begone Bisree, we resist thee!"

Nothing happened, so we tried again.

"Begone Bisree, we resist thee!"

Again, nothing.

"Command them as one, Pippy," Howie encouraged.

At that point, what was there to lose? So, I did, as loudly as possible, I said, "Begone Bisree, I resist thee!"

The response to my Begetting them was immediate. The remaining haunting whistles and trumpets that appeared as only illusions melted away like liquid mercury flowing into an opening in the floor that sucked them up like a drain. The drums and cymbals began ricocheting off the walls like ping-pong balls, and after a couple of collisions, they were slowly absorbed into the walls without leaving a sign they had ever been there.

I stared at Howie briefly and then at my palimals, wondering who would speak first. I expected to hear a wise quip from Howie, but he was preoccupied with checking Tahoe's saddle and petting her while Kitty Joe was tongue-grooming Feathers. It was like nothing happened at all, though I learned two things for sure: one, the power of Begetting was real, and I, I alone, had that tremendous power. Second, I also felt that maybe Howie's cool demeanor was actually for real.

***

We moved silently through the tunnel, all of us watching and listening. I thought deeply, recalling the many variations of Begetting and Loofiting training. Now that I knew it worked, I thought about how I might have used some of these options with the Bisree. But the reality around the next turn extinguished the luxury of such fantasy.

Suddenly, the walls started weeping flames. The fire surrounded us within a minute, and I grabbed my hair and rolled it up next to my head. Terrified, I recalled when I was five years old, my long hair caught fire while roasting marshmallows on one of our camping trips. My dad grabbed me, ran me into the river next to our camp, and dunked me to douse the flames. But unfortunately, I had blocked that from my memory, and it was in the tunnel with us all at once.

"Follow me," Howie ordered. "It's the Pulwings at work. C'mon, we can walk through the fire."

"I can't," Tahoe whimpered as the Pulwings group of Ghosts shot flames and sparked fires throughout the tunnel. Immediately, I realized that while the Ghosts were focused on me, all of us were being threatened by their actions—another change in the rules of Spooner Pond—something Truggles warned me about.

Feathers cowered on her back along with Kitty Joe, and again, I stared at Howie like he was crazy, forgetting how I was amazed by his extraordinary moments earlier.

"Can't you feel the heat?" I said, my heart pumping like I was running a race. "The flames are wicked-looking and getting bigger! Don't you hear their crackle?"

"But are you sweating?" he challenged. "No, and there's no smoke, either. No smoke, no fire. It's all pure Ghost illusion. We can walk through the fire, and it won't harm us unless we think it will." He took a deep breath, grabbed my hand, and said: "C'mon. Stay right next to me."

With his right hand, Howie held my left hand, and with his left hand, he grabbed Tahoe's long mane and marched the five of us through the flames. "Blow lightly as we pass through the flames, so you don't forget to breathe," Howie instructed us.

Remarkably, we did pass through the flames while my hands tightly covered my hair.

CHAPTER TWENTY-FOUR

From Coffin to Noggin' Nudger Moment

We were nearing the end of the tunnel, and right before the exit, we stopped to assess how we were doing. Feathers hadn't uttered a word the whole way, nor had Kitty Joe. Tahoe was shaken but strong, and Howie was, well, Howie, my super guy.

We opened what we thought was the exit door only to find what appeared to be a movie screen playing a terrifying movie...and I was the lead actor.

The scene was a university youth camp last summer. There I was in my knee-length animal-print pajamas with my bunkmate, GracieAnn. I glanced over at Howie, grinning as he eyed me. "Nice painted toes," he said. I lowered my head in disgust and embarrassment.

"This isn't real, Howie."

"You were at camp last year. Wasn't GracieAnn your bunkmate?"

"Yeah, but it's not what we see right now."

"Looks pretty real to me," Howie said.

I didn't realize how I was getting sucked into this illusion, but I knew I didn't want it to go on. But it did.

GracieAnn was sixteen and a camp counselor. It was her seventh year at camp, and right before us in the cave tunnel, she spoke as if speaking to all of us, telling us with emphasis that she had stayed in this same dorm room for each of the past three years and that this dorm room was special.

There we were, lying on our beds talking about girl stuff, definitely not what I wanted Howie to hear because he was part of the conversation where I admitted I liked him but disliked his macho attitude. Again, I glanced at him, nodding approval of my comments, as an innocent grin crept across my face.

The expression on his face turned to a horrified look as he stared at the cave tunnel wall. I peered at the image, and there I was, going into a trance as my clothes or outer skin had become the walls of a coffin where my awake body was lying.

I then started trembling because the image on the wall revealed a dream I had with GracieAnn, but one I hadn't told anyone about, and she said she was afraid to tell anyone about it. I thought of taking it to Dack but never did. At my lowest point last year, I was even tempted to take it to Mrs. Sopher, but I never got enough courage.

The five of us fixed our eyes on the tunnel wall as we watched me lying face up in a coffin that appeared to be a part of me. The scene changed on the wall without warning; it became three-dimensional and now, from my point of view, in the dream. It was like we all watched it as if lying in a coffin. The image on the tunnel wall was a close-up from my point of view of lying in the coffin, and the three-dimensional image drew us in more.

Together, we watched as the coffin lid was placed over our heads as if we were there. Tahoe closed her eyes, and Feathers jumped into Howie's arms, an absolute first. Next, however, Kitty Joe hopped into my arms and rubbed his head against my face. It felt like we were all in a coffin, and right there before us, a force we couldn't see was hammering nails into the coffin's lid to trap us inside. The horror for me was that what we watched on the tunnel wall was just as it was in my dream. The three-dimensional image on the tunnel wall drew us in; while the lights dimmed, the nails were pounded in, first at my feet, then my legs, then my waist, then around my upper body.

As it continued, we watched my hands and arms reach up in the coffin to prevent the wooden lid from being nailed together. Finally, it became clear the coffin was made of old rotten wood with black streaks of fungal rot. Slivers of light shone through the cracks in the wood. My level of panic was clearly depicted on the tunnel wall, and I could feel I was perspiring excessively there in the tunnel as I watched.

The harder I pushed up on the lid, the louder the hammering became. I struggled to keep the lid from being sealed down, and Tahoe started crying while Howie cheered for me. Eventually, I stopped it from being closed and shoved the top off the coffin with one swift push. We watched as the image on the tunnel wall shifted perspective, and I triumphantly sat up in my bed and peered around the dorm room. The coffin had disappeared, but we could see GracieAnn buried under her covers and a group of four spirits dancing around my bed.

"You don't believe all that, do you, Pippy?" Howie asked.

"I can't seem to hide from it," I said, shaking away from the wall. "This really happened, and I *don't* want to know what it means. I didn't think anyone would ever find out."

"Calm down," he said. "The wall's gone blank."

And it had.

"Let me help," said my feline palimal, who hadn't spoken a few words this entire journey but didn't sound like Kitty Joe.

I stared at him, still holding him in my arms. He peered back at me, but he was certainly different. I held Kitty Joe up to my face and gazed into his eyes. He remained silent. I remembered what B.C. had said and asked my Kitty Joe.

"You've been called, haven't you?"

He stared at me intently. "Yes, but not as Kitty Joe," he said, hopping down to the tunnel's floor.

"I'll be darned," Howie said, marveling at the transformed feline.

"As far as I can tell, you're still a kid," Joe Kitty began, "and you're troubled. That qualifies for Joe Kitty to step in." He grinned at me and nodded. "Ready to rip apart this dream?"

"That's how fast you can change?" I asked, remembering how awkward Kitty Joe's transition to Joe Kitty was in South Sideways.

"Actually, it's pretty much at will. I just threw in that troubled kid thing for effect."

"So, you believe me that it was a dream?"

"Oh, definitely; it was a fine demonic dream."

"Demonic? Then let's not relive it and get out of here."

"And not get through Courage Cave?" Howie interrupted. "See, I told you we should have taken Back Trail."

"You don't understand!" I snapped at Howie. "Sa Jo—"

"*Stop, Pippy!*" Howie grabbed me and put his hand around my mouth.

"*Gross!*" I said as I caught a whiff of his sweaty armpits as he squeezed me, and I felt the sweat on his arms.

"You can't bail out so easily, Pippy. This isn't that scary. No demon dream is gonna keep us from getting to High Stones."

"You don't get it, Howie. It's not about being afraid. I just want out. *Now!*" I insisted, refusing to look anyone in the eyes.

"But you're so close, Pippy," Joe Kitty said.

"Yeah, c'mon, Pippy," Tahoe urged. "You were smart enough to bring him along, so use him."

This wasn't my plan for Joe Kitty, I thought to myself.

"Okay, okay, we'll go on," I acquiesced, peering around at my eager troop.

"Good," Howie said, putting his arm around me.

"Ah, Howie?" I flashed him a smirk. "About the arm..."

"Okay," he said, backed away, and stood beside Tahoe.

"Look," Joe Kitty began. "Let's all settle down. We've still got to get through this section of the tunnel. The Ghosts are extraordinarily kind to us; we better take advantage of it. So, let's get back to your dream, Pippy. I assume you trust me to go on."

"I do."

"Good, because although its demonic presence was high, from what I've seen thus far, there's a good intention to this dream."

"Really?" I remembered how afraid I was when I had the dream—how I'd even dreaded thinking about it.

"I've got to know," Joe Kitty said. "Did you see GracieAnn buried under her covers, or did you dream she was under her covers?"

"I was sure I was awake while I watched the spirits dance, and at the same time, I saw GracieAnn bury her head under the covers."

"What did you do?" Joe Kitty asked.

"I covered my head, too, hoping they'd go away."

"Really? And you were sure you were awake and weren't dreaming by then?"

"Yeah, I'm sure. That's what's been so weird all along."

"What?"

"Well, I dreamed about being in the coffin, but then I was awake, watching the dancing spirits." I said, "But it got a bit hazy when two other spirits joined the four spirits. I think I started getting afraid because the two new spirits were larger and overpowering."

"Were they evil-looking?" Joe Kitty asked.

"Not exactly, but they were at least twice as large as the others."

"What happened?"

"This is what's so weird. None of the spirits appeared to care about me, but they did seem to care about each other. It seemed like they danced for five to ten minutes before leaving, and the room returned to normal. I glanced at GracieAnn; her head was still buried under the covers. I called out to her, and she asked if they were gone. I asked her what she meant, and she referred to the spirits as Ghosts. She removed the covers from her head when I told her they were gone.

GracieAnn said a bunch of ghosts were running around my bed and that she had heard for many years that our dorm room was haunted and had long been trying to see ghosts out of curiosity, but that she had never imagined it'd be so scary."

"You knew those four spirits, didn't you?" Joe Kitty asked.

"Do we have to go on?" I asked, blushing and embarrassed. "There's nothing on the wall, anyway. Can't we get out of here?"

I wanted to leave, but as soon as I stepped forward, the wall came alive with the images of the six spirits running around my bed.

"I guess not," Joe Kitty said. "Now, did you know the four spirits or not?"

"Weelllll," I said, peering at them running around my coffin.

"You have known those spirits for years, Pippy, haven't you?" Joe Kitty noted.

I gazed around the tunnel at my troop of palimals and discreetly glanced at Howie, all fixed on the images on the wall. "Well, yes. But I'm not possessed."

"For how long?" Joe Kitty asked.

"Yes, how long?" Howie echoed.

"For about six years," I reluctantly admitted, taking note of Howie staring at me like I was a total loon. Then I added, "But this was the first time they had been anywhere but home in my bedroom."

"And they've become your friends," Joe Kitty concluded, pointing to the four spirits. Two were about four feet tall, while the others appeared a foot or so shorter.

"Yeah, I guess," I said, twirling my fingers through my hair. "I feel comfortable with them, but dancing around my body in a coffin with those two gigantic spirits was too weird," I said, pointing to the eight-foot-tall spirits.

"Have you ever talked about them to anyone," Joe Kitty asked.

"No."

"Have you begun talking with your spirit friends?"

Wham! Now I knew Joe Kitty, Howie, Tahoe, and Feathers would soon learn about what I thought was my secret for the past six years.

Not even Sarah knew about my spirit friends, though I suspected Truggles knew about them because they arrived in my life soon after Truggles appeared in my dreams. I'd always called them 'my guys,' and I'd been talking to them for at least the last two years. They'd been my companions all the way through elementary school. Remarkably, though, I felt relieved, even liberated from keeping 'my guys' a secret, and with that release came a feeling of comfort I hadn't ever known. I was proud of my four spirit friends and no longer afraid to speak about them.

"Some is talking from me to them," I said, "but not to me. That night, though, I swear I heard them speak two words, not to me, but to the two huge spirits."

"They did? Hmm? Let's watch." Joe Kitty grinned, and the five of us watched the dream play out on the wall.

From what we watched on the wall, it was clear more than two words were spoken. I didn't remember 'my guys' talking so much to the two large spirits, maybe because my head was covered.

"They're organizing your thoughts and emotions, Pippy." Joe Kitty marveled at the display of supernatural teamwork. "They were preparing you for this journey all along."

"Like getting the butterflies to fly in formation before a race?"

"Butterflies?" Joe Kitty asked.

"At home, it's a term we have for getting nervous before something important we're doing. For example, when I ran track, my dad had always taught me that when I got the 'butterflies,' I should *not* try to get rid of them but learn how to get them to fly in formation."

"Excellent example," Joe Kitty grinned. "Then the two spirits came to get your thoughts and emotions to fly in formation for the events yet to come in your life."

"But how does all of this relate to my coffin dream?" I asked. Watching the spirits dancing on the wall, I realized I was no longer troubled by the notion of the coffin. Instead, I was fascinated by the prospects of 'my guys' working with other spirits.

"In a moment, Pippy, but do you remember the two words spoken by *your guys* to the two huge spirits?" Joe Kitty asked.

"Yeah, the words have stuck with me, though I never knew what they meant. Truggles is the only one I've ever told."

"And what did Truggles say?" Joe Kitty asked.

"Just two words: 'very good.' And then Truggles grinned and dismissed the subject."

"And what were the words?"

"They sounded like *thagh* and *moowenda*."

As I said these words, the tunnel wall went blank, and Joe Kitty's smile turned to a huge grin.

"Your dream was an actual dream, meaning something really happened. 'Your guys' came to rescue you from your life's demons and demonstrate their power over evil. Only after 'your guys' gained dominion over the evil spirits could the two giant spirits enter your life to team up with your spirits to prepare you for the next big moment in your life."

"Big moment?"

"The moment we're in right now!" Joe Kitty said.

"The journey?"

"Yes, and from that day last summer to now and forever more, Thagh and Moowenda will be united with your spirits as long as you aspire to know and live the words and will of High Stones."

"Are they with us now?" I asked.

"No, nor are 'your guys' with us during this journey."

"Will I see them again?"

"They wait for us," Joe Kitty assured me.

"Then what were the evil spirits in my dream?"

"Wouldn't you rather we get on our way to High Stones?"

"Yeah, c'mon, Pippy," Howie urged, troubled by the shift in focus.

"Just tell me a little."

"Okay, but..." Joe Kitty gave me one of his impatient stares like he'd do when I kept Kitty Joe from hunting Peigts. "We've got to be quick about it."

"Okay," I said, happy to have gotten my way.

"The demons of depression and sorrow attempted to possess you through the movement of your coffin," he began, "but 'your guys' gave you the strength and inner resources to resist the demons as they attempted to seal you in the coffin. Had they succeeded in sealing you in, you would have had no choice but to craft a deal with the demons to regain your freedom from their day-to-day influence."

"What? Are you saying I'd get depressed or sad all the time unless I traded with the demons?"

"Odd, huh? But yes. It's never a desirable position in which to be placed because demons don't always deal fairly. If you don't have some anti-demon smarts when you try to strike a deal with them, you're bound to be outsmarted, and your life is likely to be one with plenty of sorrow, doubt, fear, and unhappiness."

"Without my guys, I would have been toast," I said.

"That's one way of looking at it, but you have been called to High Stones. You have been chosen, and you have been prepared, and through your preparation and allegiance to Truggles, you have gained other protection from the evil ones," Joe Kitty explained.

"Wait. Now you're complicating things. Do my guys work for Truggles?" I asked.

"In a manner of speaking, as Joe Kitty works for Truggles," Joe Kitty hopped onto Tahoe's back and then onto her head. "Time we get going."

"Heck, that was nothing," Howie complained. "I thought Courage Cave would be more challenging."

"I'm afraid that was only a warm-up," said Joe Kitty.

"What do you mean?"

"Howie's half right, I think," Joe Kitty began. "It only dawned on me this moment. Huh..."

"What?" I wondered.

Joe Kitty smiled and nodded. "Definitely a noggin' nudger moment for me." He paused. "The Ghosts were never meant to keep you from High Stones but to prepare you for the next stage of your journey. Always remember, no matter what, that Truggles has dominion over all the Ghosts of Courage Cave."

"So that's good news," Howie said, "because we'll be able to avoid the Hooded Ones and MOTs now that we've gotten through Courage Cave."

Howie looked agreeably at me and added, "I guess you were right, Pippy; Courage Cave was the best approach."

"Whoa, you two, you're missing the point of Truggles' teaching here. Pippy isn't ready to take on the Howlers. As soon as we walk out the door of Courage Cave, I guarantee that we'll find ourselves instantly transported to Rock Castle Mountain. From there, our real journey to High Stones will begin." Joe Kitty sat motionless for a moment and stared off into the dark hollows of Courage Cave. "Your final journey to High Stones will begin at Rock Castle Mountain, and you will travel along the Back Trail to the Threshold of High Stones and finally through the valley."

"That's not fair!" Howie protested.

"*Calm down*," I ordered. "Joe Kitty, explain. What do you mean?"

"Simply this: if you are ever to have actual dominion over the Ghosts of Courage Cave, the Hooded Ones, the Monitors of Temptation, and the Howlers and achieve your destiny, you must face and overcome all of these on your journey to High Stones. Though Truggles has prepared you to avoid serious harm, there are no protections for those who do not heed his word, nor will they meet you in High Stones until you have succeeded in this journey. Remember, you are the first of your kind."

"And I am the second," Howie blurted out.

"There is much yet to come, Howie Yeary. Remember, *your job is to get Pippy to High Stones*." Joe Kitty said this with measured precision.

"Yeah, I know," Howie said, half-embarrassed. "But I was kind of ad-libbing."

"Stay focused!" Joe Kitty said, and the five of us exited Courage Cave. Unfortunately, we weren't immediately transported to the North Thwortal in Rock Castle Mountain as Joe Kitty had predicted. Instead, we walked on an archway that spanned the divide between Courage Cave and Rock Castle Mountain, leading us to the soft, spongy, hideaway rocks.

As we traveled across the archway, all of us on Tahoe's back, Joe Kitty having assumed his place of honor on her head. Tahoe led a discussion reflecting on the evil souls and demons we would face in the days ahead, again amazing me with her quiet but almost mystical understanding of things around her.

"The evil souls and demons challenge all who strive to get to High Stones. We'll know when we are getting close because it will get nasty," Tahoe nodded, almost knocking the black and white feline off her head.

"Ey, watch at, ya bag pony! And watch out fir dose nasty nostril drippins."

"Glad you're back, Kitty Joe," I said with a smile. "I was starting to miss you."

"Yap, I'm back. Now's ease up, Tahoe."

"My pleasure, little guy," Tahoe grinned and raised her eyelid to glance at Kitty Joe as he groomed himself.

"You understand, Pippy, the strongest of evil souls and demons were once in High Stones themselves, and ever since they were cast away, they have been angry and vengeful. They know you have become a force against them, and Thagh's and Moowenda's presence in your dream mocked the evil souls and demons and showed them how favored you are by High Stones. So be certain they will be after you."

"You know about Thagh and Moowenda, Tahoe?" I asked.

"I have for a very long time, but not about 'your guys' or you."

"Hey, wait. What's going on here?" Howie chimed in. "There is too much spirit talking and not enough talk about you being a marked person on this trip, Pippy. The same demon souls and mean spirits after you will also be after us."

"Unless, Howie, you outsmart 'em," Feathers teased. "Isn't that why Pippy chose you?"

"Why, you little pipsqueak," Howie, with love, pinched Feathers's ear. "You're right. Bring on those wimpy spirits, and I'll have my way with them!"

CHAPTER TWENTY-FIVE

Feathers, What Were You Thinking?

There wasn't anything too unusual about the trees and boulders busting out around us at Rock Castle Mountain. Our archway took us to the spongy hideaway rocks on the exterior perimeter of Rock Castle Mountain and not the North Thwortal itself, avoiding the need to go through the tunnels, which would have been all but impossible with Tahoe. Looking at the action of those boulders, though, it appeared they were either teenage MOTs making mischief or Hooded Ones preparing to challenge us.

"Be still and stay together," I said as we walked among the rolling boulders and trees that sprouted out of the ground at will around us. Feathers rode in the backpack Howie was now wearing, leaving the appearance that there were only four of us. As much as we tried to stay together, the boulders and trees maneuvered among us, creating barriers that divided us.

Each of our steps became a dodge among the active boulders that positioned themselves to direct and redirect our intended paths. Soon, the only option for moving forward was to follow the trails created by the active boulders and trees. The entire area soon became a dense boulder and tree forest maze where we were trapped. The trees worked in partnership with each other and the boulders as the trees intertwined their branches and wrapped their uppermost roots around the boulders.

First, we called one another to reorganize our group. I was still with Tahoe, but Howie and Kitty Joe had jumped off to try to find a way out, and Feathers was still with Howie. They hollered; we hollered, but it was pretty tricky. Our voices grew closer and farther apart for at least thirty minutes. None of the five of us ever gave up, although there was a moment when Tahoe and I stopped hollering to listen and move toward Howie's sound, and it worked. Within five minutes, our group united, a bit hoarse and frustrated.

"What do you think, Pippy, MOTs or Hooded Ones?"

"Don't really know, Howie. I should have remembered the first rule: sniff 'em." And just as I readied to sniff the closest tree, the trees and boulders began to separate. One by one, the trees changed into hooded evil souls that hovered around us as the boulders emitted an eerie array of moans and groans.

As they encircled us, they formed groups of three, not saying or doing much, yet I think they were trying to intimidate us. In staccato fashion, I Begot at least six groups of three, only to have them replaced by eighteen more Hooded Ones. Mysteriously, though, they didn't do anything except occupy the space around us, suffocating us by exhaling heavily and forcing us to breathe their musky, skunkish air.

We wrapped wet cloths around our faces, something Howie packed along on the journey to neutralize Hooded Ones' breath. They seemed agreeable to letting Howie, Feathers, Kitty Joe, and I pass through. Then, all of a sudden, they seized on the most critical member of our group, Tahoe, our transportation for a very long journey. Spectacularly, the Hooded Ones materialized something Tahoe had longed to have: a Spanish Arabian horse companion beside her.

Then, as if possessed, Kitty Joe leaped from Tahoe's back. He sank his claws and long, sharp teeth into the leg of the materialized Spanish Arabian. My feline palimal must have known something none of us knew because his bite was enough irritation for the Hooded One, who had created the materialization to maintain it. The Spanish Arabian materialization was quickly abandoned.

"That was some awesome fighting," Howie said.

"Waell, as Benny calls 'em, dose ol' robe heads can't have it both ways. Dey can't make stuff and be free a feelin' a bite."

"That's good to know," I mumbled aloud, then noticed the sad look on Tahoe's face. "Tahoe, when we get to High Stones, I'll ensure you get a real Spanish Arabian companion with you forever."

"And I'll help her," piped Feathers as he popped his head out of the backpack.

"I can only hope," Tahoe said with determination. "Now, hop aboard, let's get out of here!"

Howie had left the backpack hooked to Tahoe's saddle horn, and thus, after Kitty Joe and I climbed aboard, all of us but Howie were ready to go. I should have expected it to happen and knew it was fine, but Howie was about twenty yards from us having fun with the Hooded Ones, who tried to trade him parlor trick powers for his clandiram. Though he was flippant at times, I never once doubted his loyalty. Kitty Joe seemed to favor playing with them as much as they attempted to entice him. He taunted them and refused to surrender the clandiram, upon which they focused too much attention. Maybe it was that they thought there were venoms or potions in the clandiram, I don't know, but it was like they were a bunch of bloodhounds sniffing out the fox. It was amusing that these creatures were so timid in Howie's presence.

Without warning, a large tree emerged from the ground in front of Howie, and an extra-large Hooded One materialized and spewed vapors in Howie's face, "Surrender the pouch," the tree demanded. "It is ours!"

"Take a bath, Hooded One!" Howie fired back.

"I demand the pouch!" the Hooded One erupted.

"Can't have it, Hollow Face."

While brave, Howie's strategy didn't mean much to the Hooded One. Within seconds, a cascade of fluid, life-like giant maple leaves the thickness of a baseball mitt surrounded Howie, moaning and moaning and groaning as they squeezed him as if to crush him.

I saw what was happening, leaped off Tahoe, and shifted into a superpower girl role. It was a role Sarah was much more comfortable with, but this was my group, and I had to act fast. So, recalling another dimension of Begetting, I raised my arms and swept them across the giant maple leaves, and with full faith and certainty, I commanded: "Begone, I resist thee all—*implode!*"

Instantly, the maple leaves aged, dried, and crumbled apart, and a quiet breeze blew them away, freeing Howie.

"Awesome move, Pippy." Howie grinned. "Wow!"

"It worked just as Grandma Goat taught me in Mystasanctim."

"Just awesome..." Howie smiled, then offered me a hand-clasped stirrup to board Tahoe.

CRACK!

The sound smashed into us, knocking Howie to the ground and leaving me hanging onto Tahoe's saddle horn, the back-pack beneath my grasp.

A woman with a beautiful face and long blonde hair pro-truding from her shiny jet-black cape and hood stood there, peering down at Howie and eyeing me.

"I am here for him!" she said.

"Here for who?" I asked.

"For the mouse."

"Who are you?"

"Barney knows me," she said with a bedeviled look. "I am his good Hag."

Knowing Feathers was Barney before becoming Feathers and that it was an old Hag that made it happen, I was stymied. I was not to lie to anyone or get sucked into a trap that would jeopardize my group.

"There is no Barney with us," I asserted.

"I smell him; I know he's here."

Howie bolted in front of her and tried to distract her. "My goodness, you're beautiful!" he said.

"Young man," she began, "you are such a boy," and she ex-tended a finger in Howie's face, and as she touched him, her face vanished, her robe and hood turned off-white, and her finger disappeared. She was nothing less than a Hooded One, albeit a large one.

"Ugh," Howie said.

"Now, give me the mouse!"

She reached for the backpack. I reacted and summoned the power of High Stones to be with me as I commanded and thrust my hands at her, "Begone, we resist thee—*shiver!*" Having never tried it before, we were all amazed by the strong stream of sparks that flew from my fingers.

Before our eyes, we watched the robe and hood freeze, with the Hooded One shivering into pieces, crumbling apart, and falling to the earth like crushed ice.

"I'm impressed," Howie said. "But I think they're only toying with us and testing your powers."

"You think so?"

"Don't show them too much of what you've got because they seem more interested in Feathers than us."

"Yeah, what's that about?" I asked.

"Don't know, but it's weird," Howie said. "The Hooded Ones act like they own Feathers."

"So, we ready to go on?" I asked.

"Yep."

"And you're not jealous of my power?" I asked, grinning and nudging him in the side.

He eyed me for a moment and looked me up and down. "Pippy, I'm glad you've got the guts to use your powers."

As we rode off, Howie pried open the backpack and whispered to Feathers, "You know those Hooded Ones?"

"Nope," Feathers said shyly.

"But Barney, we know you," came a voice from above. We gazed up to see a bird that flew over us, and as soon as it had appeared, the bird was gone.

Walking along, I couldn't get this Barney thing off my mind. In addition, I felt a bit haunted by the Hooded Ones' obsession with Feathers, who was one-fifth of my arsenal for this journey. Still, no further intrusions, and I stepped behind Howie, placing him in the lead during this walking phase of our trip, and flipped open the flap on the backpack, exposing Feathers.

"What was all that about, Feathers?" I asked.

He stared sheepishly at me and answered slowly, "Sorry, Pippy, but that was the voice of the old Hag who gave me the ability to fly."

"You traded with a Hooded One?" I asked.

"She seemed like a nice Outsider old hag," Feathers said.

"With powers outside Points Afar? What were you thinking?"

"I wanted to fly."

"Fine," I said, angry and frustrated. I realized my uncontrolled emotions were diminishing my reasoning. That was a sure way to lose the use of my powers in Spooner Pond.

"What do we do now?" Howie quizzed me like I'd know.

"I'm not sure," I said, taking Feather's head and peering into his eyes. "Alata. Sorry, Feathers, we won't abandon you." I turned to Howie and said, "We just go on as planned."

"Good, I agree," Howie said as he reached over his shoulder to pat Feathers. "So, what that Feathers traded something else for the ability to fly. Big deal. The Hooded One old Hag doesn't own him. To heck with them. Our concern is you, Pippy, and getting as many of us to High Stones as possible. So, yeah, I agree, go on as planned."

Howie removed the backpack and, while tugging on one of Feathers's ears, whispered to him, "Don't worry, I won't let anything happen to you, little guy." Then, a smile on both of their faces, Howie cinched up the backpack and hung it on Tahoe's saddle horn, Feathers still inside.

CHAPTER TWENTY-SIX

Entering the Bend
of Back Trail

Howie and I strode together with Tahoe in the lead, with Joe Kitty sitting on her head and the backpack hanging on her saddle. As we neared the junction of the trail out of Rock Castle Mountain and Back Trail, we could hear the gravel crunching under our feet. The boulders had been crushed by a horrific force and laid out like a carpet for us to follow. The problem was that I didn't remember the junction looking like this, yet we stuck to it like puppies to peanut butter and made our way to Back Trail.

It was a casual stroll, though my mind wandered with thick cascading clouds dotting the sky over Bend of Back Trail. Some appeared to have fingers diving toward us, getting closer to us as we got closer to the Bend of Back Trail. I anticipated an escape plan where these clouds would erupt in a downpour, causing a flash flood in the low-lying Bend of Back Trail.

"Pippy? Hello. Anybody home?" Howie grabbed my shoulder, interrupting my thoughts.

"Oh, sorry," I said, catching myself. "I was just thinking about how weird the sky and the trail are. Aren't you worried about rain?"

"Rain?"

"I've never seen clouds so thick at Spooner Pond," I said, staring at the increasingly menacing-looking clouds forming over us.

Howie stopped and grabbed my waist, which, surprisingly, didn't bother me. "Are you okay, Pippy? There aren't any clouds."

For a moment, I thought he was crazy. The clouds were there and intensifying by the moment. Although Tahoe might have gotten fifty yards ahead by this time, a group of three Hooded Ones descended upon Howie and me. Led by an extra-large one the size of the One who had earlier materialized into Feathers's old Hag.

"We all know where you are attempting to go, Pippy," the Hooded One began, "and no need to Beget us, for we are many, and you are few." The other two groaned and stunk up the air as they chanted, "We are many, and you are few."

"And those of us who stop you," the Hooded One continued, "will be rewarded."

I stared at the Hooded One, my eyes fixed with determination and my face sure. I was ready to take them on.

Tahoe turned, saw the commotion, and reared up to begin her sprint to get back to us. Unfortunately, two groups of three Hooded Ones surrounded her before she could move. In a rare show of aggression to protect her little friend in the backpack and to get back to assist us, Tahoe reared up many times, casting authority in all four directions of the compass, and dashed right into and through the Hooded Ones to get by our side.

"Our rewards are even greater if we can stop a Chosen One," the larger Hooded One gloated.

216

"That must be you it's referring to," I scorned the Hooded One and shifted my attention to Howie, who had grabbed the backpack off Tahoe's saddle horn.

Howie reached into the backpack. "Here, freshen up!" And Howie grabbed a handful of lulu berries and tossed them into the open hood of the tallest Hooded One.

Digging in the backpack for more, he said, "C'mon, help me, Pippy. You said it before. There's a risk for Hooded Ones when they materialize into anything, so let's give 'em something to laugh about."

Was Howie ever right because their speaking ability made their vocal mechanism vulnerable? I followed Howie's lead in a well-conceived plan.

We went on the offensive with lulu berries, tossing all we had into the openings in their hoods. The Hooded Ones were burping quickly, and bubbles spewed from their hoods. Unfortunately, their giggles weren't like ours, sounding more like squealing pigs; when the giggles set upon them, they lost control, and the other Hooded Ones drifted away. We left the three in their silliness and moved onto Back Trail, convinced we were done with them for good.

Howie was right. There were never any clouds, nor was there a hint of anything but spectacular Spooner Pond weather, but I would have sworn otherwise. Peculiar how the mind tricks you, even if you're a chosen one. The most fantastic thing about the ordeal was that Howie and I worked well together, even for a moment. There, I was the needy one. So yeah, I was exceedingly happy I chose Howie to accompany me to High Stones.

As we entered Bend of Back Trail, we descended into the earth. It was like walking into a ravine sliced through time with layers of rock and fossils displayed throughout its steep walls and monstrous vines overhead, at times seeming to reach their tentacles down the trail. Finally, the outermost perimeter of the thickest of the overhead vines, about fifty feet into this five-hundred-foot-long section of Back Trail, the course began to darken. With Howie standing watch, I reached into the backpack he had now strapped to his waist and shoulders for our passage through the Bend of Back Trail. I pulled out two necklaces of Wonder Stones that Grandma Goat helped me to string. The order of stringing of one set of Wonder Stones bestowed discernment to the wearer; the other necklace was ordered to sensitize the wearer's ears to sounds.

I placed the brilliant rainbow-colored banded Wonder Stones necklace around Kitty Joe's neck. His intention was to sensitize his already great hearing to super hearing. Next, I placed the necklace with two red-speckled white Wonder Stones on each side of twelve long orange-cream-colored Wonder Stones around Howie's neck, intending it to be for discernment. Together, I figured Kitty Joe's critter-sniffing self with extra sensitive hearing would help root out Hooded Ones in the Bend of Back Trail. At the same time, Howie's resourcefulness would be heightened if he could psych out the competition.

As I fitted Howie's necklace, I had to satisfy my curiosity. "How'd you know about the lulu berries, Howie?" I asked as I tickled his neck with the Wonder Stones and then spun his head to see face to face, raising my eyebrows like Mrs. Sopher.

"I sort of thought that sack Kitty Joe had when we picked him off Happy Trail had some lulu berries. It *was* stuffed to splitting."

"Very observant, and a good thing, too." I smiled. "But how'd you know the lulu berries would work?"

"Didn't you once tell me that once a lulu berry enters someone's mouth, it must be eaten? That it was impossible to spit out lulu berries?"

"What? You remember that; that was years ago, and I think I may have been wrong. I'm not sure if that's true about lulu berries, but right now, I guess it doesn't matter 'cause we emptied the sack on those three rascals."

"Your backpack served a useful purpose, and now we no longer need it."

"Your life we don't," I snapped back.

"Just kidding, just kidding," Howie weaved around me. "The backpack's a part of me now, Pippy. So don't worry, I'll take care of it, and besides, this is way too much walking for a big-eared mouse."

He was okay, that Howie Yeary. And at that instant, I felt confident he would take care of my backpack and my little guy within.

Giant hands appeared formed by vines. The limited lighting-streaked shadows on the thicker tentacles that seemed lifelike vines. I'd swear there were faces behind the translucent outer walls of the vines, and like the clouds I imagined, I was sure the vines were speaking to us in some sort of gibberish that didn't make any sense. I climbed onto Tahoe's back to get closer to the vines to determine what they were saying.

I felt a lot more secure being within a hand's reach of the lower-hanging vines, yet I was most compelled to get closer to the thickest of the vines. I would have sworn they were alive, but even as near as I got, I couldn't be sure they were saying anything.

"They're just roots and vines—the sounds are no more than a distraction."

"Maaybeee," I said, staring inquisitively at the vines I wanted to believe had faces, catching myself twisting my hair between my fingers during my analysis.

While riding through the Bend of Back Trail, Howie trotted alongside me with Feathers tucked away in the backpack. Kitty Joe remained ahead of us, darting in and out among the ancient plant life and rocks along the way.

As we continued to stroll along, we seemed to be of one mind as we worked through the Bend of Back Trail. We began our climb out of the depression in the earth to continue along the Back Trail to the Threshold of High Stones. Although we hadn't encountered any strenuous activity from mature MOTs, I was pretty sure they had influenced much of the action of the Hooded Ones. I mean, it made sense that they were orchestrating the repeated assaults and setting us up for something, and to tell you the truth, I was incredulous about us getting out of the Bend of Back Trail without more than a whimper from the vines.

Eager to climb out of the shadows of the darkness, we hurried toward the brightly lit Back Trail at the end of the Bend of Back Trail. It was like running out of a giant dark cave to get to the opening, where the sky was blue and the sun shone.

As we approached the exit of the Bend of Back Trail, we froze as a giant figure appeared silhouetted in the exit against the backdrop of the sunny blue sky. It had to be a warrior of some kind, with sabers and weapons hanging from its sides. All was deathly silent...but Feathers.

"Hey, guys, what's the hold-up? I need to get some fresh air and get out of this backpack!"

"Shhhh," I said and gave the backpack a nudge. "Take care of him, Howie."

"I don't think he's the one we have to worry about right now," Howie said as he pointed up at the opening where four more warrior types had joined the original one. They began to strike their weapons against their armor-plated suits, creating an echo in Bend of Back Trail.

"Let's turn around," Tahoe offered.

"I ain't scared," Kitty Joe added.

"Pippy?" Howie asked.

I was tongue-tied. I didn't know what to do until I recalled what B.C. had taught me about fear and MOTs. *Remember,* he said, *it's your fear from which they draw their power to control you.*

"Stay here," I ordered. I tossed Kitty Joe into Howie's arms and charged off toward the opening with Tahoe in full gallop. There's nothing like riding a Spanish Arabian with twishloc in her mane.

I approached the five warriors as if they were mere illusions. Unfortunately, they were anything but illusions, and they raised their blades at our arrival. Charging fast and believing wholly in my twishloc—that I had been called to High Stones and would be protected—I Loofited Tahoe and me over the warriors' outstretched weapons. They spun around to face us, shields over their faces.

"Yantu sam oppitum!" Their apparent leader commanded this, and they raised their weapons and started growling at us.

"Can't see you, fellows," I hollered, hoping they'd lift their face shields. "Nothing to be afraid of; we have no weapons."

"Yantu sam oppitum," the leader roared, and they came at us with full force, face shields down.

"I surrender!" I yelled as I hopped off Tahoe and ordered her to return to the others. It gave them pause, but as they hovered around me, they snorted and grumbled until their leader spoke.

"Yantu sam oppitum, Pippy."

I couldn't believe they used my name. By making this mistake, they confirmed that they acted as instruments of evil souls and demons much sooner than I had imagined. Still, I needed to see their eyes to Beget them with a summoning of the power of High Stones.

"Do you want me?" I said, standing open to them, my hands outstretched, forming a 'T.' "I'm all yours," I said, utterly awash in my twishloc.

As they approached, their shields still down, I closed my eyes and tried to remember the song I learned in Mystasanctim. I went blank. I heard them draw their swords, the metal of their sheaths seeming to sharpen the blades of their weapons as they pulled them free. I glanced up. Their shields were still down, and their swords were drawn high over their heads. *Pippy, if you cannot see their eyes, tune in on the focus of their effort.*

Of course, I had forgotten. It was as if time stood still for a split second, and all motion slowed as I opened my eyes and faced the five of them. Their swords were poised to strike me. I stared them directly in the face-shields and shoulder, raising my arms to chest level. My eyes were wide, and my hair was blowing as a wind circled about us. I trembled and shook, not with fear but with an immense welling up of power. Chills raced through me. The skies darkened, and the ground seemed unsteady.

My focus was crystal clear, and I was filled with the will and power of High Stones. I believed! I made two fists and cocked my arms at the elbows to capture all the energy circulating within me, and summarily commanded the warriors, *"Begone, we resist you—twist into knots!"*

I straightened my arms and opened my fists as I let the energy fly. It was like mega fireworks; lightning bolts flew from my fingers, and I roasted them. As their metal sizzled, they bent and twisted like pretzels, intermingling with one another, forming a pile of useless hardware that disappeared in a puff of air upon cooling. Though I felt exhausted and emotionally spent, I had once again claimed dominion over the evil souls and demons and witnessed the real power of being in the will of the High Stones.

However, I realized that while I was attacked by an army of MOTs, more of them had come along and trapped the rest of my party in the Bend of Back Trail. At least one hundred demon warriors were surrounding them.

I knew to run towards my friends, fearing not for me but for them. Oddly, the demon warriors gave me free passage and pretty much ignored me, but by the time I got to my group, Howie was surrounded by three of their leaders.

"Howie," I called as I tried to get to him, but the demon warriors who had let me in now blocked my movement by forming an impenetrable wall between Howie and us.

"I'm fine," Howie hollered. "Be still; it's my turn to deal!"

What else could I do but trust him to do whatever he felt was necessary to get us out of this mess? It must have been something spectacular because of what happened next.

For thirty minutes, we stood huddled together, Tahoe, Kitty Joe, me, and the backpack hitched to Tahoe's saddle horn. I glanced at my palimals and patted the backpack to reassure Feathers, but I did not hear a whimper from him. I peeked inside, and he was gone. In his place was the necklace Howie always wore around his neck with a metal emblem hanging from it.

Kitty Joe looked at me and said, "Howie took Father's wath ham undar has cap."

"Great," I said, thinking, *Howie traded my secret weapon for his necklace.*

We watched as Howie and his captors wrestled with words and hand gestures. It didn't look good, and my mind was overloaded. I was actually starting to lose focus. Loofiting, Begetting, Telekinesis...nothing made sense. I could always resort to my backup plan of transporting the five of us to an escape thwortal or back to the North Thwortal if we wanted to try Back Trail again. But I had never told anyone of my backup plan. With Howie and Feathers in the throes of their predicament, my backup plan was only three-fifths of a plan.

"Why did Howie do this?" I asked impatiently.

"He said he heard a voice inside him," Tahoe explained.

"A voice?"

"He called the voice Shardam, and off he ran to halt the invasion and take on the leaders, his sword drawn and waving your scarf in his other hand."

"Sarah's scarf?" I asked. "The red and black one that was in the backpack?"

Tahoe nodded.

I was disappointed. Sarah and I had always shared trinkets and bits of clothing for good luck, and now Howie had Sarah's scarf. What a weird thing to bother me at the time when the thought of Howie hearing Shardam's voice was far more mysterious.

Seeking physical comfort, I hung close to Tahoe, stroking her mane and petting Kitty Joe as he sat in her saddle. "Sarah gave me the scarf to carry for good luck; let's all believe it will work for Howie," I explained. But I was preoccupied with the thought that Howie now seemed to be our only hope, and if Shardam was indeed communicating with him, what a blessed day that was. Howie would soon become Shardam's apprentice. As the reigning Champion of Points Afar, Shardam was pledged to be the supreme protector for High Stones until another defeated him in competition.

It was indeed an odd sight watching Howie standing with the group of mean-snorting demon warriors against the backdrop of the shadow-streaked confines of the Bend of Back Trail. Steamy vapors rose from their bodies, shrouding their discussions in a mist highlighted only by an occasional ray of light streaking through the vines.

My fate, so controlled by my swift use of certain powers and tricks, was now in Howie's hands. I could never have tried to save only three of us and left Howie and Feathers on their own. Their conversation appeared to be anything but calm as Howie raised his sword more than a few times, and they theirs, and indeed some were pushing and shoving, but at a point, it all ceased, and it seemed they had come to an agreement, and it was apparent Howie was insistent on the terms.

They didn't shake hands like many people, but they butted the handles of their swords and separated. As Howie strode confidently toward us, his weapons swaying with his arrogant swagger that always irritated me and that I hadn't seen the entire journey, the demon warriors appeared to retreat, all hundreds of them. It was the strangest thing: it was all so awesome, yet unbelievable. I felt like shouting joyfully but was afraid to show too much emotion, thus weakening my concentration.

"What happened, Howie?" I asked. "Are you okay?" Sweat beaded on his forehead, and his gloves were wet and clinging to his hands from wielding his sword. "Did you have to fight them?"

"Of course I did. Didn't you? I mean, what else was I going to do? You were gone."

"Yes, gone fighting off those Hooded Ones on Back Trail."

"And leaving us here to be trapped," Howie said.

"I know," I said, reflecting. "We need to stick together as a team."

"I was scared, Pippy, so I did what I needed to do, and I know it was right. But now we're free to go to the Threshold of High Stones, and I'm certain there'll be no further interference."

"Are you certain?" I looked askance at him. "Do you know this because the Hooded Ones, MOTs, or whatever told you so? Did you take the word of the demons? Really, Howie!"

"Pippy," he said steely-eyed, "I am certain."

"Okay," I said, staring at him, both proud of him and worried about him. "Let's take care of your cuts and bruises and move on."

Howie had some scratches on his arms, having chosen to wear only the swordsman inner gloves instead of the long-shanked gloves I had advised him to wear, but most apparent was a rather pronounced scratch just below his left clavicle. I cleaned the wounds with alcohol, dabbed antiseptic, and put on a couple of band aides. However, the wound on his clavicle was too jagged for standard band aides and required gauze pads stuffed in my backpack first-aid kit.

Settled and ready to move on, we all climbed aboard Tahoe. This time, I wore Sarah's scarf, and he wore his necklace, which, he corrected me, was not his necklace but his amulet. Feathers? He stayed in the backpack because I still had plans for him...just in case.

CHAPTER TWENTY-SEVEN

A Chat about Howlers

As we left the Bend of Back Trail and approached the long stretch of Back Trail, I wondered about Howie's attitude change but couldn't get over his heroic actions. I even considered giving him a hug, but his post-fight body was sweaty. And although he was quiet throughout the ride, his moans and groans from the deep-cut wound were the sound of someone enjoying himself in a victorious battle.

At a very winding, tall tree-enclosed portion of Back Trail from the Bend of Back Trail to the Threshold of High Stones, we stopped and sat on the grass to eat our ration of snacks: half a chocolate bar, half an apple, and a handful of cashews, and sip water from our canteens. It'd be another ten minutes before arriving at the Threshold of High Stones, unlike the trail between Courage Cave and the Threshold of High Stones, which is only about a five-minute walk.

"Any idea what we can expect from the Howlers, Pippy?" Howie asked as he chewed on a bite of his chocolate bar.

"I really don't know," I answered, sipping water. "Howlers can do about anything. They have the power of physical illusion, they can control the elements of nature, and they have all the powers of the Hooded Ones, Monitors of Temptation, and Ghosts of Courage Cave. So if anyone can find our weak points, it'll be Howlers."

"Tahoe, you ever seen a Howler?" Howie asked, peering up before switching to his left boot.

"Never."

"You, Kitty Joe?" Howie asked as he stood.

"Nope."

"What about you, Feathers?" Howie asked as he picked up the long-eared mouse and held him up head high.

"Not I."

"So," Howie said as he put Feathers back down, then scratched his head and took a bite of the apple. "We don't have any experience with these Howlers at all."

"Well, that's not exactly true, Howie," I said.

"Reeeally?" he said, acting somewhat indignant. "Why, did you meet one in your dreams?"

"Hardly a dream, Howie," I said, suddenly remembering how much I hated this attitude thing Howie would spring on me. "Actually, it was quite real."

"Well? What did you learn?"

"Okay, Mr. Big Shot," I began with some fire in my eyes. "Three things: one, wind announces a Howler's arrival, and it can be tornado force, but it does stop; two, Howlers are much grander than anything we've seen thus far, and their potential is *huge*; and three, I'm sure we'll encounter them."

"Okay." I could see him making several mental notes.

"Oh, and there's one more thing," I said, smiling. "It's four. I'm *sure* you'll help me overcome the Howlers and get to High Stones."

"How do you know that?" he asked.

"It is what I see." I grinned.

"Then I will be sure to wear my amulet."

"And I sure to wear Sarah's scarf."

With that, we climbed aboard Tahoe for the remainder of the trail to the Threshold of High Stones.

CHAPTER TWENTY-EIGHT

Take Feathers, but Leave My Backpack

As we rounded the second of the last two bends in Back Trail, we came out of the trees and came to a halt. We stared up, awestruck by a massive wall. The wall was enormous; it was all we could see, as if nothing up or down, right or left, could be seen but the wall. If we turned around, we could see trees and forest along the Back Trail, but every other way we looked was a pure, awesome wall!

I remembered the wall from my dream travels as the wall that separated High Stones from the rest of Spooner Pond, but I never remember seeing it as large as it is, nor did I ever see High Stones on the other side of the wall. All I saw was the trail that led to my encounter with the Genie Howler—during one of the tours with Truggles.

The wall was far more daunting up close, and that awesomeness was magnified by the fact it took us five minutes to walk along the base of the wall to get to the Threshold of High Stones entrance. It was like walking along the bottom of a giant concrete dam that reached high into the sky, but it wasn't concrete. It was indeed the most spectacular wall of rock imaginable. I don't know exactly, but maybe it was at least eight stories high. I can't say for sure because it disappeared into the dense, thick clouds found over this part of Spooner Pond. We could see no beginning and end in its width and breadth.

The dirt trail along its base was easy to follow, as the path was lined by large boulders that looked like tiny peas when contrasted against the backdrop of the massive wall. That the trail was well worn was evidence that many travelers had gotten this far, which surprised me because both B.C. and Grandma Goat had led me to believe very few ever made it to High Stones. So, either they were fibbing, which I'm sure they weren't, or the Howlers up ahead were as bad or worse as everyone said.

When we arrived at the Threshold of High Stones, it was just as I remembered it from my guided tour—a ten-foot-high triangular opening, like a mouse hole in a vast wall. The top portion of the triangle opening was maybe ten feet across, and the bottom was about twenty and a half feet across. Looking into the door, it was clear that although we could never see the width of the wall from the trail, this visitor's hole was about seventy feet long, making it at least that wide. We dismounted to enter.

It was a bit eerie inside, and even though it was clean, dry, and lit, there was this weird feeling about the entry. The surface of the interior walls was shiny and mirror-like, reflecting our images as we walked through the opening. But walk through, we did, and after several nervous minutes, we found ourselves on the other side and at the top of a steep, narrow trail that led into the valley below—a valley teeming with lush plant growth amid spectacular gold columns.

A wisp of wind ruffled my hair not more than fifteen feet down the long trail. I was conditioned well, and my first thought turned to Howlers. Were they announcing themselves? We stopped walking, and the wind stopped as well. We took a couple more steps and were teased by the wind again. Finally, we stopped, and the wind ceased.

We all stood there, staring at each other in silence. Then, taking a deep breath, I gazed at the uncertain faces of my palimals, including Feathers, who had poked his head out of the backpack, and at Howie, who had taken his knife out of its sheath and was flipping it from hand to hand, and asked, "Sure you're all ready?"

"This is what I've been waiting for," Howie said confidently as he re-sheathed his knife, tied his ponytail, licked his lips, and put on his long-shanked gloves.

Before my palimals could respond, a sudden wind cracked like a sonic boom. It became a violent swirling wind that churned up the earth and natural debris around us like a tornado, blinding us from seeing anything around us. The harsh sounds it generated pounded our eardrums, and an incredible pressure in our inner ears got close to the point of aching. We huddled together. Then, we were lifted off the earth one by one and sucked into the swirl of tornado-like winds. We were tossed about in the funnel in complete disorder, but it seemed like we were moving in slow motion compared to the vicious speed of the winds.

I saw Tahoe float by on her back with a blank look. Kitty Joe was tumbling like a gymnast out of control, and Howie floated by me, clutching the backpack and Feathers close to him. The episode lasted maybe five minutes before it quit as abruptly as it began. It took a few moments for the dust to settle, and when it did, we were standing as we were when the violent winds hit, surrounded by what looked like an army of maybe a thousand children, teens, and adults just like us. They crowded behind us and all along the trail, standing on its steep sides. They didn't say a word, only stared at us and made gestures with their mouths like they were trying to communicate, but no sounds came out.

It was eerie, but they hugged our clothes and arms as they approached us. It felt as if they might swallow us up in their swarm. The closer they got, the more they smelled like old, musty clothes; you'd find them stuffed in the back of a closet or an old chest in the attic, but I never sensed they were trying to harm us. *They couldn't be real*, I thought to myself, but they looked and smelled *very* real, but not smelly like Hooded Ones, and their tugging on our clothes was real.

I noticed Howie put his ear to the mouth of one of the more unique-looking females. She had an angelic, even a bit majestic air about her. The girl stood taller than the rest and carried herself confidently...shoulders back and head high. She seemed to be trying to mouth words to Howie as he strained to listen. He then turned to read her lips and study her facial movements as she tried to communicate with him. Then, Howie turned to me and asked me for the backpack.

"Why?" I wondered.

"We need the backpack," Howie said with urgency. "I need Feathers and Tahoe. Now!"

"Wait! I need Feathers and Tahoe."

"You've got to trust me, Pippy, and I've got to get going! If you're ever to get to High Stones, I've got to get back!"

I remember feeling strange about agreeing to Howie's request, but it must have been my twishloc telling me within that his request was okay. I had since experienced the power of twishloc when I was Begetting the Hooded Ones and B.C.'s words about twishloc being all about believing and having faith that I was called by High Stones.

"Take Feathers, but leave me the backpack," I said.

Howie grabbed Feathers and hailed Tahoe. Forever loyal to me, Tahoe glanced at me for my okay, and I nodded and gestured that she go with Howie. I had no idea why he needed Tahoe and Feathers, but he had been so right about strategy on this journey, and getting too analytical at this point would have contradicted my twishloc.

Howie leaped aboard Tahoe with Feathers tucked in his shirt against his chest, and they raced away through the throng of creatures. Howie didn't even bother to dismount Tahoe as she raced through the triangular entrance we had just entered. Instead, he ducked and yelled, "Go girl. Run, Tahoe, run!" as Tahoe ran back through the entrance and onto the Back Trail.

I hadn't thought of them leaving me alone with Kitty Joe in the Threshold of High Stones, but as much as I was tempted to yell at them, my twishloc tugged on me to stay calm. Good thing, as that was the last I saw of them. It was now Kitty Joe, my backpack, one thousand creatures, and me.

"Walk on, Pippy," Kitty Joe's Joe Kitty persona said, peering up at me, catching me off guard. "Don't worry, Kitty Joe is no longer with us on this journey; it's Joe Kitty the rest of the way in," he said as he hopped up into my arms.

I nodded, stroking his head as I gawked at the creatures, then looked at my silly kitten palimal and realized how challenging things were. As cuddly as Kitty Joe had been when I felt overwhelmed and needed a friend to sit with, Joe Kitty wasn't the cuddly type. I'm sure he accommodated my petting him to help me through this transition, but I knew he'd instead be analyzing and figuring, and I also needed Joe Kitty more than Kitty Joe because of his smarts.

CHAPTER TWENTY-NINE

Joe Kitty, a Backpack, and Me

I took the two necklaces made from Wonder Stones out of the backpack and placed them around Joe Kitty's neck. "Okay, my kitten," I said as I bent down to pet him a final time before we continued our journey. "I am counting on you to discern and listen. We're it."

"No problem, Pippy," he assured me, as mature and confident sounding as I had ever heard him be.

We continued down the trail, and the whole time, I thought I could always resort to "Sa Jo!" though using it would take us back to the Bend of Back Trail. But, of course, that wasn't an attractive option either. I also had my Black Fire Opal ring, and we could ditch the place and go back to North Star Ridge, but then I'd be worried about leaving Howie in Spooner Pond without me.

"Remain in the will of High Stones, and carry Truggles in your heart," Joe Kitty said as he nudged up against my leg and winked at me.

Yeah, I thought, *that's what B.C. always said.*

Like a hot knife cutting through soft butter, we strode through the throng of creatures. In the back of my mind, I was sure they'd vanish like all illusions in Spooner Pond because the illusions always drew their power to control us from our fear of them. I had no doubts at that moment that as long as I remained in the will of High Stones, I'd have nothing to fear.

The creatures didn't appear to bother Joe Kitty as they parted the way for him as he led us down the trail. It made no sense for me to be intimidated by their sheer numbers because we had no reason to believe they meant us any harm, though they were a bit of a nuisance. We persisted and moved through them, facing no physical resistance, determined to ignore them. They let us pass through them and then lined up behind us and followed us down the trail like we were their leaders. The tall, striking females walked right behind me.

Joe Kitty peered up at me. "They're not illusions, Pippy."

"Then what are they?"

"Don't know, but they're here to stay. I sense their permanence."

I stared suspiciously at the throng. It was odd. If the creatures weren't illusions, then what were they? They didn't look like what I thought of as ghosts, but they weren't people who just couldn't speak either because none of them appeared to react to our gestures or communicate except for the tall and angelic-looking one. I thought maybe they were spiritless humans, though I based that assumption on a program I saw once, and I had no idea what it meant to be a spiritless human. I needed to know more, and as much as I didn't want to be alone, I had to send my Wonder Stone-laden palimal off into the throng to do his discerning thing, leaving me with only my backpack.

I continued creeping down the trail as Joe Kitty ventured into the throng. It was a complete, nerve-wracking five minutes before I made it to the valley floor, with every single one of those creatures right behind me. I assumed Joe Kitty was somewhere in their midst.

In stark contrast to my dark mood, the plant life and colors in the valley were more spectacular than I ever imagined, and the golden columns grew out of the ground like trees. Unfortunately, however, they lacked branches and leaves, which seemed almost liquid in their appearance but were as solid as a rock.

I decided to have a snack ration while waiting for Joe Kitty to catch up before taking off into the valley. Standing as calmly as I could while eating a chocolate bar and being stared at by hundreds of spiritless eyes, a tortuous gust of wind roared through the valley and knocked me off my feet. The chocolate bar flew out of my hand, and my backpack blew away into the throng of creatures. Then, as quickly and violently as the wind arose, it stopped.

"Stand up, little princess," said a thundering voice.

"Oh, great," I said, peering up, feeling as defenseless as possible, "it's you again." That forty-foot-high genie I met once before was back. Same ol' mean scowl and decorated robe. He extended his gigantic hand, inviting me to climb aboard, but I wouldn't buy it.

"Come on," he taunted me, "you have nothing to fear. You have twishloc!" He laughed, mocking me. "And I see you've brought along a group of friends to help you," he said, as his scowl deliberately turned to a big grin.

Okay, Howie, where are you when I really need you? Where is anyone? I said to myself. *Do not doubt the power of your Twishloc.* I heard a deep voice in me. *Do not surrender the power of your Twishloc.*

As if I was a skilled veteran of Spooner Pond wars, I Loofited up to face the giant genie eye to eye, hovering some thirty-eight feet off the ground. He seemed surprised by my ability, and for just a moment, I thought I had the advantage.

"Begone, I resist thee!" I said, staring the genie in the eye.

"Ha, ha, ha," he laughed. Then, it knocked me out of the sky and caused me to lose my Loofit and make a soft landing on the earth below. "Didn't they teach you, little princess, that you cannot *Beget a Howler*? Ha, ha, ha."

"Then try this," I said, standing and kicking the big fat toe of his three-toed foot. It was a juvenile move for sure, but it worked.

"Ouch!" he grumbled.

I kicked his other foot.

"Pesky little princess, aren't you? Trying to hurt me. Your kicks will only tire you, and your folly will soon make you *mine!*"

All the while, I'm concentrating hard, trying to send telepathic communications to the Peigts nestled in my backpack: *I need the backpack, I need the backpack,* I thought over and over again, adding the plea: *Please direct others to fetch me the backpack, please direct others to bring me the backpack.* I kept kicking, hoping the genie would succumb to my magical powers.

"This is pointless, pretty girl. Come, join me," he said as he extended his hand. "You cannot hurt me."

"No!" I exclaimed. I summoned all the energy and power I could, raised my hand shoulder high, and said, "Begone, we resist thee!" I let go with a few sparks from my hands.

He scoffed in response. "*Enough*, little princess!"

A nudge in my shoulder blades spooked me, and I spun around, ready to fight. However, the majestic Missy extended her hand to offer me my backpack. For an instant, I made eye contact with her as if to thank her, and though she remained expressionless, I was sure we had communicated. I opened my backpack and released a pair of Roogers I had stowed away. They darted out, climbed up the genie's toes, and seized his ankles with their teeth.

"Ama lama," I said.

The genie instantly cowered before me, shrinking to a height of four feet. The genie fell to the ground knees, head peeking out of the robe piled up and spread out on the valley floor.

"Why, I don't know what to do with you, oh great genie?" I sassed the shrunken oaf. Remember that one's clothes don't shrink from Roogers' bites, only the body. "Nice material," I began, petting the deep fluff of the robe. "Now, what's that rule you have here in *Howlerland*?" I asked rhetorically. "Get shown up by a mere mortal, and you lose your power and crawl under a rock?" I ridiculed him.

The genie only moaned.

"Nothing to say, big stuff?" I quizzed him and then yanked him from the robe.

Still, not a word or a whimper was uttered from him as he lay on the ground. I looked at his pathetic face and asked mockingly, "Don't you think it's time I take my twishloc and get to High Stones, Genie?"

He glared at me and stood, still not uttering a sound. Then, with his head hung low, he crept away and disappeared into a hideaway rock, a structure I thought existed only in Rock Castle Mountain. I believed he'd crawl under a rock, not into one, but I was still only a visitor to Spooner Pond.

I shrugged. Realizing I wasn't correct, I cinched up my backpack and threw it over my shoulder just as Joe Kitty arrived.

"Nice of you to show up," I said, waving my hair and teasing him by turning my back on him while grinning because I knew everything was okay.

"So that's what you cooked up with Kitty Joe," Joe Kitty said. "I saw the whole thing, Pippy."

"You knew about the Roogers?" I asked.

"No, but how'd Kitty Joe get them to go along?"

"He made a deal with them: two Roogers for our journey in exchange for Kitty Joe's solemn pledge to never again hunt Roogers, rodents, or insects of any kind in the Big Trees Area of the Wooded Forest."

"That ol' Kitty Joe sure loves you."

"Yeah, and I miss him sometimes."

"So does Joe Kitty miss him...and so does Joe Kitty love Pippy," he grinned.

I lifted my kitty friend and held him in my arms as he surrendered and appeared to enjoy my tickling his head. I grinned at him before a scolding look crept on my face, "But you gave me a heck of a scare, Mr. Joe Kitty."

"Be thankful the Peigts heard you," Joe Kitty began, as proper as ever, "and be thankful our soulless followers aren't spiritless at all."

"They aren't?" I wondered.

"They all have spirits, but all lack souls. It's why they appear so lost."

"That's what you discerned?"

"That's what took so long. In fact, I discerned soulless creatures all have an inextinguishable spirit to survive, but their souls have been stripped from them. They can't connect their spirits and bodies and thus appear mindless. The truth is their spirits yearn for the connection, and that yearning, most powerful in the majestic one that assists us, enabled her to communicate with the Peigts and help you."

"Think that's how Howie communicated with her?"

"Or she with him."

"But what could she have said for him to take off with Tahoe and Feathers?"

"I have no idea."

"You're sure they have no souls?" I mumbled, still confused.

"Spirits, yes; souls, no," said Joe Kitty, adding, "but I am certain they mean you no harm."

"Then why are they here? Are they not the work of the Howlers?" I asked.

"I don't know for sure. Maybe the soulless creatures were dumped in your lap to test your cleverness or confuse you, making you more vulnerable to attack. Unlike the typical illusions of Howlers, these humans without souls are no illusion. I think the baby tornado that heralded their arrival was the illusion that made you doubt these creatures. Other forces are at work here, but I'm unsure."

"Then do we continue to take them with us?" I asked.

"Right now, you're their only connection to survival, but you do not need them."

"But they need me?" I asked.

"Apparently, they have the spirit and desire to be with you regardless of your will. Your challenge is to remain focused regardless of them. And that may be it—the more they occupy your mind, the less able you are to focus on the journey. Remember, you walk with twishloc; never give it up."

"Think Howie and the others are okay?" I asked as we picked up the pace.

"I can't imagine Howie's not got things under control, though there's a good chance we'll never see him again."

"*What?*" I said, staring at Joe Kitty.

"You can't look back. So don't be thinking about Howie."

"It's not just Howie. What about Tahoe and Feathers?"

"You may not see them either."

"Ever?"

"Noooo," Joe Kitty teased. "They're not here right now on this journey, but your eternity has just begun, and they will be part of your eternity."

"Well," I reflected, "that's not so bad."

"It's quite good, Pippy. But you don't have to worry. Howie's a mighty warrior. He will take care of Tahoe and Feathers. *Your* destiny *and your attention* must be on High Stones. You have been called to follow and cannot lose focus."

"Follow Truggles?"

"Yes."

Feeling a touch of melancholy over Howie's absence yet knowing the power of what Joe Kitty had said, I continued, as did my entourage of soulless creatures.

CHAPTER THIRTY

Esiarp Eht Drol, Ronoh
High Stones Right Here

The more we descended into the valley, the more apparent its vastness. Ironically, though, the more expansive the valley, the narrower the trail. Soon, it dove into the valley floor, and we found ourselves walking on a tree-lined path, deep with vegetation well over ten feet tall. We were surrounded by white-barked aspen-like trees showing splendid green and yellow colors. The trail of soulless creatures behind me was four long soccer fields. After a short climb through the trees, the course opened to a plateau overlooking yet another spacious valley full of colorful wildflowers. It was as if the wildflowers had been placed before us to create what looked like an artsy quilt with a detailed etched trail winding through it.

Not long after that, we descended into this well-flowered valley, where the flowers' colors and variety of shapes yielded an almost hypnotic effect; their fragrances were nothing short of dreamy.

"We must be close to High Stones, Joe Kitty," I said as I patted my palimal.

"It seems that way, doesn't it? This is spectacular. Even our soulless friends seem more animated and lifelike."

And they did. Odd, but we were ready to find High Stones on the other side of the valley where the wildflowers ended. Joe Kitty got a little more excited than me and was prepared to run down the trail. I asked him to hold back while I picked a bouquet of flowers. Mom always said that bringing flowers is always welcomed when you visit someone for the first time. I wasn't sure who'd greet us in High Stones, so I stepped off the trail to pick a rather colorful bouquet of purples, oranges, reds, and some violets.

I bent over to pick my last flower. It was a massive bright yellow flower, more delicate than a sunflower but equally magnificent. It appeared to be a pair of rather large and conspicuous nostrils sticking out of the ground at the base of the plant on which the flowers grew. They looked like crocodile nostrils and must have been at least eight inches high.

I stepped back and stood staring at this odd sight. I wasn't inclined to run, and where would I run anyway? Certainly not back to Howlerland. I inched myself back to the giant yellow flower plant to see if the nostrils were still there; maybe I had imagined them.

But they were still there. My first instinct was to ignore them like I didn't see them, but my curiosity got to me. I bent over and touched the top of one of the nostrils with the tip of my finger.

"Yikes," I yelled, stepping back. "It's alive!"

"And I discern, warm, moist, and hairy," added Joe Kitty.

"No way," I insisted, shaking my head.

"I am certain," Joe Kitty said. "Leave them alone."

I know I should have listened, but I was feeling pretty tough by now, and I leaned over to examine them a little closer.

As I was about to touch them again, they snorted at me, and I must have jumped three feet into the air. Not only was the snorting real, but a rush of warm, moist air also pelted my jeans, soaking through my legs and under my socks all the way through to my ankles.

A retreat was now the only thing I could do, but when I turned around, I faced an impossible barrier in my soulless companions. I could have run through the wildflowers, but I was worried about Joe Kitty. I glanced back at the nostrils—a good thing—and just about gagged when a large snoot emerged from the ground to which the nostrils belonged. The force of the earth cracking and opening up forced me to back up further, and I watched as a magnificent specimen of primordial dinosaur and modern-day dragon mixed into one emerged out of the earth.

It was like I woke the beast from a deep sleep, as rich red earth and wildflowers rolled off its massive body and giant wings as it stood upright. The once expansive wildflower quilt was disorganized and ragged. There was dirt and crushed flowers all about us, some more striking flowers clinging lifelessly to the creature's scales and horns. The beast's eyes were deep and intimidating, and it stretched and groaned as it shook off the earth and flowers lying on its scaly skin. Then, as abruptly as it rose from the ground, it took notice of me and reared up on its hind legs, spreading its wings and zeroing in on us with its penetrating stare.

It was spooky. Joe Kitty was hiding between my legs, and my Rooger buddies had scattered. My soulless friends were kind of just there. The beast and I stared at each other. It didn't speak, nor did it breathe any fire. This dragon, however, was much more ferocious looking than the genie, and I didn't have any sense that I'd be communicating with it as I watched it stretch out and straighten its neck. Just listening to it breathe was scary enough.

As I backed away from the dragon and inched my way closer to the trail, the dragon's main body didn't move, but it followed me with its head about ten feet from me, its neck stretching at will and getting as long as needed to keep its head near me. I'd say the dragon's head alone was two or three times my height, and its eyes were the size of hula hoops. It was like I was a specimen in a jar, and the dragon was watching my every move. The further away I got, the more it strained its neck to follow me. Its neck was about thirty-five feet long and taut, with its head so close to me I could see my entire body reflection in its eyeballs.

The next thing I knew, it groaned, and its neck snapped back close to its body. I thought I was rid of it until the dragon flapped its enormous wings, lifted off the ground, and hovered over me on the path. It blocked the sunlight from my eyes with the shadow it cast. Then it hit me...all the dragon needed to do was set down on me, and my adventure would be over.

I grabbed Joe Kitty and ran toward a group of trees for shelter, but the dragon pursued us. There was no doubt the dragon was yet another of my adversaries, probably another Howler, but I wasn't sure. The thousand soulless ones scattered as the dragon bore down on me—all but the Missy. Finally, I glanced at Joe Kitty and said, "I'll use the ring to get us out of here."

"Don't be foolish," he said.

"I can't Beget it, and there's nowhere else to run," I said as we hid among the trees.

"But to give up High Stones...you can't!"

"What else can I do?"

"Talk to Truggles."

"But I can't."

"Try."

I tried my very best, but there was nothing.

"What about the song of B.C.?" Joe Kitty asked.

"Yes, the song! B.C. said I'd know when to use it; maybe this is the right time."

"Get with it, Pippy!" Joe Kitty said with an urgency I had yet to see expressed from this otherwise very cool palimal.

"Lift your eyes to the stones," I began to sing, "from whence on high my help comes. For stones so high that made all here we know, will not let your feet be harmed. Will not ever..."

Suddenly, my mind went blank, and the dragon got closer.

"Come on, Pippy. *Think!*" Joe Kitty said.

My mind was empty. I couldn't muster another thought, and I flashed back to a time I, an 'A' student, failed one of Mr. Daniel's tests, and he told me not to take it too seriously, saying: "*Sometimes, even when you're sure you know something, you can forget it, and even when you're confident, you can still be in doubt.*" Well, that's exactly how I felt.

The striking female, who never left my side, nudged me hard and grabbed my head. I tried to push her away, but she persisted, and all I can remember is going into this trance of sorts and remembering the song in its entirety. I sang it as loudly as I could, but nothing happened, nothing at all. I sang the song again. Still, nothing happened. The dragon circled overhead, and as if on cue to fulfill my most feared expectation, the dragon began breathing fire—spitting huge flames that sang through the trees around us.

"B.C. said it would work," I said, peering at a somewhat dejected Joe Kitty.

"I might as well be Kitty Joe."

"What's wrong?" I asked, worried I was losing my only cogent partner.

He said, defeated and dejected, "I forgot the song of B.C. works only on Hooded Ones and MOTs."

It definitely was not what I wanted to hear. So, instead, I watched the dragon swoop down even closer to the tops of the trees. Then, as feared, it began to set the tops of the trees on fire.

"I don't know what else to do?" Joe Kitty said. "Maybe we've run out of tricks."

"Oh, fine, so now *you're* giving up," I scolded him.

"Well, it doesn't look too good."

"Phooey," I replied. "You guys are all wimps. Next time, I'll put together a team of girls."

With no choice but to trust my instincts, I tilted my head upward and Loofited myself to face the dragon head-on. I perched on its nose, right behind its fuming nostrils. We flew together as it circled over the trees. Although it was a bit dizzying of a ride, it helped to slow down the dragon, even calm it somewhat. I had no idea what the dragon was thinking, but I just knew if it was a Howler, there was no way I would let an evil spirit or demon soul keep me from High Stones!

It played with me like a Howler, and it almost got to me because it's true that, like Hooded Ones and MOTs, Howlers want you to lose faith in High Stones. But my will was strong, and I knew that just like the genie. Howler's physical manifestation was vulnerable to physical attack; the same had to be true for the dragon if it was a Howler.

So, as I was staring at this creature, I remembered something Truggles told me about non-human form Howler manifestations. Apparently, they are nearsighted and can't see distant objects very well. So maybe this dragon was a Howler. It could see me up close, which explained why it was staring at me, but as I got further away, the dragon either followed me with its head or smelled me out and descended on me.

So, I'm thinking, what better place to be than sitting on its nose, looking it straight in the eyes, and giving it just what it wanted. But, of course, I was Loofiting, so I wasn't worried about falling, and I had one of my other secret weapons in my hand, but not for the reasons Joe Kitty, or I expect the dragon, was thinking.

With the pad of my left thumb over the Black Fire Opal ring, I closed my eyes and said, *"Esiarp eht Drol, Ronoh High Stones Right Here!"*

As I gave my command, an explosion of bright light flashed in the dragon's eyes, momentarily blinding it. I remained on its nose until the dragon stopped to the side and went belly up as it descended rapidly toward the ground. I leaped off, still in the air by Loofitting.

Just before it crashed into the trees below, it reversed itself and flew back up to meet me in the sky over the burning trees.

"Very well done, little princess," the dragon said in a deep, scratchy voice, the warm, moist air from its nostrils engulfing me.

I Loofited myself out of the path of his nostrils and stared hard into its eyes. "You know me," I asked. "Do I know you?"

"We have a mutual acquaintance," the dragon said in his scratchy voice.

"Truggles?" I quipped.

"Oh no," the dragon snorted and grunted. "Nor your High Stones."

"Then, who?" I asked, thinking this was the first time I'd ever gotten a hint that High Stones might be a person...

"I think now," the dragon said, "you must figure that out on your own. We have a much-undone business, little princess, and you have so few resources left."

And with that parting word, the dragon sped away from me, flying high and out of sight, leaving me Loofited above a grove of once-burning trees that were now a brilliant green color.

I Loofited back down next to Joe Kitty, who had since run out from under the trees.

"Brilliant, absolutely brilliant, Pippy," Joe Kitty said. "Fascinating use of the blinding light, but then it looked like you were talking with the dragon."

"Yeah, it was kind of weird. We talked, sort of gibberish, about our mutual friend."

"Really? You and the dragon have a mutual friend; that's odd."

"Yeah, I thought so as well."

"Indeed. Hmm. Howlers will do whatever they can to throw you off," Joe Kitty said with a grin.

"I know...but I'm not sure right now that the dragon was a Howler."

"It behaved just like one, Pippy."

"Yeah, sort of, but something about it didn't make sense."

"But your explosion of light worked on it."

"I know. You're right," I said. "I've got to admit: it worked just like I learned it from Grandma Goat in Mystasanctim."

"She taught you well."

"We both learned it accidentally, but she worked with me to perfect it. I promised not to tell anyone about it until I had to use it in the most necessary circumstances when battling evil, yet only when I was sure no one could get hurt from the light."

"Light as a weapon to battle evil," Joe Kitty remarked. "That's never been done here, but then I know only so much."

"Yeow!" I screamed.

"What?" Joe Kitty asked.

"Look!" I pointed to the opening across the meadow from which the dragon had emerged. "What do you know of that, Joe Kitty?"

"Oh nooooo!" Joe Kitty exclaimed. "Come on!"

Joe Kitty and I scampered away. Below, coming out of the hole in the earth from which the massive dragon had emerged, a line of small immature dragons marched forward. They fell all over one another and spit little plumes of fire. I didn't bother to do a head count, but I'm sure at least a dozen popped out of the hole in just a handful of seconds...and they weren't slowing down.

"They've got to be young Howlers," Joe Kitty said.

"Oh yeah, you think so," I said as we ran, hoping to leave the young Howlers in disarray. "Let's leave them alone to be someone else's problem!"

CHAPTER THIRTY-ONE

Spirits in Tow

We didn't stop running until we were clear of all the trees and bushes in the valley. There, we came to a lush field of low grass, and in the near distance before us, I could finally see what I had longed to cast my eyes on: the golden gateposts that served as the start of the final trail to High Stones.

It was just as B.C. and Grandma Goat had told me. They'd also told me I would be safe...forever once I arrived. Yes, it was just like they had explained it would be, and we were about three hundred yards away. Taking a few breaths, we broke into a full sprint, but before we could celebrate, the young dragons from which we had run had matured, as if magically, and were airborne, flying in formation about to descend on us. Hundreds were still small in stature but big in numbers and spitting plenty of fire.

I was out of tricks. I had a handful of Peigts, some regular and some anointed, and a few snacks in my backpack. Unfortunately, in the throes of the chase, I had forgotten about the soulless beings who had tagged along with us for some time now, yet a glance back revealed they were still tagging along, making us an easy target for the young dragons.

Two hundred yards away from the gateposts, the dragons stopped. For a split second, I believed we had outrun them, but once again, I was reminded never to ever make such assumptions about Howler types. With the presence of an emperor leading his legions into battle, the massive dragon I first met reappeared from above, diving at us like a stunt pilot, casting a great shadow over us, and sweeping in to lead the legion of smaller dragons against us.

They were everywhere, like a swarm of angry bees. My arms were pinned to my sides, and I couldn't free either arm to get my left thumb or palm over the Black Fire Opal ring. My mind was racing a mile a minute, trying to figure out what to do. It sickened me to think of using the coward's way out. I did it once and swore I'd never do it again. But then I thought I'd be selfish not to use it to save Joe Kitty, and that bothered me even as we were being smothered by what I assumed to be young demon Howlers. I knew it was up to me to get us out of there.

"Sa, Jo…" I began.

"*Stop!*" Joe Kitty screamed. "What's that?" He pointed behind us as we lay entangled in the fire-spitting dragons.

And just as I was about to complete the rescue command, *Sa Jo*, we both thought we heard angels singing, though poorly off-key.

"*Atta nom, summa! Atta nom, summa!*" the chorus rang out.

As it turned out, it wasn't a choir of angels.

It was Howie and Tahoe hollering at the top of their lungs. Howie rode my palimal Mustang headlong into the swarm of dragons, wielding his sword. The sun's reflections on his amulet struck the dragon in the eyes. Right then, he looked like a hip prince charming—my knight in sweaty clothes with his hair full and flowing, ablaze with the energy I had never imagined possible.

In tow behind was what looked like a giant flock of black-birds. However, as they neared us, it was clear they were not birds but a dense collection of very alive shapes and images that reminded me of ghosts making groaning noises, some high-pitched, some low-pitched, some in between.

Howie rode Tahoe like a mighty war stallion covered with plates of protective armor as she plowed through the young dragons. She knocked some down and even galloped over those who wouldn't move to evade her charge. All the while, Howie yelled, *"Atta nom, summa! Atta nom, summa!"* Those were the words I used to summon the powerful spirits at Mystasanc-tim. However, Howie's command of them was different than it had ever been for me.

Just then, the massive dragon leader swooped in on Howie. Howie stopped, as did the enormous dragon. Howie drew his yanlookie. They froze, as did all the dragons near them.

"You're the next one, aren't you, young Yeary?" the dragon asked, taunting Howie in its deep, scratchy voice.

"Next one?" Howie responded, continuing to hold his yan-lookie steady, pointing at the dragon's under the chin—the most vulnerable place to strike it.

"Next to become a Lusean Master," the dragon said and grunted.

"You are no dragon," Howie insisted.

"And you are not yet Shardam's student," the dragon bel-lowed and flung fire at Howie's feet. "Put away your toy!"

Yet, as it scolded Howie, the dragon rose, commanded his legion of dragons to attack us, and then flew off.

What followed was a ferocious volley of spitting fire and flailing tails and more than expert yanlookie wielding by young

Yeary. I watched, astutely impressed, wondering if I could get away with calling him *Young Yeary* from now on.

"*Atta nom, summa! Atta nom, summa!*"Howie bellowed as he waved the yanlookie above his head. He swung it like an expert to chop off the heads of any dragon within arm's reach. Then, as the massive dragon had exited, Howie reached into his clandiram and tossed a bright red powder behind him. The flock of shapes he had in tow burst apart and scattered to merge with the thousand soulless creatures, bringing them to life.

My troop of four was magnified by an army of a thousand, and although weaponless, my new army would confuse and battle the hundreds of dragons. My newly energized army, led by Howie's expert use of the yanlookie, decapitated and smothered the dragons. As the genie Howler had done into the rock, any remaining dragons retreated into the earth.

Exhausted and spent, yet feeling victorious, I stood amidst my troops, dumbfounded, looking admiringly at Howie and Tahoe. I first gave her a big kiss right on her lips and then stared for a few seconds at Howie, who proudly displayed and waved the yanlookie in victory. I shoved my arms around his sweaty neck and under his arms, glad to smell him instead of the stench of burning dragon flesh. He let the yanlookie rest against my back as we hugged to celebrate our conquest.

"Back-ups, Yeary?" I pulled back, my arms still around his waist, and looked deviously at him.

He just stared at me and smiled. "I couldn't let you down. We each have our journeys, but you are first; you're my girl."

"So, you think this macho rescue means I'm your girl?"

"No. You've always been my girl, the only girl I've ever wanted."

"Huh," I stared hard at him. "And your journey?" I stepped away from him and turned to avoid his eyes, unsure if I was more uncomfortable with his 'my girl' comment or if I felt like my journey had never been his. Then, looking for a way to worm my way out of those feelings, I asked, "Is your journey with Shardam?"

"Apparently, it's the talk of the demon and dragon world," Howie said, referring to the words of the massive dragon.

"Yeah, sort of threw me off, too...that dragon talking."

"The voice was familiar."

"Maybe in your dreams, Young Yeary. Just a typical mean 'old dragon' voice, don't you think?" I said.

"Maybe..." Howie mumbled to himself, his blank, distant stare a clear sign something way beyond me was on his mind. He glanced once at me again and then proceeded to slowly and deliberately sheath his yanlookie.

With the conflict over, we convened my entire entourage, including the army of once-spiritless beings, and assessed our losses. We all had scratches and bruises, but many were injured more severely, with maybe fifty of my army killed and carcasses of dead dragons still littering the meadow. I hadn't really known about human death in Spooner Pond. Although I had heard tales of outright disappearances, particularly in the Dark Seas and High Pass, I had never seen this devastation in Spooner Pond. It was disturbing that this place I thought was so close to High Stones was full of violence and danger.

"This was a battle, Pippy," Howie said, "and someone is surely opposed to you getting to High Stones."

"Yeah, I guess." I gazed over the destruction and carnage of the once beautiful meadow.

"What will we do with our dead and injured?" I asked.

"I'll take care of that, Pippy," the striking, formerly soulless female, now fully embodied and of strong spirit, said in a sweet voice as she handed me my backpack. "We wait for you to lead us to High Stones."

I glanced at her, holding that eye contact connection we had already established, and stared quizzically at her, asking, "You've heard my name enough to know who I am, but now that you speak, just who are you and why do you look to me to get you to High Stones? I'm not sure I'll get there myself."

"Oh, you will, Pippy, you will," she answered delicately. "I am Lynsa."

"You seem like the leader of your people, Lynsa, not me."

"No, *you* are our leader," Lynsa said with force.

"Look, I know you helped us defeat the dragons," I said, a bit perturbed, "but at this point and based on all I have been through, I don't really know if I trust you, believe you, or think I'm able to take anyone to High Stones."

"I know you can trust us," Lynsa said in a soothing voice. "But even more, Pippy, I am grateful you rescued us from the entombment of the vines. As Truggles said, 'Those who listen to my words and believe in my origin from High Stones will have eternal life and free passage to High Stones once they have overcome the challenges of Spooner Pond.'"

Lynsa paused and took hold of my hands. "We have believed Truggles, and it was revealed to us you were to be successful, Pippy, and would lead us to High Stones."

"But I cannot be your leader, and I did not free you," I protested, unsure what I heard. Truggles had never told me about any Lynsa or a legion of soulless beings.

"Howie freed us by uniting us with our souls, and he is under your command, isn't he?"

"Yes, but..." I stared at Howie, who nervously stared back at me.

"But now we can get to High Stones," Lynsa urged as others clamored nearby.

"They await us, Pippy," Tahoe said, distracting me from Lynsa as she swung her head and neck toward the gateposts to the final trail to High Stones.

"But wait," I argued. "I'm still not sure of the forces we just encountered. I think there were too many deaths and injuries for typical Howler challenges."

"I have seen it before, Pippy," Lynsa said. "Few overcome the dragons."

"So, the dragons aren't Howlers?"

"I don't know for sure, but they are destructive."

"Like what, you've seen them a couple of times?" Howie interjected.

"Oh, no...maybe thirty or forty times in the past one hundred years," Lynsa said.

"What?"

"Yes, I'm quite sure of that. But, unfortunately, the last one of your kind, Truggles, who could have rescued us, could not overcome the last hurdle. After that, our souls were imprisoned in the vines for almost fifty years. That is, until now."

"Okay, this is starting to make sense," I said, staring at Lynsa. "You *were* in the Bend of Back Trail vines when we passed."

"No, not us exactly, but our souls were held prisoner in the vines. Our bodies were cast into the Threshold of High Stones to live in beauty, without the souls to appreciate or enjoy it. Without our souls, we could only live through others with souls, like you and Howie."

"Okay..." I said, shaking my head, still trying to figure things out. "So, you're not Howlers, but are you controlled by them? Isn't this their homeland?"

"Pippy," Tahoe interrupted, "they are calling us."

And across the field were two tallish beings standing alongside the gateposts to the final trail to High Stones.

"It is their homeland, but without souls, they cannot control us," Lynsa said.

"*Pippy...*" Tahoe persisted.

"Okay, okay, Tahoe," I patted her and thanked Lynsa, whose whole attention was also on the gateposts across the field. "Just one thing before we go, Tahoe and Howie," I said, glancing at him. "Where is Feathers?"

Howie and Tahoe exchanged glances, and Howie's face grew red with embarrassment. "Well, let's just say he didn't ride back with us but that we're sure he's okay," Howie said.

"He better not be hurt."

"I think he's fine, Pippy," Tahoe chimed in.

"He is, okay?" I said, staring at the two of them.

"Sometimes you must trust your friends just because," Tahoe said.

"I guess," I said, glaring at them. "Even if your friends wait until the *last second* to show up!"

"Timing is everything, Pippy." Howie grinned.

"Yeah, but I still don't understand what you did."

"Don't ask. I can't explain it anyway." Howie glanced at me and then cast his attention to the throng of bodies who expected me to lead them to High Stones. "All I can say is that I did as I was told."

I stared at Howie and then Tahoe, seeking something more.

"I can't explain either," Tahoe said, "but Howie had me run like I'd never run before, and it sure seems we did the right thing. Look at all these smiling, happy people around us."

"Yes." I smiled. "They do look happy."

I prepared to mount Tahoe for the ride to the gateposts when I noticed two tall, inviting figures standing by them.

"Thagh and Moowenda?"

"They await you," Tahoe said.

My doubts turned to confidence because I knew Thagh and Moowenda were excellent and close to High Stones. It was like the feeling I sometimes got when finally figuring out a tricky algebra problem. Or, when you get how to do something you've been trying to learn, it happens. I felt like the pieces of this High Stones puzzle were finally starting to fall into place for the first time. I remember glancing over at Lynsa, not saying a word, but thinking, *Maybe I can lead your people into High Stones?*

"They are pleased to see us," Tahoe said, flicking her tail high in anticipation of our arrival at the gateposts.

"Then let's go!"

I smiled, and the four of us, plus a pair of Roogers who had just shown up, a couple of pairs of mixed Peigts, and my army of followers began walking the remaining two hundred yards to the brilliant golden gateposts.

CHAPTER THIRTY-TWO

Flight of a Hero

Fifty yards to go, I could almost see the smiles on Thagh's and Moowenda's faces as they stood next to the gateposts, seeming to glow like human light bulbs. I couldn't imagine a happier time, though Feathers's fate never left my mind. Another five yards closer, and the ground trembled. We stopped. I hopped off Tahoe as Howie and surveyed the area around us. Again, the earth shook, and then again, like a heartbeat. We attempted to move ahead, but the ground was unstable.

"Let's run for it!" Howie yelled.

Nodding, I turned around and yelled at everyone to follow us. We broke into a dead sprint for maybe twenty yards before the earth erupted beneath us, tossing us onto our backsides. Our fall was broken by the masses in our army. They caught us and prevented us from landing on our backs. Amidst the lifesaving hands and arms matrix, we struggled to right ourselves and prepared to move on, but that wasn't to be.

One more shake of the earth and an ancient serpent's head the size of the massive dragon we had previously encountered emerged from the ground. He was twice the size of the prior dragon. Heat blew from its nostrils like a fiery wet wind as it exhaled, so hot I feared the hairs on my head would burn. As the ancient serpent rose further out of the ground, the fire in its eyes was almost hypnotic. Then, section by section, its body emerged. I had never imagined any living creature, fantasy or otherwise, being so gigantic. Finally, as it lifted its feet from the earth, rocks, and dirt flew like artillery fire, and my army was showered with debris.

Taking a step toward us, a large crater created by its exit from the earth was visible. We dared not get close, though Howie's curiosity almost caused him to fall in. Then, the unthinkable happened. The monstrous ancient serpent was so enormous that nothing else but its massive body was apparent. It took a mighty breath and exhaled, blowing away my 950 soldiers, leaving Lynsa, Howie, Tahoe, Joe Kitty, me, and my backpack standing at its feet, each of its scales the size of Tahoe.

Howie glanced over at me, confused and afraid. "Any ideas?"

"Join arms with me," I ordered to the three of them. I then looked painfully at my newly dispersed army leader. "Sorry, Lynsa, you'll have to wait another fifty years. But here," I said, removing the straps from my shoulders. "Take my backpack. Where we're headed, it will be of little use."

"No way," Howie said, grabbing the backpack. "We're not giving up."

"No more hero warriors, Howie. We're done with Spooner Pond. Now give Lynsa the backpack."

"Can't do it," Howie resisted me.

"He's right, Pippy," Tahoe implored. "Think of Truggles' teachings."

"Resist, Pippy," Joe Kitty said.

"Lead with your twishloc," Tahoe said. "We will follow you. Stand for High Stones, and no one can come against us."

"Let me blade this big Howler," Howie said. He pulled his yanlookie from its sheath and ran it into the ancient serpent's foot, drawing nothing but a gust of hot steam.

"Pippy, get me up to his head," Howie said.

I peered at him like an absolute loon, but he insisted, egged on by Joe Kitty and Tahoe. Lynsa urged him on, too, having come to life with her encouragement: "Loofit, Loofit, Loofit Howie, way up high, don't let him fall."

Maybe they knew better than I did? So I Loofited Howie and me to get close to the ancient serpent's head, and he whipped out his clandiram, took out a handful of a grayish-green powder, and flung it in the old serpent's eye.

First, one eye blinked, then the other, and then the two in unison. Then, I reached into my backpack and invited Howie to do the same, and we each grabbed two thorn projectiles from the Enchanted Forest Maze. Finally, we plunged four large thorns into the ancient serpent's temples.

"And here's two more for good measure," Howie said as he pulled a couple of smaller ones out of his clandiram.

Together, we had plunged six projectiles into the temple region of the ancient serpent, hoping to cause it to itch in this sensitive place, but all we got out of the mammoth beast was a violent shaking of its head and a quick trip back to the ground.

"Good try, Howie, but when did you get those projectiles?"

"When you and Sarah were figuring out the final maze problem."

Howie stared up at the ancient serpent settling down after the projectile attack.

"Come on, I'll show you what she'd do," I said. "All of you, huddle with me!"

As the four of us came together, I began to hum a tune B.C. often sang. The others joined in, even Howie, who never could carry a tune.

I can't say how long we huddled, but it calmed me down. The fear was gone, but I had no idea what to do. The ancient serpent seemed to ignore us, but we became oblivious to the old serpent within seconds. The tune had stilled our fear, and because we were at peace, we grew quiet, and the only sound we heard was the slowed breathing of the ancient serpent. Breath after breath, maybe eight in all, before the silence was broken.

"Hey, hey, hey. Time to whip it up," a shrill voice rang out. "It's show time!"

Only one other creature had a voice like that, and it was Feathers. We broke the huddle and peered up, and above us, flying like a stunt pilot and swooping down to join us, was Feathers, a grin on his face that was a joy to see.

"Feathers," I said as he flew into my arms and snuggled close to my face. "I love you, my little friend."

"Love you, Pips!"

"I made it, Howie!" Feathers said excitedly.

"Made it big time, little guy!" Howie grinned and gave him a tug on his ear.

"I flew everywhere, K.J.!"

Joe Kitty smiled.

Finally, all of us were together again. I was relieved because I had always felt responsible for my palimals and Howie. I was determined that no ancient serpent would ever take this feeling away from me.

And as if it had read my mind and was ready to dominate me for good and forever more, the ancient serpent roared and stretched high into the sky and let a deafening roar. We covered our heads at first, but the old serpent's cry was drowned out by the sudden and much more powerful sound of wind. A huge, grinding tornado appeared as if out of nowhere.

We cast our eyes upward and high above the ancient serpent and covered as far as we could see to the right. On the left was a massive volume of water swirling over us, spitting out waves around us. It was like a gigantic tornado in shape, but it wasn't pulling anything up, only driving the water down.

Its touch-down point dove directly down to the ancient serpent's fiery and angry face. Howie cupped his hands over his ears to cut down on the harsh sounds, but I stood there transfixed by the awesomeness of the funnel of water and its dominance over the ancient serpent. In fact, I heard no sounds and felt no pain in my ears, as was the case when the water arrived. Even so, the closer the water got to the ancient serpent, the louder its churning sound became, yet the less I was affected. Finally, the water funnel stopped descending further, hovered over the old serpent's head, and all grew eerily still.

And then Truggles' voice was in my head, still and peaceful.

Even the spirit of truth you cannot see, Pippy, even though you know Him, He will forever dwell in you and guide you. Through Him, I will never leave you without comfort and security; through Him, I will always come to you. Even though it has been a while since you have seen me, you now know I am here, and because I live always, you shall live also. Very soon, you will learn about Him and my Father. Now go to the two....

I glanced at Howie, my palimals, Lynsa, and all those I could see with me. Except for Lynsa, there was a look of bewilderment, like I was the target of their confusion. Yet, somehow renewed and invigorated by the words I had heard and feeling again that I was called to lead, I summoned all of them to begin running toward the gateposts as if the mammoth ancient serpent wasn't even there.

It was like watching a 3-D movie. As we all moved, the ancient serpent and water funnel became motionless and still. All nine hundred fifty-five of us, plus a backpack of Roogers and Peigts, marched ceremoniously toward the gateposts. We must have looked like ants marching by a 3-D statue of a giant ancient serpent and a water funnel over the sky behind us.

Then, as we neared the gateposts, a deafening voice rang out from the water funnel above the ancient serpent. As they both came back to life, we halted in our tracks.

"Begone all demons and evil souls of this valley. Begone, we resist thee from this time forth and for evermore!"

The words were deafening, and the look on Howie's face and the chatter of my troops was even more evidence that this wasn't something anyone could ignore. Though, bewilderment returned to their faces.

I felt a power flow into me, an absolute power that made me feel like I could move a mountain. Guided by only instinct, I glanced at the massive, disabled ancient serpent and Loofited up to face it at eye level.

As I faced the ancient serpent, I held my right hand with my Black Fire Opal ring glistening and my palm facing the old serpent. With a wave, I guided a resistant ancient serpent back into the crater from which it came, pushing it along as if with an enormous energy field. Then, holding my hand still in such a way to keep the old serpent in its place, I took my other hand and waved it across the meadow to gather all the displaced earth and rebury the ancient serpent. As I did, the field returned to its original beauty. I had, indeed, taken mastery over the ancient serpent and valley.

I Loofited back down to my group, and we watched as the massive water funnel diminished. Then, gazing at the clearing skied and return of the spectacular light of the valley, I wondered...

Had Heliotroppe the power to create a massive presence and take dominion over the entire valley and all its evil spirits and demons? And if not, who would have such an ability? Truggles never displayed anything like this. Maybe it was an outsider like Shardam who had such incredible powers, but how would it have been given to me?

In my quandary, two hands were set on my shoulders from behind. I spun around and was startled at first, only to see it was Lynsa, standing there smiling angelically at me. "It *was* Heliotroppe," she said, then stroked my hair like only Sarah and my mom were allowed to do, and I was surprised I enjoyed it.

I acknowledged her caring touch with a smile. Then, I turned toward Howie for reasons I did not understand. As I did, these other words were spoken, ringing out through the skies: "*I have sent you Him who you shall never see but must always know as your protector, for He comes from High Stones where He resides in eternity and from Me. Although Heliotroppe has come to bring you to me safely, He shall now and hereafter teach you all things and bring all things to your remembrance, so you will know all you have* been taught. *No more fear, worry, or sadness, for you have heard and now understand. I went away and have yet to return to you, but now you come to Me, for even there is more excellent than Me in this place. It will be for you to have faith and believe like never before."*

I watched Howie's face twist and turn as if he were aching with confusion, peering around to find the source of the voice. That same bewilderment was in his eyes. Lynsa, however, was calm. Again, the words continued to flow:

"We understand, and your success is you have not become divided among yourself, yet you have divided the one who seeks to divide all to cause them to fall. If you keep the evil one divided against himself, the legions and the ancient serpent's kingdom will not stand. Know your strength to cast out the evil ones through your words and the tools we have given you, assigned to you from the High Stones who have chosen to do this work through you. Stay wary of the evil ones who will come upon you from all places, close and far, and attempt to take away all your power by dividing you from your friends and family to cause spoils. Understand always and in every way. All those who know High Stones yet do not stand with him are against High Stones and will be scattered. Yet when all that drives you from High Stones is gone, you will walk safely through all places and always find what you seek."

I understood and found great joy in the words.

"Is um un con tanni," Lynsa said as she smiled and grasped my hands.

I stared at Lynsa and asked, "What's happening?"

"Everything we have waited for after so many years."

"I can't take it anymore!" Howie interrupted with a burst. "Is this some game I don't know about? All I'm getting is a bunch of gibberish? First the 'yah, la, la, la' from the skies, and now you two yacking," Howie said, looking perturbed for the first time on this journey. "I haven't understood a word you're saying or any weird sounds coming out of the skies."

"He can't hear yet," Lynsa said, further irritating an already frustrated Howie.

"You mean you didn't hear anything we heard?" I asked Howie.

"I told you, just a bunch of gibberish."

"You didn't hear anything about High Stones?"

"Nothing! Just a bunch of chatter coming out of the skies."

"Really?" I asked.

"Yes, Pippy...really!" Howie paused, a smile returning to his cranky face, "But no matter, because at least it scared the fire out of the ancient serpent."

"You really haven't heard anything?" I said, disbelieving him because the words were so clear and powerful.

"Accept that he is not ready to hear these words, Pippy," Lynsa said. "It comes in time to all who are chosen."

"As you were chosen?" I asked.

"Yes, at one time."

"Pippy, uh, Lynsa...hello? I'm still here." Howie was shaking me by the shoulder and nodding at Lynsa. "Don't you think we'd better get going? The gateposts are right over there. And with the way things happen around here, a monster could pop out of that rock," he said, tapping a nearby stone with the tip of his yanlookie.

I paused, stared long at Howie, then Lynsa, and motioned my palimals and the others to follow us. Together, we began our triumphant walk through the gateposts.

950 Bodies in Tow

At the gateposts, Thagh and Moowenda gathered all of us together on the valley side of the gateposts. My original team stood together with Lynsa and the others behind us.

"No more troubles or challenges ahead, Pippy," Thagh began. "You and two of your palimals have succeeded, and Lynsa and the others may follow you to High Stones."

"What?" I said, confused. "What about Howie? And why only two palimals? You don't expect me to choose two out of the three. That doesn't make sense." I was incredulous over Howie not making it and wondered how a palimal could be left out.

"These choices were made long ago, for Feathers, even before the journey began."

"And as for Howie," Thagh explained, "when he made a choice in the Bend of Back Trail."

"What choice?" I asked.

"I had to deal with some souls, the Hooded Ones and MOTs," Howie said.

"*What?*"

"This is your journey, Pippy," Howie said. "I had to make sure you made it. I promised you." Smiling, he lifted Feathers into his arms. "We'll see you when you return."

"We'll be okay, Pips," Feathers said.

"Wait, wait... what's going on here?" I asked.

"It is time for Howie and Feathers to leave," Moowenda said.

"*Wait!*" I demanded. "At least let me understand what happened at Bend of Back Trail."

Moowenda glanced at Thagh, and the latter nodded approval.

Howie explained as well as he could. "At Shardam's advice, I traded my opportunity to enter High Stones for Lynsia and the nine hundred and forty-nine other souls imprisoned by the Hooded Ones, Monitors of Temptation, and the Howlers in the vines in Bend of Back Trail. The deal was that freeing the souls would ensure the soulless bodies we found here in the valley would be loose, presumably to help us—to give you an army!"

"So, when was this deal made?"

"That time when I was with their leaders."

"And you waited until now to tell me? You knew these bodies would be waiting for us in the valley?"

"It was at Shardam's advice that I make the deal and not talk about it, and he is now my Teacher of the Lusean Arts."

"And so, you do whatever he says, like trading your soul?" I asked with a tone of anger.

"I am to learn from Shardam; He is High Stones' protector."

"But what was the deal with Feathers?"

"I don't know exactly. Pure instinct, I guess, because after we got through the wall entrance to the Threshold and began back down Back Trail, I launched Feathers at full gallop, encouraging him to fly like he had never flown before and to seek out help."

I glanced at Feathers.

"And my instincts, Pippy, led me to Heliotroppe," Feathers said.

"So that was Heliotroppe in the water funnel," I said.

"We flew together," Feathers said, "and the closer we got to you, the larger Heliotroppe became."

"You did all this, Howie?"

"It was for my girl," he said lovingly.

"You're nuts," I said, but I was at peace with him and the situation as if his words stilled me. Then, finally, I looked at Moowenda and asked, "How will Howie get home?"

"He will have safe passage."

"Well, I want Howie to have my Black Fire Opal ring."

Thagh and Moowenda stared at each other, conversing in a language none understood until Thagh addressed me, "Go ahead, it is your ring."

I placed the Black Fire Opal ring on Howie's index finger and explained how to use it, then flung the backpack over his shoulder and clipped it around his waist. I turned him around and looked him in the eyes. I thanked him and gave him a big kiss on his lips for the first time. Definitely not too romantic, but not repulsive as the thought at times had been.

"This really is goodbye," I said.

"For now," he said. He nodded, and Feathers began walking away as the others entered through the gateposts and started the trek up the trail leading to the majestic mountain before us. It was many times taller than the Threshold of High Stones wall. Its broad base stood gallantly in the forest of trees surrounding it, and its rich brownish-red color looked metallic. Then, perhaps only five hundred yards up, the mountain disappeared into an impenetrable fog, hiding from view the place that was our destiny.

Moowenda pointed at the thick fog surrounding the mountain's upper reaches and asked, "Would you all like to fly the rest of the way up to High Stones?"

I glanced back, hoping to glimpse Howie and Feathers, but they were well down the trail. Finally, exhausted, I peered up at Moowenda. "Are you kidding? Of course, but how?"

"We shall give Tahoe wings." She chuckled.

"Easier than running," I said, patting Tahoe on her neck.

"Ah ha, sure," Tahoe joked. "Nope, I don't think so."

"Don't worry, Tahoe, we don't have the power to give wings to palimals," Moowenda began, "and Pippy is some years away from doing so on her own."

I queried Moowenda with a 'what-the-heck-you-talkin'-about' look. "But right now, Pippy, your dominion grows, and you have the power to Loofit all of you to High Stones," she said.

"I knew I could Loofit at least Tahoe, and I imagine Joe Kitty's nothing, but what about Lynsa and the others?"

"You can Loofit all," Moowenda said. "Now, you and Joe Kitty climb aboard Tahoe, and remember, the essential thing is to maintain physical contact with the both of them as you Loofit, and they will fly with you."

"And the others?"

"It will be up to Lynsa to hold onto Tahoe's tail, and they will hold onto each other." So, with Joe Kitty in my lap, my arms wrapped around Tahoe's neck, and Lynsa hanging onto Tahoe's tail, I stared at the path ahead leading up the majestic mountain before us and willed us to Loofit. Nothing happened.

"Even those with dominion get tired," Thagh said.

"Tired," a voice behind us bellowed, "not Pippy Natalie Hyland."

We all turned around, and an elegant lady stood wearing a full red velvet dress trimmed in frilly white lace. I stared at her long silver-gray hair flowing across her shoulders and down her back. My heart seemed to drop, and the world spun. Could it really be...?

"Mrs. Sopher? Is that you?"

Among other things, her hair was not so perfectly in place atop her head as it had always been, and she was not wearing her distinctive, weird eyeglasses either.

"It is I, dear," she said as she stretched her arms toward me.

I jumped off Tahoe and ran over to hug her. As I threw my arms around her, I got the surprise of my life. I felt a familiar face hidden from view and positioned behind Mrs. Sopher.

"Sarah!" I said, smiling broadly.

"Pips!"

Together, all three of us hugged. I was speechless.

"You're wondering about all of this, yes? It's not up to me to explain," Mrs. Sopher began, "only to remind you to follow Truggles obediently, and he will guide you to all you could ever want and do in life."

"But how did you get here?" I asked. I began to wonder if I was perhaps dreaming.

She chuckled and grasped the necklace she wore. "You had your ring; I have my pendant."

"And Sarah?"

"She came along as my guest," Mrs. Sopher said, nodding. "I assumed you'd want Sarah to go to High Stones with you."

"No way; you're not..." I stared at her with anticipation.

"Take Sarah with you, Lynsa, and all your palimals. Go on, be on your way. Rullen is waiting as well."

"But we already tried, and it didn't work."

"Of course, it didn't work. It was not quite your time...not without Sarah being with you." Mrs. Sopher stroked my hair. "Now it is your time, Pippy, and it will be for all time to come. Follow Moowenda's advice, and she will tell you what to do."

And with that, Mrs. Sopher grasped her pendant and uttered *Esiarp eht Drol, Ronoh High Stones, West Thwortal*, and she was gone.

I stood there with Sarah holding hands, staring deep into her eyes, and she into mine, whispering, "Are we ready?"

With a chuckle, she replied, "Have we ever not been?"

Yeah, she was my Sarah, and yes, we *were* ready.

Moowenda motioned us to climb aboard Tahoe, and Sarah sat behind me and advised us. "Sarah, place your arms around Pippy and hug her closely. Then, Pippy, close your eyes and see the center of the mist. When you can see it in your mind, Loofit all of you to the center, and you will fly to High Stones."

And as we took off and floated into the fog, Sarah held fast, as did Lynsa and all 950 other bodies in tow—all in one very long line behind us. Thagh and Moowenda remained at the gateposts, smiling and waving farewell.

Once we arrived in the mist, I heard Sarah breathing profoundly and the sound of the water crystals that formed the clouds colliding with one another. It was as if all the water crystals were made of expensive glass crystals, and the melodic sounds they made as they crashed echoed all around us. Collectively, they created a subtle vibration that touched every sense organ in my body. I temporarily lost contact with Sarah, Joe Kitty, and Tahoe and was treated to a movie screen much like the one I saw in Courage Cave, only this time, the actors were Feathers and Howie.

There they were in real-time, trotting down the trail out of the Threshold of High Stones, Feathers riding in the backpack with the flap open, his ears flopping in the breeze. It seemed not a bother or care between them, and Howie spent much of his time flashing the Black Fire Opal ring in the sun to reflect on the rocks and trees along the way before stopping at the base of the trail leading out of the valley.

"So, you're ready for this, Feathers?" Howie asked.

"I suppose so," Feathers said as he jumped out of the backpack. "We're in this together now, boss."

"That's how I see it, little guy." Howie closed his eyes, placed his left hand's palm over the Black Fire Opal ring, and said, "*Esiarp eht Drol, Ronoh High Stones, West Thwortal.*"

"Our destination, boss?"

"Let's explore the Northwest boundary of the Wooded Forest first."

"And then?" Feathers asked.

"Then I'm off to Montrose to join Shardam."

The sounds ceased, the skies calmed, and Sarah whispered to me, her head still against my neck.

"Howie loved you, you know."

"Yeah, maybe, but we're so young," I said.

"Yeah, but we can love at any age."

"I suppose, but I don't know if we can know what it is to be loved at any age?"

"Maybe you'll find out in High Stones?"

"Maybe, but I'm unsure what *we'll* find in High Stones."

"No, Pippy, what *you'll* find in High Stones," Sarah said as she hugged my neck and floated away from me into the mist, her voice tailing off. "I have to earn my way to High Stones, and when I'm called, I will make my way through Spooner Pond as you have."

Then, her voice paused, "I love you, Pippy..."

And I was on my way into High Stones.